About the Author

Sun Chara, a multi-published, JABBIC winner for *Manhattan Millionaire's Cinderella*, writes sexy, hip 'n fun contemporary romance, high adventure historical romance, and any genre that knocks at her imagination. Globetrotting for lore while keeping tabs on Hollywood leads, she loves the challenge of creating stories for book and screen. Designer frappuccinos with whipping cream and sprinkles on top make everyday a celebration!

https://facebook.com/suncharaauthorpage
@sunchara3

A Match Made in Heaven?

SUN CHARA

A division of HarperCollins Publishers
www.harpercollins.co.uk

Harper*Impulse* an imprint of
HarperCollins*Publishers*
1 London Bridge Street
London SE1 9GF

www.harpercollins.co.uk

A Paperback Original 2018

First published in Great Britain in ebook format by Harper*Impulse* 2018

Copyright © Sun Chara 2018

Sun Chara asserts the moral right to
be identified as the author of this work

A catalogue record for this book
is available from the British Library

ISBN: 9780008145118

Typeset by Palimpsest Book Production Ltd, Falkirk, Stirlingshire

Printed by CPI Group (UK) Ltd, Croydon CR0 4YY

MIX
Paper from
responsible sources
FSC **FSC® C007454**
www.fsc.org

This book is produced from independently certified FSC™ paper
to ensure responsible forest management.

For more information visit: www.harpercollins.co.uk/green

To all the believers ... may you catch a glimpse of the angels at work in your life ... feel the breeze light as an angel's wing fleeting by ... cherish.

Thank you! to superstar editor, Charlotte Ledger for her shining example in all things books.

A special thank you! to brilliant assistant editor, Eloisa Clegg and superb HarperImpulse team for working at supersonic speed to make this book sparkle.

"Be not forgetful to entertain strangers: for thereby some have entertained angels unawares." Hebrews 13:2

Prologue

May Day! Meddling mamma's about to bust…

"What now?" Mirabella slapped her hands over her ears and shifted for a comfy spot at the base of the poplar. With her combat boots as pillow and her frizzy braid wrapped around her like a blanket, she'd been about to indulge in some off-duty snooze time.

May Day!

A niggle persisted, and she tuned into the call. "What d' ya got?"

Matrimony emergency.

"Where?" She yawned and, lifting her lashes, glanced at the rain-drenched heavens. A crystal drop slid from a leaf; she opened her mouth and it landed smack on her tongue. "Mmm … not bad."

Your turf.

"Uh, uh. Came to California for a little R&R remember?"

Take a rain check.

"Don't mention rain." She sprang bolt upright. Southern California was supposed to be sunshine, beaches and cute guys. Huh!

His chuckle crackled through the airwaves, tickling her ears.

"This is very inconvenient," she grumbled.

Be a trooper, Bella. Shouldn't take you long to wrap things up.

She hugged her knees and propped her chin on them, the fabric of her fatigues chaffing her skin, but she barely noticed. "Must I care about these humans?"

You must.

"What's it this time?"

The usual.

"Send a cadet from the rookie force."

No can do. I need experience. Yours.

"Flatterer," she muttered.

'Tis truth I speak, Mirabella.

Sheepish, she grinned. "Okay, okay." She tossed her copper-red plait over her shoulder. It clashed with the pink bandanna knotted at her throat. "Specifics?"

Mother meddling in the match.

She groaned. Didn't He know she didn't do well with busybody mammas?

Of course, He knew.

"Another agent ..." She tried again. "I'm due forty-eight hours leave."

After the assignment, the voice boomed in her ears.

"Do I have a choice?"

She could almost hear him grinning. *Always.*

"Cover?"

Bartender at the local Pub 'n Grill.

"Wha-a-at?!" she asked. "Isn't that a little risqué?"

He chuckled. *I need reps where lost souls congregate.*

"Designer water, here I come."

I knew you'd set a good example.

"Huh! They hardly ever listen."

Ahh, don't I know it. He smiled, lighting up the skies.

"This better be worth it."

Enjoy ... and yes, it's worth it.

"Wait! Names ... addresses. I don't know who ..."

Chapter One

Sam Carroll skidded to a halt at the church entrance in a cloud of Valentino lace and satin. Too bad. The groom had showed up after all.

A bead of moisture slid between her breasts, and her heart hammered so fast, she bet it'd put a hole in her new Victoria's Secret bra. A brave breath, and she adjusted the double veils that kept her face hidden, but also made everything a blur. She clutched her father's elbow and squinted down the aisle. He was still there. Argh!

It made her insides shrivel at the thought of saying 'I do' to Michael Scott ... instead of—instead of—but he'd skipped town. She whimpered and almost turned and fled. Her father patted her hand, and she nearly screamed.

That'd be a shocker to the stiffs at this upper crust event. A giggle won out at the thought, and she felt better. Another pat to her hand. The scream scratched her throat, but got outclassed by the wedding melody filling the church.

Samantha froze in step and prayed for dissolution of these nuptials. Her ingenious plan of hours ago zoomed through her mind at supersonic speed. Her stomach swayed. Suppose it back-fired?

Her father smothered a cough with his fist.

She must've been in another dimension to have allowed mamma to railroad her with her dramatic groanings of a flailing business. Sheesh, she'd only had a latte or two with golden boy to appease her, and here she was the lead in the society wedding of the season.

Gulping a mouthful of air, she let it whiz out between her teeth. A delicate situation, but time to snuff it out … in style … er … not that exactly, but it should have the groom snapping up the right of first refusal. With that thought in the forefront of her mind, she tightened her fingers on her father's arm and stomped forward in her galoshes.

The guests' muffled murmurs followed her down the aisle, grating on her raw emotions and compounding her doubts. The chatter grew louder, and abruptly stopped when she stepped beside the groom. An odd sensation teased. She dismissed it, not daring to glance at him just yet.

"Oh, my," someone said. "Mrs. Carroll's about to pass out."

Her father plunked down beside mamma and held her upright. "Not another word out of you, woman." He chuckled, pleased.

"Are we-e-e rea-a-ady?" The wiry priest sneezed, pointing to the burning candles. "All-ll-ergies."

Samantha nodded in empathy, and the groom curled his fingers around her hand. His heat zapped up her arm, through her bloodstream and straight into her heart. Her pulse zinged her ribs.

"Dearly beloved …" the priest began the sermon.

Oxygen spiraled in her throat. Pressure pounded her temples. Perspiration dampened her forehead and prickles chased up her spine. She crinkled her brow and twitched her nose at the hint of a familiar scent. Cool spice. She shook her head. Stress of the situation must be causing this crazy speeding of her vitals.

The priest droned on, "… why these two should not be joined in holy matrimony, speak now or forever hold your peace."

4

"I wish to spea-a-ak." A man stumbled into the church, his hair standing on end, shirttail hanging out and torn tux sagging at the shoulder.

Dang the veils. She couldn't see his face clearly, and in the commotion, couldn't ID his voice. But she could smell the splatter on him … phew, heavy-duty stuff. She held her breath and grinned. Good timing.

"Tha-at" –he pointed to the groom— "is-is an impostor … a-aah!"

Samantha exhaled in a rush, and her veils fluttered.

A Doberman snarled at his heels. He shrieked and jumped onto a pew, setting off a myriad of sound effects from the guests.

A parade of yelping canines raced inside, and a pot-bellied man huffed and puffed after them. He stumbled to a halt, and dolled up babes of all shapes and sizes hyperventilated, groping for their hubbies in the pews.

"What's the meaning of this?" the priest demanded. "We are in the house of God."

"What's going on?" Sam glimpsed her mother swoon a second time, her gargantuan hat tipping. Her father was too slow in catching her, and she slithered to the floor.

"Wasn't 'bout to let prissy boy scoop you up, Sammy," the groom whispered in her ear, his eye on the dog keeper.

"He got away in the pick-up with the dogs in back," the dogcatcher muttered.

"Who?" Samantha yanked the veils over her head and blinked, her contacts nearly popping from her pupils. "You?!" She narrowed her eyes at the two-day stubble shadowing his jaw. "How?"

Johnny gaped, then tossed back his head and laughed. "What've you done to yourself?"

"You should talk … you … you no good, stubborn mule." She couldn't use the choice words itching to spill off her tongue. She was, after all, in church; she cringed at the blue streak whipping through her mind.

5

Air crackled.

She looked him over from head to toe. His work shirt slouched beneath his waist-length jacket and a chauffeur's cap was tucked under his arm. Faded jeans hugged his legs, a tear exposed one of his knees and scuffed boots were visible beneath his tattered cuffs. His shoulder-length reddish hair was combed though.

"Didn't have time to change." He cupped her chin and gazed deep into her scarlet eyes, squinting to see through the blood-red lenses to her blue irises. "Sorry."

He touched the dark paint beneath her eyes and smudged his fingers.

She slapped his hand away.

Not easily deterred, he pushed a gaudy green lock off her golden brow and goop smeared across her forehead. "You clash, sweetheart," he teased.

She sniffed, nose in the air.

He dabbed at the smudge, but heat from his hand made it worse. "You know I love you as you are ... er ... were." He tried to caress her cheek beneath the layers of ruddy foundation, but only scraped the crusty surface. "You didn't have to morph just for me." He winced at the gaping hole between her teeth. "I would've preferred you hadn't." His grin widened. "It's washable?" His query was hopeful.

A soft growl in her throat, and she turned, sinking her small sharp teeth into his hand.

"Hey!" He yanked his hand back. "Glad to know you still have all your teeth, princess."

"Don't you sweet talk me, you ... you ..." She swung away and clipped his jaw with her bouquet of dandelions.

He staggered back, tumbled over a yelping Chihuahua, and sprawled on the floor. Appalled at her behavior, she dropped to her knees beside him, heedless of squashing her gown around her. "Johnny, are you all right?" She slapped his face, and his bristles scoured her fingers. "I didn't mean it."

He mocked a moan. "If you could just cradle my head in your lap, sweetheart, and kiss ..."

"Ooo!" She caught the twinkle in his brown gaze. Struggling to her feet, she swished to the side and stomped her foot. The hem of her dress brushed his temple and his head plopped back to the floor.

"Rubber boots, Sam?" He winked. "Setting a new trend?"

She ignored the hit, and favored him with her stiff back.

"We'll have none of this." The priest ran a hand around his collar, patted his thinning hair and sneezed.

He squinted heavenward through his wire rim spectacles. Sam could swear ... oops ... perhaps not swear exactly, but could bet ... not that either ... see, yes, she could see the man was offering prayers for deliverance from the lot of them.

She took a step closer, about to whisper to him that a long vacation after this might help, but she staggered to a stop. Something Johnny said smacked her in the pit of her stomach.

"Good thing the floor's carpeted." Johnny rubbed the back of his head, his eyes fixed on her. He inhaled, and the air blasted from his mouth in frustration. Her heat hinting of roses had his temperature rising and his belly tensing. He was tempted to grab her by the boot and topple her onto his lap. His groin tightened, and his jaw did the same. He wanted to touch, taste ... feel ... If he had to marry her prematurely to nix that bozo's attempt to get her in the sack, so be it.

He pushed himself up to a sitting position and stroked his chin with the back of his hand. Whether he could keep her without exposing his secret was another matter altogether.

"Red here picked me up in a limo ..." The jilted groom loomed above him and shoving a finger in his face, distracted his thoughts. "... and dumped me off at the dog pound."

Sam swiveled around, her brows shooting upward.

"A slight detour." Johnny bounced back up and a burnished lock flopped over his brow.

7

"I could have you arrested." Michael wiped dirt off his chin with his torn sleeve, and an Irish setter pawed his chest. "Down, boy, down," he strained a croon.

A rotund man elbowed his way through the crowd and confronted Johnny. "You are finished at Global Bank, young man." He puffed out his chest and grabbed his wife by the arm. "Gertrude, Michael, let's go."

"Yes, dad." Michael tripped after him, trying to extricate himself from the beasts, and shot Johnny a lethal look. "Coming."

Johnny glanced at Sam smoothing her gown; glad she missed Michael's hostile darts. Her head snapped up, and she pinned him with her sharp gaze. His heart sank. She must've caught on, and the game was up.

"What did you say?" She took a step, then another.

Air whistled from his mouth, and he backtracked.

She advanced.

He leaned back against the church organ, and the keys sounded off cue but nobody noticed.

"When?" He bolted up and averting his eyes, straightened his shirt cuffs. "Did I say what?"

"A couple of minutes ago."

"You mean when you landed a right hook on my mug?"

"Yeah."

He feigned a cough; relieved she wasn't referring to the exiting buffoon. A grin curved his mouth. "I would've preferred you hadn't changed."

"No." She shook her head, veils flapping like wings on either side of her shoulders. "Before that."

"I said that I ... uh ... love you."

"You do?"

"The woman still questions my word." He slapped a hand to his forehead and rolled his eyes heavenward. "If she but knew what I went through to get here—" He blinked, once, twice. Nah, he must be seeing things.

8

Angels didn't flitter about the church ceiling chewing bubblegum and dressed in fatigues—hey, did she just wink at him? Must be the stress of the scene, but he could've sworn ... Chuckling, he shook his head and dismissed the illusion. Just as quickly, a sobering thought flashed through his mind. There must've been one tapping on his shoulder earlier, when he made that pit stop at Lucky Lou's on the Nevada state line.

"You do." Samantha flung herself into his arms.

"Mmm." He rained kisses all over her face, hoping he wouldn't regret the tough decision he made to keep his finances under wraps, for the time being. "Yum, this goop's candy flavored."

"Belgian chocolate, lite ... low carbs."

"Could get used to the taste ... you."

"I love you, Johnny Belen."

The priest coughed. "Is there a wedding to be had?"

"Just a minute." Sam twisted aside and popped the red lenses from her eyes. After tossing them behind her, she turned to him and looked every inch the radiant bride. Johnny gulped, and hauled her back into his embrace.

"Did you really drop Michael off at the pound?" She muffled a giggle with her veils.

Michael was pressed flat against the back wall and inching his way to the door. A Doberman Pinscher pawed his chest and slurped his face.

"Willie's Doggie Salon, sweetheart." Johnny caught sight of his buddy scrambling to round up the animals, and his mouth twitched at the corners. "Start up in Goodsprings, Nevada."

"Never heard of it—"

"Well, that's because it's—"

"Johnny, you trekked across the desert to find me," she whispered, delighted.

"I did," he murmured. "The Mojave Desert no less."

She laughed, the sound ringing off stained glass windows like the bells of St. Mary's. "Funny man."

9

"Yeah." He swallowed the lump in his throat before it explode into a confession he might later regret.

"Do you want a wedding or not?" the priest asked in exasperation, but his mouth twitched a smile.

"I do," she said.

"I do," he said.

"I pronounce you man and wife." The priest breathed a sigh of relief and blotted his moist brow with the back of his hand. "You may kiss the bride."

A sliver of doubt pricked his heart, but when she threw her arms around his neck and smiled, it dissipated. Amidst shrieks and snarling dogs, the sweetest serenade he ever heard, Johnny kissed his Sam.

****

Two years later ...

"Honey ..." Samantha stood at the kitchen counter mixing pancake batter in a plastic bowl.

"Mmm." Johnny wrapped his arms around her protruding belly and pushed aside the collar of her sweatshirt, nuzzling her neck.

"Someone's at the door." She leaned back against his chest, breath checking in her throat. "Uh ... will you get it?"

"No." He nibbled at her earlobe.

"Jo— "

He nipped the tip of her ear. "If I must."

Smiling, she watched him stride from the tiny kitchen. She pressed one hand to the small of her back and rubbed her swelling abdomen with the other. A sigh of contentment slipped from her mouth. The baby was due in three months.

Johnny walked back, pulling the letter from the envelope.

She plopped the spoon in the batter. "What is it?"

10

He remained silent, perusing the page.

"Johnny?"

"Special delivery."

"What's it say?"

He glanced up, not quite meeting her eyes, a wry twist on his mouth. "You don't want to know."

Chapter Two

Samantha leaned over his shoulder, and the words hit her like a sledgehammer. "Not married!" She snatched the paper from his hand, her gaze riveted on the black bold-faced type. **"Not legally married."** She raised her eyes and collided with his look of consternation.

"Is this possible, Johnny?"

He stuffed his hands in his pockets. "Dunno."

Laughter bubbled from her, first softly, then growing louder. She swallowed the hysteria and her shoulders drooped, her face crumbling.

"Sam?"

"We-we're not married." She swiped her damp cheeks with the back of her hand, sure her mascara, her one luxury, and pancake batter blended on her face. "A-nd I'm six months pregnant."

Johnny reached for her, and then let his hand drop by his side. "We can clear this up … sure it's some kind of mistake."

She groaned. "Mamma'll have a royal fit."

He scowled. "More like she'll boogie woogie."

"Wish you two would get alo—" She bit off the words that'd trigger an argument between them and spread her hand across her big belly.

"You okay?" He stepped closer.

"No."

"Is it the baby?" he asked, his voice uneasy.

"Yes … no … what I mean is … yes, baby's okay."

A whistle of relief sounded from his mouth, but got snuffed by her next words.

"But I'm not okay with this bombshell you've dropped." She lifted the spoon from the bowl. "What am I going to do?"

He slitted his gaze. "You mean we, what are *we* going to do, right?"

Blobs of batter dripped at her feet, adding a new dimension to the scruffy linoleum. "No." She considered him for a long moment. "What are *you* going to do, Johnny?"

Her challenge, a gauntlet hurled at his feet, and he swooped it up.

"I'll get a new license … I'll sign this one … I'll—"

"Signature on wedding license does not match groom's identification," she read. "Document false. Signature forged." She stared at him, sure her eyes were huge and accusing. "What were you thinking?"

He straddled a chair. "I was thinking about you."

"Huh?"

"I was mesmerized by your … er … beauty if you remember."

She shook the spoon at him. Minute batter missiles sprinkled his face and his shirt. "Johnny Belen, I'm warning you …"

He ran a finger down his cheek and licked the drop with his tongue. "Mmm, this is good."

"Johnny."

"Okay, Sam." He leaped up, a sheepish grin on his lips. "Guess I forgot … but I was sure—"

"I don't believe it." She plunged the spoon back in the batter. "You don't forget a thing like that." Swinging open the cupboard, she grabbed two plates, shoved them at him and slammed it shut.

He set the chipped dishes on the bottle-cap sized table. "You'll recall ours was no ordinary wedding."

Sam sighed. "Yes." For a fleeting moment, her wedding day replayed at speed before her eyes and emotion swelled inside her. Abruptly, she crammed the memory aside and opened the refrigerator, welcoming the frosty air on her hot cheeks. "I re-re-remember."

"It was easy to overlook—"

She took out the butter and banged the fridge door shut with her elbow.

"—a thing like that." What could he say? It was a rhino-size blunder and he felt like a heel for it. He bashed a tuff of hair dangling on his forehead back with his fist. Thoughts of cuffing snoboy into cyberspace had distracted him, and subconsciously he must've scribbled Scott's name on the wedding doc.

He shot Sam a covert glance.

She shot one back.

Until he checked the copy in their safety deposit box at the bank, he'd be in the doghouse under lock and key. "There is a funny side to this, Sam." He tested the waters, his words half question, half statement, his lips tugging at the corners.

Silence.

"Sam?"

"Oh, you're impossible." She set the bowl on the counter, crumbled the letter in a ball and took aim.

"I wanted to get you away from that jerk fast and—"

The paper missile ricocheted off his chest, and she gripped the wooden spoon, stirring the batter. "One." She paused for emphasis. "I've put up with your chronic unemployment—"

"Reverting to high and mighty socialite are you?" His eyes darkened. "I couldn't just be temporarily between jobs?"

"Tempo-perma is what you mean," she let fly, her words stinging.

"Aww, Sam, that was a low blow."

14

"You're always out of a job, Johnny." She absent-mindedly created figure eights in the batter with the ladle.

"Nope." He fixed his sights on his very pregnant wife, and his gut hitched. Fool, to think love could bridge the gap between them.

Love never fails.

The silent message lit his brain. He wrinkled his brow but couldn't recall where he'd heard those profound words. Was what they shared enough to transcend social status pressure? He smirked and nearly guffawed at his naiveté, even at thirty-four. At a loss, he gulped down the self-deprecating sound, thinking it might be time to 'fess up. "I've bought ... er ... working ... I've wanted to tell you about—"

"Heard that before, Johnny."

Her words were like ten-pound weights crushing his shoulders.

In the heavy silence, the batter sloshed in the bowl, keeping time with the ticking cuckoo clock above the stove.

"Two." She smacked the ladle on the batter, speckling the counter. "I've put up with living in this drabby matchbox for two years."

"It won't always be that way, Sam." He stepped closer, encircling her shoulder, but she shrank away. "I thought it was our home ... and I've wanted to tel—"

"Oh, it is, Johnny. It is." Her tone softened a tad, giving him hope.

He pulled her into his arms, and she laid her head on his shoulder. "Then, what is it?" He stroked her hair, the motion soothing...arousing. "I've wanted to tell you about my, our good fortu—"

"Not legally wed." She jerked away and grabbed the frying pan off the shelf and banged it on the stove.

He rubbed the back of his head and breathed a sigh of relief she'd found another target.

"What will people ... I mean—"

"Mamma …" he inserted for her.

"… think." She turned on the gas element and it flared to life.

"You made a choice on that score when you married me." He flexed his shoulder muscles. "But if that matters so much to you, Sam, maybe you shouldn't have said 'I do.'" He'd just given her an out if she wanted it, and his heart faltered.

By social standards, he was an ordinary guy from the poor 'hood, and she was high society from the ritzy side of town. His roots stemmed from Irish farmers tilling land for survival. Her ancestry was linked to the English aristocracy. While he'd pounded the pavement for work during the day and studied for a business degree at night, she hung out at the café on campus, sipping designer lattes with her socialite friends.

Maybe he should've joined her there … maybe that's where he'd made his mistake. Regardless, it was time he found out the truth about why she married him. He'd been putting it off until after the baby came, but the grenade in that letter was about to blast them apart. He'd have to toss in his ammo prematurely and either neutralize or detonate matters between them.

'Rich debutante jilts catch of the season to marry poor boy Belen.' Isn't that how the society page read in the Beverly Hills Weekly? His tone sounded empty, his heart padlocked.

"Doesn't matter, now." She scratched a dried disc of batter with her slipper.

"Why's that?"

"We're not married."

"Easy to fix."

"No, it isn't." She yanked open the cutlery drawer, took out a knife, sliced a slab of butter and tossed it in the pan. It sizzled.

"Why not?" He removed the knife from her fingers, placed it on the countertop and closed the drawer before she could slam it shut.

She shrugged, not quite meeting his searching gaze.

Johnny plowed a hand through his hair, breath blasting from

his mouth. Heck, she still thought him the peasant barely making enough to keep a roof over their heads. Of course, his pad in North Hollywood couldn't compete with her family's Beverly Hills mansion. The recent news of their union, or lack thereof, had her speed-redialing about their life.

"Why'd you marry me, Sam?" An air pocket jammed in his throat, and his pulse jerked off beat.

"Because ... I ..." She twisted her wedding ring around her finger.

"Maybe it was to get back at your mother and get away from that bozo, Scott."

"Leave my mother out of this," she snapped. "And as for Michael, well ... you could be kind."

"You defending that circus clown?" he bit out.

"Not exactly." An unbidden smile brushed her mouth, and then vanished in the onslaught of their verbal shoot out.

"I'm supposed to know what that means?"

"He's a family friend."

"And that makes this" –he pointed to her and himself, then slashed his hand through the air— "all right?"

"No ... yes ... I dunno."

"Maybe it had nothing to do with me—feelings for me." He drilled, wanting to read her ... get answers. Maybe the nuptials had been a set-up for self-serving purposes; the notion flogged his mind ... his gut.

Samantha blinked at him, aghast. How could he think such a thing, and with her carrying his child? Maybe love and marriage didn't mean the same to him as it did to her. She muffled a hiccup; she'd even given up lattes to save them money. Well, she'd better find out what kind of man she married ... er ... thought she married.

She glared at him.

He glared back.

"Johnny Belen, that's a rotten thing to say." She twitched her nose at an odor filling the kitchen, but was too upset to identify the source.

"What?" He rubbed a hand across his jaw and pushed open the window above the sink. "That Scott is a buffoon or a circus clown?"

"No."

He rolled his shoulders. "You mean about feelings, etc.?"

She didn't answer.

"Isn't it true?"

She compressed her lips.

"Want to make this marriage legal or not?" He challenged, loosening his tie and folding his arms across his broad chest.

She scooped up a ladle full of batter.

"Guess I've got your answer." He spun around to leave.

"Hey, Belen."

He glanced over his shoulder. "Wha-a-"

She tossed the batter at him like a lacrosse ball and it smacked his forehead, dribbling down his face.

"Not funny, Sam." He wiped the back of his hand across his eyes, and she glimpsed a storm brewing in them.

"You're right, it's not." She scooped fresh ammo and pitched ladle 'n all at him.

He ducked, and the wallop landed beneath the cuckoo clock on the wall behind him. The utensil rattled to the floor. He kicked it aside and stomped forward to do battle, the cuckoo clock chirping the ninth hour to the tempo of his steps.

A low growl in his throat gave way to the amused twitch on his lips. He advanced one step … two … until his muscled torso brushed her belly. "If you weren't six months pregnant, I'd turn you over my knee."

"And what?" Sam raised her chin, her lip trembling and her eyes stinging. At any other time, he would've played along, washing her face with the flour mix, then lifting her in his arms, he'd climb the stairs and dunk her beneath the shower to make up. A catch in her throat, and erotic memories zinged through her mind, sensitizing her body and spiking her pulse.

Now, the playful antics backfired, fueling anger and lengthening the distance between them.

"Sam—" He sniffed, and a string of choice words rambled off his tongue. "You trying to burn us down or what?"

Smoke billowed around the pint-sized stove.

"Oh my!" She shuffled to the sink.

"No!" Johnny turned the element off and grabbed the pan lid. "Can't snuff a grease fire with water." Slamming the cover on the pan, he extinguished the danger. "Gotta suffocate it."

Like our marriage? He frowned, the thought zinging through his mind.

"Wasn't that hungry, anyway," she murmured.

He shook his head and stomped from the kitchen. The shrill sound of the doorbell startled her and made him pause in stride. She waddled close behind him, hugging the mixing bowl to her bosom.

Johnny yanked the front door open. "What the—"

"Have I come at an inopportune time?" Michael Scott stood on the doorstep, dressed in a designer suit, his blond hair slicked back and his arms laden with red roses. Glancing from one to the other, he preened like a peacock. "I've come to claim my stolen bride."

Chapter Three

Oblivious to simmering tension, Michael skimmed his pale blues over Sam's soot-streaked face, a notch lower to the plastic bowl in her hands, and up again, zeroing on Johnny's batter-stained shirt.

"A domestic dispute?" He grinned like a Cheshire cat and took a step closer, pinching his nose in distaste. "Not trying to cook, are you Irishman?"

"You're outta line, bozo." Johnny lunged and landed a right hook on his jaw. "Beat it."

"Johnny!" Sam grabbed his sleeve to pull him away but by then, Michael lay sprawled on the walk, scarlet blooms flying every which way.

"Should've done that two years ago."

She squinted at the sunlight and shoving past Johnny, wobbled down the two steps to the fallen man. "Are you all right, Michael?"

"Yeah," he grumbled, reaching for her outstretched hand. "That freckle-faced leprechaun better watch his temper or he'll land in jail."

"I think not." Johnny advanced like a man with a mission. "You're trespassing."

"This is Samantha's property, too."

"Yeah, and she's my wife."

"Not anymore." A triumphant grin split his mouth. "She's mine."

"Michael …" Samantha glanced at Johnny and sucked in her breath, allowing it to slowly filter between her teeth. His shoulders were rigid, his jaw steel and a flush slashed his cheekbones. He was spoiling for a fight. "Johnny …"

"We'll see about that." Johnny pushed up his sleeves and in one long stride came at him.

In fluid motion, reminiscent of his former ballet training, Michael grabbed her outstretched hand, leaped up and raised his fists.

"Right, put up your dukes, then."

"Bang on, mister," Johnny muttered.

"No!" She kept him at bay with the bowl she held and pushed Michael back with her other hand. "Stop it, the both of yoa-aa-h!" She doubled over and the bowl cluttered down the steps, pancake batter splattering the cement walk.

"Samantha!" Johnny reached for her, his whole body seeming to pale. "What is it?"

Michael Scott stood locked on the step, mouth hanging open. "What ca-a-an I do?"

"Shut up!"

"A-agh … I've got to …" She leaned against Johnny's shoulder. "Not to worry." She took a deep breath and exhaled in puffs. "I-I need to lie down for a minute."

Samantha lowered her lashes, hating to worry Johnny and panic Michael, but she had to do something to diffuse the situation. A woman could take license at a time like this, couldn't she? She felt a twinge of uncertainty; was that a niggle pricking her conscience?

"Sure, honey." Johnny scooped her up in his arms, climbed the steps, kicked the front door open and strode into the living room.

"Michael," he bellowed. "Fluff up the cushions, will ya?"

Michael thawed to life and pranced behind him.

He placed Sam on the sofa and knelt beside her, holding her hand. "You okay, Sammy mine?"

Michael grabbed a magazine off the coffee table, fanning himself.

Johnny shot him a frosty look.

Michael froze in mid-motion, and then quickly turned the paper fan toward Sam.

"Thank you, both." She pushed up to a sitting position, not missing the antagonistic glances between the two men. "Now, let's talk this out."

"You okay, Sam?" Johnny brushed a golden curl off her brow, his gaze connecting with hers.

"Fine … like civilized—"

"Sure?"

"Yes, Johnny—people."

"Good." Johnny leaped to his full six-foot height, flexed his hands, and light glinted off his wedding ring. He stared Michael down. "You, get out of my house."

"For you, Samantha." Michael pulled a wilted rose from his breast pocket and offered it to her.

Johnny knocked it from his hand.

"Johnny ..." She touched his arm.

"Samantha, do you want me to go?" Michael took a step toward her but Johnny blocked his path.

"Michael ..." she whispered.

"My wife does not want you to stay" –Johnny gave her a tentative glance— "do you?"

"She's not your wife, anymore." Michael almost stomped his foot.

"Stop." She fell back against the cushions and closed her lashes. A myriad of emotions churned inside her, and she opened her eyes wide. "Out."

Startled, both men gaped at her.

"You and yo—"

"Okay, okay, Sa-sa-mantha," Michael stammered, backing away. "Do-don't get upset again, please."

Johnny grinned.

Michael glowered at him. "I'll be back for her."

"Scram." Johnny chased him out, slammed the door behind him and straightened his shirt cuffs. "Glad that's done with." In two strides, he was beside her and plunked down on the sofa, his weight pressing down the cushions. He laced his fingers with hers, his thumb stroking the inside of her wrist, his breath a sliver of sound in the lull of silence.

"It's not." She gritted her teeth, trying desperately to ignore his heat zapping into her. Her pulse leaped. Before she succumbed to the emotion and curled into him, she withdrew her hand. Not quite meeting his eyes, she snatched a cushion and hugged it to her bosom.

"No?" he asked.

Tick. Tock. The cuckoo clock sounded the half hour, the echo ominous.

"I want you to leave, too, Johnny."

Chapter Four

Taciturn, Johnny marched out and slammed the back door behind him, the sound reverberating around the room.

Samantha pressed her hands over her ears, tears welling in her eyes.

Seconds slipped by.

Silence, thick and dark, swelled around her, pressing, choking.

She had to get out. Grabbing her jacket from the hall closet, she shoved her arms into it and rushed out to the car. What had she done? Confusion clouded her mind, and she gripped the steering wheel, blinking rapidly to clear her vision. A drive might help her figure out how she'd landed in this predicament.

But where could she go? A woman alone with limited funds had only so many choices. Distraught, she buckled up and pulled out of the driveway, cruising toward her parents, and then changed direction. She couldn't face her mother's gloating. 'I told you so.' She needed to be alone. To think. Sort things out in her mind.

Her heart.

Golden State 5 North beckoned, and she veered onto it. A faint smile quivered on her mouth. Seemed no matter how bad things appeared, there was always something to be grateful for—she hadn't hit L.A. rush hour traffic. "Phew!"

The car motor hummed a soothing rhythm, and she relaxed. She kept driving.

And driving.

She stopped once for a bathroom break, to fill up the car with gas and buy a sandwich and an apple. For her baby's sake, she forced herself to eat.

Several hours crawled by, and dusk hovered, turning the horizon ablaze with color. She hoped the old turn of phrase *'Red sky at night, sailors' delight'* would be true for her as well. A grin curved her mouth; yes, the weather was on her side.

City lights blurred behind and open countryside stretched far ahead of her. Then, in a twinkling, night fell, and she couldn't get her bearings. Her heart stuttered, then sped, keeping tempo with the spinning wheels. She flicked on the headlights, and brightness illuminated her path. A sigh sounded from deep inside her. She searched for a place to turn around and head back home, but there was no exit sign. A few cars whizzed past and disappeared into the darkness. She leaned onto the steering wheel, peering through the windshield, and realized she was lost. The road stretched before her, lonely and deserted. Exactly how she felt.

"Samantha Belen," she whispered, and her lip quivered, wondering how long she'd be keeping that name. "Get a grip, girl." The smart thing to do would be to pull into the next town and rent a room for the night. A deep breath, and she exhaled a blast of air. After a good night's sleep, she'd feel better, think more clearly.

She didn't get far.

Several yards further, the Chevy coughed and sputtered. She glanced in the rearview mirror. Oncoming headlights flashed, nearly blinding and looming ever closer; the car seemed to slow for a second, then sped past.

"Don't panic, don't panic." She glanced at the gas gauge, relieved to see it was half full. A moment later, she swerved onto the shoulder, stopped, and watched the other vehicle become speck then disappear into the night.

She didn't know whether to be glad or annoyed that the driv hadn't stopped. She glanced over her shoulder. Neon signs adve tising gas and lodging had been swallowed by darkness long ag Overhead, stars sparkled like diamonds. The clock on the das board indicated the eleventh hour, and she twisted her lips in self-deprecating way. Like a dodo, she'd forgotten her cell phor on the bedside table in her rush to leave. Dejected, she laid h head on the steering wheel, and hopelessness engulfed her.

"What am I to do, Lord?" she murmured.

A rap on the window startled her, and she snapped her hea up, her pulse doing double time. A truck driver, slender in buil with hair tucked beneath a work hat, peered at her through squa spectacles. She rolled the window down a fraction and glimpse his Semi across the street.

"Ma'am," the worker's voice seemed to boom in the eer darkness. "You, okay?"

"Yes." A calmness enveloped her. "But my car's conked out."

"Want me to drive you to the next gas station?"

She shook her head and loose curls fell around her temple "You're a stranger and ... uh ..."

"S' right, ma'am, I understand." He scratched his nape an smiled, his teeth sparkling white. "You got road service?"

"My husb—I mean yes, yes I do."

"Give me your card number and I'll drive into the next tow and call 'em for you. Someone'll come by and tow you in to th nearest garage."

"Thank you." She rifled in her purse and jotted her AA membership code on a crumpled napkin.

"Mind you" —the man rubbed his smooth chin— "Doul you'll get anyone to work on it 'til mornin."

"How early?"

"Maybe seven, seven-thirty."

"Um, okay." She rolled the window a fraction lower and met the man's steady green gaze, his smile still in place. Was that a pink hue glinting from his headgear? A trick of the light for sure. "Here it is." She gave him the number, wondering how a trucker could look so squeaky clean, white shirt and spic and span jeans. And his hands; not a speck of car oil or dirt on them. Did Good Samaritans come looking like this? she mused.

"Shouldn't take more 'n half an hour for someone to get here this time of night," he reassured, breaking into her thoughts. "Best stay put in that car of yours 'til then."

At her nod, he touched two fingers to his temple and was gone as instantly as he'd appeared.

"A guardian angel." She chuckled at her musings, then sobered as silence enfolded her, deafening in its intensity. Resting her head on the steering wheel, she closed her eyes only to pop them open a second later.

Someone pounded on the windshield. Had the man returned? It seemed like he'd just left moments ago. She glimpsed the back of a much taller, heavier man who bent down to inspect the front of her car, his tow truck a few feet behind him.

"Lady," the driver said, pulling his red cap low over his forehead before straightening. "Put it in neutral and come on out."

He drew closer, and she glimpsed the company logo on the breast pocket of his oil-smeared overalls. The glare of the truck's lights had her shielding her eyes with her hand, and she couldn't decipher the name nor see the man's face clearly. She rubbed her eyes, thinking it must be about midnight. The man shifted sideways and pulled up the collar of his shirt against rising wind.

He smelled of gas and grease, and she wrinkled her nose in distaste. What a difference from her Good Samaritan. She shrugged and opened the door, thankful for the help. At a time like this, she couldn't be choosy.

Reaching inside the car, he snapped the knob beneath the dashboard that opened the hood. The motion had him nearly touching her, and although she shrank back against the seat, her nerve endings went on alert. Must be the chill in the air, she thought. He whipped out, moved to the front of the Chevy, and raised the hood. A flick of a flashlight, and he poked his head in the machinery.

"Not the battery." He tinkered for a few minutes more. "Alternator belt is loose."

"Can you fix it?"

"Afraid not, ma'am." With his face hidden under the hood, his words were barely audible. "I'll have to tow you in." He flicked off the flashlight, slammed the hood down and bent to hook the chain beneath the front fender. "Come on out."

She hesitated.

"Lady," the man said, his words muffled. "I've had a long day and I'm tired as a toad doin' laps in quicksand."

She didn't move.

"If you don't mind, I want to get home and bunk down for the night."

While he was busy adjusting the chain between her Chevy Impala and his tow truck, she pushed the door wider. She started to slide out, but got stuck behind the steering wheel. An embarrassed moan, and she placed her hand protectively across her abdomen, shuffling an inch or two.

"You all right, lady?" He peered at her from the shadow of his cap and pulling a rag from his back pocket, wiped his hands. "Let me help you."

Touched by his concern, she took his grease-stained hand and he closed his fingers over hers. His grip was firm, yet gentle, and somehow familiar. Heat traversed up her arm, shooting sparks into her and singeing her heart. A breathless moment, and he helped her out, his hand warm around her fingers, protective. A tremulous smile brushed her mouth, and she bit it away. But she couldn't control her pulse as easily; it bopped off beat so much, she nearly imagined the man was—

28

"This way," he said, voice gruff, relinquishing her hand.

Night chill zapped through her light jacket, and she hid her hands inside her sleeves. He led the way to the truck, his gait marred by a slight limp. Sam slowed her pace, realizing he couldn't be whom she wished him to be. His stilted walk had just blown her imaginings to smithereens. By the time she stepped up to the vehicle, he'd already opened the passenger door.

"Watch your step." He shifted and placed his other hand on her upper arm to assist her.

A current rife with sensation coursed through her, and she stiffened. "Thank you."

"Don't mention it." He brushed a hand across his mouth and walked around, climbing onto the driver's seat. "Buckle up."

She fiddled with the belt, and he leaned over to help her, his cap skimming her chin. She smelled him. Although nearly smothered by the automotive odor on his clothes, an underlying scent knocked at her memory. Her heart skidded, and she sucked in a sharp breath. Odd that this stranger should have this effect on her. Must be the anxiety of the situation.

The seatbelt clicked in place. "That should do it." He averted his gaze, fastened his own seatbelt and turned on the ignition. Then he reached up, flicked on the cab light and stared her in the face.

"Oh, you!" The words bumped in her throat, reflecting her ire.

"Yep." He winked, and stroked her arm with his hand.

She flinched away, unsure of whether to be glad or no.

He tilted his lips in a rakish grin. "Where to Mrs. Belen" ---the grin faded from his craggy features— "or would that be the ex Mrs. Belen?"

Chapter Five

"What're you doing, here?"

"You think I'd bail with you six months pregnant with my child?"

"You followed me."

"I did."

"Oh!" She grabbed the seatbelt strap and squeezed. "If I wasn't pregnant, then you wouldn't be here?"

"Didn't say that."

"Didn't have to, Belen."

He flashed her a closed look. Women ... er ... woman, he thought, and revving up the motor, floored it. Were all women so unreasonable or just the pregnant ones.

She twisted around and glanced out the window. It was black as pitch...cold and empty, so he doubted she saw anything. She shivered.

"Cold?"

"A little."

He turned on the heat, cast her a cursory glance and concentrated on the road ahead. Now he'd found her, words froze on his tongue and he didn't quite know how to break the barrier between them. A smile tilted the corner of his mouth. Music.

That should create a softer mood. He clicked on the radio and strains of 'You've lost that loving feeling' filled the cab. Man, what a choice. Quickly, he flipped the knobs for another station.

"Must you insist on that insufferable noise?"

"Thought you liked music."

"It's giving me headache. Turn it off."

He shrugged. "Yes, ma'am." He twisted the knob and accidentally turned it the wrong way, sound blaring like a siren in the confines of the cab. Next second, he silenced it with a flick of his fingers.

"Ohh," she said, her eyes blazing with indignation. "You did that on purpose."

"Did not."

"Did too."

"Did not. Scout's honor."

"When were you ever in Boy Scouts?"

He grinned. A little mystery maybe would turn the tide in his favor. "You don't know everything about me, yet, Mrs. Belen."

"I suppose not." She sent him a surreptitious glance and concentrated on the black abyss they were sailing through.

But, then again, it could backfire. Seemed like that's what happened just now, with her giving him the cold shoulder treatment. He shook his head, what the heck, and started whistling.

"Johnny, must you do that now?"

He let the whistling slip away beneath the hum of the engine. "Better?"

"Yes, thanks."

As miles whizzed by, silence stretched taut between them, ready to snap at the slightest provocation. Sam chanced a glance at him from beneath her lashes. Aloof, he gripped the wheel with one hand, the wrist of his other hand resting on top, his eyes focused on the road ahead. It appeared he'd forgotten she sat beside him. Fine by her. She was seeing a new side to Johnny; one she wasn't sure how to take.

Samantha shifted in her seat and contemplated the star-studded sky. Not a soul in sight except for her and Johnny. Not a sound except for the hum of the motor. A breath, and she released it in a sigh.

Johnny flickered a glance her way, and she glimpsed his reflection in the windowpane. He didn't say anything and she didn't turn to him. A second later, he averted his gaze to the highway. She sighed.

In other circumstances, she'd be cuddled next to him, her head on his shoulder, her arm wrapped around his biceps, dozing, knowing she was safe in her husband's arms. She squeezed her eyes shut. Tears stung her eyelids, and emotion throbbed in her throat. How could things, people, change at a word? Or, in their case, by a letter denouncing their marriage... could that be?

She pressed her knuckles to her mouth and hoped he couldn't see her. Doubts plagued her mind. Did he want out of the marriage now he had the chance? A little voice needled...did *she*? Something balked inside her... her heart. She couldn't imagine life without Johnny; the Johnny she'd known; the Johnny she thought she'd married. Had he changed so much in one day?

Her eyelids felt heavy, her heart heavier.

She glanced at him from beneath her drooping lashes. Had he always been so remote, so mercenary? Had his boyish charm and good looks blinded her to his real character? After all, he had kept silent for a whole year and suddenly showed up on her wedding day to whisk her away. Had he thought marrying her would be his ticket to easy street—a quick fix from the pauper's life?

"Why'd you never write?" She shook herself awake and forced the words between stiff lips.

"What?"

"When you were gone for that whole year."

An exasperated sigh burst from him. "Why're you coming out of left field like that, Sam?"

"Well?"

"After two years, you ask?"

"Yeah, I'm asking." She focused on his chiseled profile, barely visible in the shadow of the cab. Maybe she was the one who'd changed.

In the year he'd been gone, she'd swabbed her pain by overdosing on lattes at the café on campus and in the process, found there was something beyond herself, beyond her heartache … God.

"Why?" The word shot from him like a bullet and ripped her thoughts apart.

"Things are about to change, it seems," she blurted, her ire rising.

"Is that right?" He tossed her a covert glance and it was nearly imperceptible the way he did it without as much as taking his eyes off the road for even a split second.

Smooth. Real smooth.

She shrugged, dismissing the annoying buzz in her head.

"You didn't answer me, Sam."

"You didn't answer me, Johnny."

"Woman, you could drive a man to—"

"Oh, that explains it, then." He was fueling her emotions big time. Brushing a hand across her brow, she pretended an outward calmness, which was a direct contrast to the fervent restlessness inside her.

"I wrote Sam." A sigh rumbled deep in his chest, and she wondered what he was really thinking, feeling. "Hard copy, e-mails, text...the whole shebang. Apparently, you didn't want to write back."

"What?"

"Mmm."

"How can that be, Johnny?" she asked, her voice softening a fraction. "I didn't hear anything from you, not a word."

"I wrote, woman."

"I didn't get your letters." A quiet moment, then, "Well, you could've called or something."

He slapped his hand against his forehead. "Is there anything I do, I've done, that meets your standards, Sam?"

She didn't answer, couldn't. If she did, it would unleash an avalanche of bickering between them and she couldn't handle that right now. Another curve in the road came and went before she glanced his way. His jaw was set, his gaze glued on the road. A multitude of thoughts and emotions jumbled inside her, resulting in confusion.

And a decision.

To find the truth. Did she dare? A peek his way. Yep, she'd do it.

A test.

To see if Johnny was the man she thought she married or an illusion. Sam muffled her dizzying notions. "Where're we going?"

"To a cottage in a wood ... er ... close enough to that."

"Why?"

"Why?" Johnny hoped she'd come to her senses by then, but of course, he didn't utter the sentiment. "You wanted to be alone to think ..." he allowed his words to trail off, not voicing thoughts tearing his brain. *Like whether you want to be married to me or not.* He tightened his grip on the wheel and the metal ridges bit into his flesh.

"Yes, alone. Not with you." Her voice faltered. "Not with anyone."

Her words cut him to the raw. A muscle boxed his jaw. "You will be, but, I'll be within shouting distance should you need me."

"Because of the baby, you mean."

"Of course, what else."

Sam's heart lurched, then hammered with a thousand minuscule mallets. Is that all she meant to him? Someone to have his child? Was he a gold digger? And since he hadn't gotten his hands on her wealth, was he ready to ditch at the first opportunity? Fear clawed at her insides. Had her mother been right about him? Had he ever really loved her?

"After the baby comes?"

"You're free to go," he said, refraining from adding, if you want to.

"I see." Her stomach dipped and her pulse skittered. She breathed in a mouthful of air and exhaled without a sound. In three months, Johnny, the man she married and the father of her child, could be rid of her, and he could hardly wait. She turned away from him and pressed her forehead to the window, the vibration of the truck a balm to her shattered nerves.

Johnny tightened his abs. She'd shut him out. Could she give up on him, on them, so quickly? At a word in a letter? Had she ever really loved him? A nerve hammered his cheek. Was she thinking of Michael Scott? She'd been friendly enough with him at the pad.

Well, the technicality threatening to nullify their union gave her the perfect opportunity to opt out. A groan throbbed in his throat, but he gulped it down.

He'd wanted to believe he could always count on her, but perhaps in the back of his mind he'd had misgivings. He had the means, yet he'd allowed them to rough it financially for a time.

A test.

To see if princess loved the pauper for himself or if she'd bolt at the first sign of hardship. In three months the baby was due. He'd have his answer then.

"Do you, Sam?"

"What?" She deigned to glance his way.

"See. See what is happening here. To us."

"I do."

"That's all you've got to say?"

"You have something more to tell me, Johnny?"

He fisted his fingers over the wheel and kept his eye on the

35

line on the road snaking ahead of them. "I wanted to give you the best, Sam."

"You never quite made it though, did you?"

"Guess not." He swallowed. "Not by your standards. Not by your mother's and not by your Michael Scott's."

"I'd like a better life, Johnny. And my mother would like a better life for me." She paused. "And he's not *my* Michael Scott."

"No?"

"What d'you mean?"

"He could give you the lifestyle you want."

"Yes, he could."

A shard of ice stabbed his heart. "And so could I." The words tumbled from his lips, but the droning of the engine made them inaudible. Not wanting to buy her affection, he didn't repeat them.

"Yet, you do nothing?"

"You call working two jobs nothing?"

"You're not working two jobs, Johnny." She shifted in her seat. "You're constantly *between* two jobs."

Air blasted between his teeth. Did she think so little of him? Disappointment overlaid the resentment rising in his chest. He'd soon know Samantha's true colors.

Fool. He'd busted his behind working odd jobs to get a down payment to buy the kennels from his buddy, Willie. Then, unable to afford help, Johnny 'd single handedly made them pay, but knowing that wouldn't be good enough for society girl, he risked all in expanding them to attract higher end customers. Putting him in a higher income bracket, he'd measure up and offer for her hand.

However, his business plan got axed when Willie had shoved the Beverly Hills Weekly society page in his face, announcing her wedding to rich bankboy.

Johnny 'd burned rubber on Interstate 15 that day. A quick

pit-stop at the Lucky Loo had him tossing a vagrant at the door a handful of coins for a Big Mac at McDonald's.

His random act of kindness had been rewarded.

By the time it had taken Johnny to cross the floor and back again on his way out, the man had busted the bank. Chuckling, Johnny hurried to his car but the man hobbled after him and handed him a check for five million. It had thrown Johnny in a quandary. He'd put the windfall on hold these two years, while he made sense of their life.

Although he'd made several attempts to come clean with Sam, she'd jabbed him about his ability to provide for her that he'd clammed up. Now that the baby was due, he'd planned to surprise her with their good fortune and eliminate her doubts. But before he confessed all, the letter arrived denouncing their marriage.

Had he lost her? Had she regretted marrying him? Was she missing the glitz and glamour of her single life? Did she regret not marrying Michael Scott? Sweat dampened his palms, and he slid his hands along the wheel for a drier spot. He tossed her a covert glance, but all he got was a view of her stiff back.

Shoving down his disappointment, he drummed his fingers on the steering wheel, his thoughts drifting.

"Stop that."

"What?"

"That incessant noise."

"What noi—"

"You're drumming." Samantha reached over and stayed his fingers on the steering wheel. A jolt of energy charged into her, and she snatched her hand away. He attracted her like a magnet. Yet, she must remain resolute. Disappointment and anger sizzled inside her. How dare he think her so shallow...a ritzy lifestyle was not all she wanted. She could rebut his ridiculous statements, but that wouldn't prove anything. Only time would show his true colors.

He laughed. "Is that all?"

"No, that's not all," she murmured, her words brittle.

"That's right, Missus," he muttered, pursing his lips. "We got things to rap on."

"Yes, of course." She ignored his sarcasm, her polite words more aggravating than if she'd responded in kind.

"What d'ya know, we finally agree on something." He pressed on the accelerator, climbed over a slight incline on the highway and onto a level stretch of seemingly endless asphalt.

"Do we really, Johnny?"

There was an explosion of lights in the horizon, but she barely noticed the glitter of the Las Vegas landscape.

"I don't know, Sam." He drew his eyebrows over the bridge of his nose.

"Do we?"

An exasperated sound burst from her mouth. "Must you always answer me with a question?"

"Huh, I'm not the one who—" He bit down on his irritable words and rephrased them. "Sure thing, Sam."

"Stop patronizing me."

"I wasn't—"

"If this is how our talk is going to go, it shouldn't take long."

"I'll make sure of it, then," he retorted in a dry voice. Could she not stand a few hours of his company and was already finding excuses?

"Why bother, then."

A saucy grin split his lips, and he scored his point. "Because that's what grownups do." The woman was provoking him, major league.

She laughed, but it cracked like thin ice on the surface of a pond. Unsettling.

He couldn't fathom her true feelings beneath the apparent merriment.

"And you're suddenly behaving like a mature adult, Johnny?" The tinkle of a giggle. "I'm impressed."

"Now who's patronizing whom, Sam?"

"You started it."

"I did?" He rubbed a hand over his face trying to make sense of what they were saying to each other, if anything.

"You're on the defensive, again."

A guffaw pushed up from his chest but got snared in his throat. "Me, again?"

"Seems like it."

The chuckle finally burst from his mouth, but it sounded galling, even to his own ears. "Whatever you say, my love."

"You are so maddening," she said, her words frosty.

"Because?"

"Because ... because ..." She folded her arms across her breasts and muttered, "There's just so much, I don't know where to begin."

He clicked his tongue. She had him there.

He drummed on the steering wheel, and then abruptly stopped, recalling her ire of moments ago. "Just blurt out what's bugging you—"

"Nothing is bugging me, Belen. Except—"

"We're almost there." He maneuvered around a narrow curve that brought them to the last mile of their journey. "Try and control your temp--"

"I'm not the one who has to control—"

"It won't take long. Another two min—"

"You can bet on that, Belen."

"Fine." And what did you get with that interchange, you pigheaded Irishman? You want to push her into that simpleton's arms? A sigh erupted from the pit of his stomach, and he swept his hand through his hair. Could he hope to bridge this ever-widening chasm between them? He doubted it. Not when they were bickering like a couple of teenagers. Is this what love and marriage did to you?

A moment later, he turned into a dirt road and pulled up in

front of a rickety picket fence. A hand-painted sign with the words *Canine Resort Kennels* hung askew from the gate.

"Here we are," he grunted.

She glanced at him in disbelief.

"Welcome home, Sam."

Chapter Six

By the time Samantha collected her thoughts, Johnny had grabbed a flashlight from beneath the driver's seat, jumped out and shut the door. He walked around to her side, yanked the door open and extended his hand to help her down. Shifting the flashlight's handle between his fingers, he slipped his hands around her middle, and she nearly fell on top of him.

He staggered backward, and her giggle mingled with his chuckle. Joy filled her heart, and she caught it mirrored in his gaze. The turmoil that had invaded their lives with a vengeance the last twenty-four hours vanished for a moment. She glanced over his shoulder and it all came rushing back.

"It's not what you've been accustomed to, Sam." He clicked the flashlight on and slid his fingers to her elbow, guiding her to the building.

"It's not," she said in an awed voice. "It's a real house and not a shoebox."

"I meant it's not luxury—"

"I know what you meant." She wiggled her arm away from his hold and traipsed onward, wishing he'd get that she didn't care so much for luxury as for plain old-fashioned comfort.

Posh and glamour she'd had, and it left her cold. Unless one controlled it, it often took control, playing the person like a puppet on a string. She wanted a warm, cozy home with a rose garden and a white picket fence. Where she could live with her husband and play with their kids...build a future with Johnny. A chance peek from beneath her lashes showed he'd gone quiet again. She itched to reach out and stroke the crinkle from his forehead, kiss—of course, she couldn't do that.

What if she was wrong about him? About everything?

She faltered in her step, her heart rejecting the idea. Air constricted in her throat. She coughed, and then filled her lungs with oxygen, regaining her equilibrium.

"Something wrong, Sam?" He stepped to her side, his words full of concern.

Real or feigned?

"No." She walked a few paces, stopped and screwed up her nose. "What's that smell?"

He sniffed and lifted the corner of his mouth in a grin. "Dog."

"Isn't he ever cleaned?"

"Don't let them hear you say that." He placed a finger to his lips. "They're sticklers for cleanliness." Tilting his head, he considered her a moment...a long moment. "Now that you're here you—"

"If you think I'm—"

"You're so industrious, Sam."

"Not in my condition."

"Thought a little exercise was good for pregnant women."

"Yes, but—"

"This is light stuff, Sam."

"Uh, uh." She raised her hands, shaking her head.

"You can handle it." As soon as the words left his mouth, Johnny cringed, knowing he'd made another blunder. "Didn't quite mean it that way."

With a slight toss of her head, she walked away, side-stepping

42

a brown mound. "No." The word floated over her shoulder and drifted away in the night breeze.

"Come on, Sam." He stomped after her, stopping so close behind her, he nudged her backside with his thighs. Her rose perfume heightened by her body heat wrapped around him like a warm caress, stirring his blood. He almost yanked her into his arms but instead used the tense energy to fuel his words. "You want to be independent, self-supporting. Here's your chance to make good … show mamma—"

"This is not what I had in mind."

"Of course not." Society girl would skip out by morning. His heart rejected the thought, but his mind accepted the possibility. "And going home to mamma when the going gets tough is?"

"Yes … no." She threw her hands up in exasperation and marched past him to the house. A moment later she stopped, bristling with indignation. Slowly, she turned and squinted at him. "How did you know I was going to mamma?"

"I … er … well …" He brushed a hand across his brows.

She closed her eyes and swayed.

He grabbed her.

She pushed him away. "You didn't, Johnny?"

A heartbeat of silence throbbed between them.

"You had me trailed?"

"You bet I did."

"Why?"

"You were distraught … I wanted to ensure you and the baby were all right." A pause. "I couldn't be in two places at the same—"

"It's the baby you were concerned about." Fiercely, she blinked tears welling in her eyes.

"Of course." He stepped closer to her. "And yo—"

"Who did you sic on us?"

He closed his eyes and counted to ten. His blood began to simmer, then iced over at her accusing tone. She didn't believe

43

him. "I asked a friend to watch out for you and let me know—"

"He did a good job spying."

"I'd done him a favor in the past."

"Naturally. One favor deserves anoth—"

"I bailed him out when his marriage busted." He didn't go into the details of buying the kennels from Willie so he could pay alimony.

"How apt." She smirked. "Let's see, he's a trim and fit trucker, with a commanding, gentle voice and the kindest eyes." She pressed her finger to her temple as if thinking. "Oh, and he has a penchant for pink hats."

"He must've morphed since I saw him last."

"What do you mean?"

"Willie's about five foot six and round as a barrel." He grinned. "You met at the wedding." A heavy beat. Maybe it was not such a good idea to remind her about that. Quickly, he regrouped. "He's a joker most of the time and yeah, I guess he's kind. To the animals at least." Then, he copied her gesture, running his finger down his cheek as if in deep thought. "About the pink headgear, gee, Sam, I dunno."

She dismissed his mocking words and hit the mark, instead. "He wasn't the one who called the tow company for me." She eyed him up and down. "He was supposed to wasn't he, Johnny? But someone else got there first."

He remained quiet for so long, she thought he hadn't heard her.

"If it wasn't Willie who helped me, who was it, Johnny?"

"Beats me." He scratched his head. "Somehow he knew who I was and signaled you were up ahead."

"So you did plan this ... this ... er ... takeover?"

"Don't be ridiculous, Sam." He laughed, and then swallowed the irritating sound. "I did nothing of the kind."

"There are those who'll disagree."

"Who?"

"Take a guess," she said in an offhand way, navigating her way up the front stairs of the rambling cottage.

He followed on her heels, not leaving well enough alone. "Michael Scott wouldn't be one, would he?" he asked, his words dry as the peeling paint on the walls.

"Think what you like." She flounced another step ahead and figured with all her extra weight, she must appear comical. She didn't care. She was too tired to get into another verbal sparring match with her husband; or should she be thinking of him as her ex? Her heartbeat swerved, and she paused on the landing to regulate her breathing.

Forcing the troublesome notions away, she focused on what was to be the roof over her head for the next couple of days. Wind whistled through the rafters. She wrapped her arms around herself and glanced up at the clouds drifting across the moon. The weather had turned, and she was thankful she wasn't stranded on that deserted stretch of freeway.

A sudden bark in the darkness made her jump. Johnny leaped up the last two steps and stood by her side. He was so close his body heat warmed her skin, but not close enough that he touched her. She bit her lip to stop herself from leaning into him. "One of your brood?"

"Yeah." He made to smile but didn't quite make it. "A welcome sound."

"Is it?"

"Thought you liked dogs."

"I do."

He cocked a russet brow as if contesting her words.

"The friendly ones," she conceded, flicking a blonde strand off her shoulder.

"Ah huh." He sidestepped to her right and almost nipped her heels. "These canines helped you marry the right man." She turned so abruptly, he bumped into her protruding belly and instantly stepped back.

45

"That's debatable." She almost retracted her words when she glimpsed pain flash across his eyes; then again, it could be a trick of the light from the flash in his hand.

In the circumstances, words were her only defense. Otherwise, she'd be falling into his arms, his eyes … him. And she couldn't do that and make a smart decision, so she allowed the verbal barrier to stand and protect her from her turbulent feelings.

"That could work both ways, Mrs. Belen."

"What do you mean by that?"

"Figure it out."

She raised her shapely brows and placed a finger on her chin. "Hmm, for better or worse was what the preacher said."

"Yeah," he said, his eyes drilling into her.

She squashed the breathless sensation, but her stomach fluttered. "That's it." She scanned the premises, breaking eye contact and swallowing her panic.

The kennels were in dire need of repair. The wire link fence surrounding the grounds sagged every which way. Posts teetered, the gate hung off its hinges, and the shed sheltering the dogs was slapped together with rotting wood. She peered through the moonlit darkness trying to see further and shivered at the cold, impersonal surroundings.

"Worse it is then."

Johnny steeled his abs. She'd just belted him in the gut with her indifferent words. He tried. More than that, he was doing. But it didn't seem to be good enough for uptown girl. In silence, he watched her waddle across the porch with head held high, about to push open the door.

"Hold it."

She twisted around, a blank look on her face. "What now?"

One stride took him to her side, and he heaved her up into his arms. His eyes caught and held hers for a revealing moment. A twister roiled inside him. A heartbeat, and she blinked away

46

the connection. He kicked the door open and walked across the threshold. "Your new home, Mrs. Belen."

She wriggled in his grasp. "Put me down."

"Sure thing." He glared down at her mutinous mouth and stole a kiss.

As he deepened the kiss, she wrapped her arms around his neck, swept away, he hoped, by the passion flaring between them.

A lonely pup's howl penetrated their sizzling embrace.

Dazed, Samantha squirmed in his arms. "Put me down."

Johnny held onto her for a moment longer, regulated his breathing, then set her on her feet. "You got it, Mrs. Belen."

Frost sheathed his heart. He withdrew, distancing himself from her.

So, she couldn't stand him touching her. He wondered what she did feel for him, if anything. Why she married him in the first place was the burning question. Until he got an answer, he'd play it cool.

She spun away from him like a top losing momentum and gaped at the scene before her. Then, she burst into tears.

"What's the matter?"

She turned on him. "I'm six months pregnant, we're not legally married, I have no idea where I am, and I'm standing in a house that looks like a tornado hit it. A-and there's a foul smell, a-a-and I'm cold and hungry." Her accusing eyes shot darts into his chest. "And you ask what's the matter?" She hiccupped.

Johnny winced. The place looked like a dump. He cleared his throat. "You're in Goodsprings, about twenty-five miles from Las Vegas and about ten from the California/Nevada state line. Soon as the kennels are hosed down, there won't be that smell." He shrugged off the navy flannel jacket he wore over his tow-driver overalls and draped it over her, his hands resting on her shoulders. Subtly, he staked his claim.

She stepped away from him and sniffed.

"There should be some food in the refrigerator." He stood

47

motionless. The long hours he'd waited and watched for her compounded the tension in his muscles. "Like you, I'm bummed at the condition of the place."

After he'd married Samantha, he cut a new deal with Willie to repair and run the kennels until he took over, pending Sam's agreement to swap urban living for a more rustic style. During that time, Willie hired someone else to manage the place while he took care of more pressing business in Los Angeles, assuring him it was in good hands.

Johnny guffawed.

Samantha sneezed.

Uncertain of how to comfort her, he rubbed the crick from his neck and motioned her to the living room.

After Michael had gate-crashed their home earlier that morning, followed by the fiasco of Sam taking off, he'd called, giving Willie a head's up that he'd be arriving in Goodsprings that night. The hired hand should've had the place ready. Instead … there was a loose screw somewhere in that man's head.

He wondered if this was what divorce and financial pressure did to a guy. Messed up his psyche. The interior of the house seemed to reflect the man's life. A wreck.

And now it looked like Johnny's life was headed that way, too.

He squinted at a moonbeam filtering through the torn bed sheet drooping from the window. Turning, he glanced down at his mud-clumped boots, sure his footprints blended with the multi-stained carpet emanating a musty smell.

He raised his eyes a fraction and breathed a sigh of relief. The fireplace was a lifesaver. Sam loved fireplaces. But then he grimaced – soot and ashes blackened the brick outlay and spilled onto the floor. Although the living room was spacious, the bare furnishings resembled discards from someone's trash bin. The tainted sofa had a big gouge on the arm; cotton puffed from it, and a matching cushion sprouted its insides. A scarred table and a busted chair were toppled over.

Wind must've whipped through the hole in the windowpane and covered everything with a film of dust and ash.

In a corner, a rocker loaded with empty boxes swayed ever-so-slightly as a clue that the caretaker had dodged just before they arrived. Johnny frowned. Something was definitely out of whack here.

A rumble worked its way up from deep in his throat, but got snared behind his set jaw. He'd have it out with Willie, but first he had to take care of Sam. This wasn't what he had in mind when he decided to bring her here, far away from Michael Scott and mamma. He booted a tumbleweed of paper into the hearth. It seemed the harder he tried to do good by her, the worse things got.

"I want to go home." Sam swatted wetness off her face, smearing dirt on her cheeks.

"This is your home, Sam."

She bawled louder.

He stepped closer, ready to wrap her in his arms, but she sidestepped him. An unsteady breath, two…three, and she stood straight to her full five feet six inches. She locked her hands across her full abdomen, cast him a steady, albeit watery, gaze. "This is *your* home, Johnny." She licked her dry lips.

And he wanted to taste, touch, hold …

"I draw the line at living in a dump."

He flinched, her words grating across his already raw emotions. "Sorry, no five-star hotel this time of night."

"Wouldn't fit your budget anyway, would it, Johnny?"

"What's mine is yours, Sam."

"This?" she snapped. "You're unbelievable."

"Copy you."

"O-o-oh!" She kicked trash out of the way, bumped into the rocking chair and waddled to the fireplace. She swept her fingers along the mantel above. A thick layer of dirt swaddled her hand, and not finding anywhere to wipe it, she rubbed it off on her sweatpants. "Point."

49

"Keeping score, are we?"

"Someone has to," she challenged and stood her ground.

His hiked eyebrow spoke volumes.

Johnny aimed the flashlight at the ceiling and glimpsed a light bulb encased in cobwebs, hanging by a single wire. Electricity. His heart lifted. A beacon in the darkness. "We have light."

In two strides, he reached the switch on the wall and flicked it on. Nothing happened. His heart sank.

"You were saying?" She tapped her foot, a wry twist on her mouth.

"The hardwood beams across the ceiling are sturdy." He pounded the wall with his fist to prove his point.

"You mean the roof won't cave in on us?

"That's right." He paced back and forth inspecting the corners for water stains. "And it doesn't leak."

"Well, what d' ya know?" She grabbed the flashlight from his hand and walked from the room. "No electricity. Dare I ask if there's water?"

"I'll check." Johnny hurried after her but she was way ahead of him.

"Don't bother," she called over her shoulder. "There's water all right. It's ice cold and rusty. The bathtub and sink are streaked with it. And the toilet— Argh! It's yellow black and horribly smelly." A second later, her voice broke mid-sob. "A hundred Mr. Cleans would have a tough time scraping through that goop."

"Aww, Sam." He sidestepped boxes stuffed with packing paper, slipped on an empty tin can, muttered sharply below his breath and regained his balance. "Hey, Sam, with your fashionista ingenuity, we'll turn this into—"

She trundled across the hall to the bedroom. "Flattery won't—" Then she screamed.

Chapter Seven

"Sam!" Johnny sprinted into the bedroom, his heart vaulting in his throat. "Are you all right?"

She stood stalk still on the middle of the floor. A mouse scurried past her legs, its icy tail brushing her ankle. "Agh!"

The moment he reached her, she fell into his arms, shaking. "I-I-I want to go home."

He stroked her hair, stumped for words. "Ah—uh—can't."

She eased out of his embrace. "Why not?"

"No place to go." He swooped up the flashlight she'd dropped on the floor when the rodent came calling. "Besides, it's three a.m. and you need to rest." No way would he let her leave at this time of night.

"What do you mean?" She retreated several more paces from him.

"Sleep, Sam—"

"Johnny …" She placed her hands on her hips, her eyes indignant.

He scratched his cheek. "I gave notice to the landlord."

"Without consulting me?"

Okay, Belen, start paddling upstream. He was treading unchartered depths of woman and about to get grilled. His shoulder blades tensed.

"You weren't there to consult, remember?" He rubbed a hand across his nape, a sardonic twist to his mouth.

After he'd booted Michael out, he 'd been stunned when Sam had asked him to leave too. He'd stomped out to their dime-sized backyard to think. When he heard her crying, he fought the urge to storm back inside and haul her into his arms. Instead, he pressed his hands against the brick wall, every muscle in his body rigid. After all, she more or less kicked him out, hadn't she?

The slamming of the front door and revving of the Chevy's engine had him spring into action. By the time he stumbled out front, he'd just caught a glimpse of the car's taillights turning the corner. He set his mouth hard. Where was she going? And to whom? Dashing back inside, he contacted Willie and had her trailed. Then he called a cab, rented the tow truck and hit the road after her.

"You'd left and neglected to say where you were headed." His eyes steady on her face. "When you'd be returning."

"I wasn't sure where I was going."

"In that frame of mind and in your condition, you had no business touring alone."

Samantha pointed her chin. "I had to get away."

"From?"

She stared him eye for eye but remained silent.

"Me."

"Yes ... no ... I don't know. From everything."

He swallowed the bitter lump lodged in his throat. "I won't be in your way here."

"Here?" She uttered the word with such distaste it would've been amusing in other circumstances. "I don't think so."

"Why not? You didn't like the apartment."

She laughed, glancing around the room. Paint was peeling off the walls, and the bed was nothing but a moth-eaten spring mattress with stuffing popping from its middle. An ancient bureau with dried bits of food strewn across the top stood opposite. She took another step toward the doorway. "Compared to this trash heap, the mouse pad was a palace."

"Sorry."

"Well, just un-give notice."

Johnny shook his head. "Probably rented already."

"How would you know?" She squinted at him, a glint of suspicion in her eyes.

He shrugged.

"Tell."

"Willie needed a place," he blurted. "Being evicted from his digs."

She slapped her hand across her forehead.

"Figured moving here—"

"Moving?"

"—we wouldn't need both." He attempted a grin, but it turned into a twitch at the corner of his mouth.

"Right. We don't need both." She kicked a soiled rag from her path. "The city flat will do."

"Afraid not." He propped his boot on a wooden crate that'd probably contained dog food and tightened his fingers around the flash's handle. Time to come clean with her. "I have something to tell—"

"I'm going home."

"To mamma." A nerve ticked along his jaw. Her abrupt words cut off his confession, leaving him cold. He didn't want a shoebox or a dump for them either. He wanted to give her a palace. One he could very well afford. He scanned the room. This place could be converted into that.

"That's right." She turned away, stiffening her back.

In the distance, the dogs howled in the wind. The windows rattled.

"Sam, you can't go now." He trudged after her, feeling like lead weights shackled his ankles. "Storm's about to break. And you're half asleep on your feet." He sure as heck was. "Wait 'til morning."

"No."

Another soulful sound from the pups, then the heavens opened, and rain pounded the roof.

"Thank God." He sidestepped empty jars, an old shoe and several soiled rags and marched across the room, shutting the window.

"I can't believe this." She held onto the doorjamb for support and her face crumpled, tears trembling on her lashes.

In three strides, Johnny stood beside her. He reached out to touch her shoulder, thought better of it and pushed his hand in the back pocket of his overalls. "I'd better go check on the dogs. When I come back, we can rustle up something to eat."

He got a sniffle and a wail for his trouble.

A puff of air built inside him, ready to burst from his lungs, and he shoved it back. He stood so close to her that the work jacket he'd draped over her earlier brushed his arm. Awareness charged into him, and the breath he'd constrained exploded out of him. He placed his hand on her shoulder.

She jerked away.

He let his hand drop to his side. "Okay, Sam." Plunking the flash in her palm, he stepped past her into the hallway. "If that's how you wanna play, fine by me." He paused, his gut twisting. "Except in an emergency, I won't come near you again." A few more paces down the hall took him to the front door. He wrenched it open and banged it shut, the screen door rattling on its hinges. She'd have to ask him next time.

Pulling up the collar of his shirt, he trampled across the grassless lawn, blobs of mud clinging to his heels. The rain shot down like pellets, stinging his face. A gust of wind cut through his clothes, turning his skin to gooseflesh. Each step he took had him sinking deeper in the mire. A grumble roared from deep in his chest.

Like his life.

As soon as Sam heard the door clang behind him, she released a heavy breath and sniffed. She brushed hair off her face and wiped wet from her cheeks with her sleeve.

"Fine by me, Belen," she murmured, her words echoing in the empty room. Patting her swollen belly, she pushed up her sleeves and determined there would be no emergency. She'd get him out from under her skin. And to do that, she'd have to avoid any and all physical contact with him. She felt her body jolt in denial, but her mind was resolute. Her heart thudded a warning, but she ignored it.

A wistful smile played on her lips. Johnny may have been out of the house, but his indomitable presence remained. Even the hint of motor oil from his jacket draped over her shoulders couldn't smother the cool spice of his aftershave; it wrapped around her like a memory, not letting go.

Until she'd met Johnny, her life had been a blueprint of what the 'elite' dictated. From a very young age she'd gone to boarding school, and unlike most children she rarely interacted with her parents. Even during vacations, she was often cared for by nannies.

Over time, under mamma's delegated tutelage, Samantha had learned to walk and talk, drink tea, dress, and even think like a 'lady'. A quick learner, she soon became exactly what her mother wanted. Samantha thought she had it all, until one winter afternoon when a brown-eyed, red-haired Irishman shielded her from a storm. Suddenly the superficiality of her life shattered, and she realized she was nothing more than a poor little rich girl. She'd had everything but love until Johnny Belen exploded into her life, turning it topsy-turvy.

A sigh dragged from deep inside her. She stepped out into the hallway and twitched her nose at the musty smell. Of course, she'd gone from one extreme to the other, from wealthy debutante to pauper's wife. Neither gave her what she wanted, for here she was, pregnant and supposedly not legally married to Johnny.

Three years ago, when Johnny tore out of town after their explosive argument on wealth and status, she'd been devastated.

With no one to turn to, mamma, fluttering amidst gaming tables and in between bets, pushed Michael at her; papa, oblivious to his wife's extracurricular games, trekked the golf course at the Bel Air Country Club, thinking he'd have money to burn upon retiring. Sam hadn't wanted to burst his bubble. And with her friends in the midst of finals and their own troubles, she'd kept her angst under lock and key.

She had never felt so empty and alone … and angry at Johnny.

A faint grin skimmed her mouth. Numerous lattes and a shopping extravaganza had masked the wound but hadn't dissolved the hurt.

A shutter banged, startling her from her deep thoughts, and she smothered a yawn with her hand.

She pointed the spray of light ahead of her in the hallway and, rubbing her arms to calm the chills, poked her head into each of the rooms. Each room seemed to be worse than the last.

A disaster, not unlike how her life was shaping up.

She wondered what lay ahead of her…with or without Johnny. The mere thought of the latter had her nerves skidding on her spine and her hands going clammy. He could still get her riled up with his Irish charm and his sexy smile. To keep a clear head about the future, she'd have to stay far away from him and keep busy.

A dry sound staggered from her mouth, and she retraced her steps to the living room. She 'd have no trouble keeping busy. Sidestepping the debris strewn across the carpet, she walked to the fireplace and picked up her handbag from the mantel where she'd left it earlier. She clicked it open, rifled through the contents, and pulled out a rubber band. A lipstick and comb followed. After she combed her hair up into a ponytail and secured it with the elastic, she outlined her mouth with a soft strawberry hue.

Amazing what a boost putting on lipstick gave a woman. She curved her mouth in a tremulous smile and, replacing the items in the bag, clicked it closed. Screwing up her face in distaste, she blew dust off the shelf and sneezed. A sniffle, and she placed her purse on the clean spot, glancing out the window.

Rain beat a savage tempo against the pane. Oddly enough, even amidst this chaos, she felt cozy being inside. An image of Johnny out in that deluge whipped through her mind, but she quickly curbed it. Instead she moved out, searching for the kitchen, determined to show that man what she was made of, pregnant or not. He'd learn a lesson.

Her heart seemed to glow, then flash like a neon sign ... another warning? Hmm. She dismissed the uneasy feeling and blew a wayward wisp of hair off her brow.

She'd leave tomorrow.

Chapter Eight

Johnny stomped through the front door, arms laden with blankets and a canvas bag. He paused and sniffed. An illusion? His taste buds went on alert, and he followed the smell of tomato soup.

Ah, the simple life. A cabin, a wife, a kid, a dog. Joy of simple pleasures danced in his head with love, warming on a cold winter night. He laughed. He married a rich society girl, accustomed to all the comforts and baubles dollars could by. Major mismatch for sure. It was time he accepted that fact. And with the 'legally not married' summons, she had an out. And so did he.

As much as he hated the thought of losing her, he wouldn't play second fiddle to the dollar bill. Would she fly the coop come morning for city lights and delights? An iron shackle squeezed his heart at the possibility.

A moment later, he stepped into the kitchen and nearly dropped the load in his arms. Sam stood at a slight angle by the stove to accommodate her condition and stirred the mixture in the blackened pot with a stick.

"Soup or me?" She fluttered her lashes.

"Can I have both?" He focused on her mouth and a wistful smile brushed his lips. Water streamed from his raingear and puddled at his feet.

She remained silent.

"Apparently not."

"Your friend cleaned us out."

"Bang on that."

He'd have a score to settle with Willie and his buddy...er...his accomplice. Johnny shook his head, more annoyed with himself than with Willie. He'd been so involved with appeasing Sam that he'd neglected his business by putting full trust in Willie. The man must've gambled away the funds he'd sent him to renovate the place.

And that explained the hired hand's quick exit. Without Willie around to take the brunt of Johnny's disapproval, and with the possibility of embezzlement charges, he must've gotten spooked.

In a position to be lenient, Johnny wouldn't go that route, especially knowing the hardships Willie had gone through recently. Nevertheless, he expected an explanation and full payback from his former college buddy and now ex-employee.

He tossed the bag and blankets in the corner and shrugged off his slicker. A quick glance showed him no place to hang it, and he draped it over the door, thoughts still jabbing his brain.

It had been his intention to surprise Sam with their good fortune and bring her to this new home to live in the style she'd been accustomed. But she'd wanted to live in the city, and he decided to go along for a time. When her mother kept meddling by throwing Michael in his face and deriding him for not adequately providing for her 'baby girl', he'd kept mum about his finances. At least until he knew for sure which way the wind blew.

And then Sam had gotten pregnant, and it changed everything. With the baby so near, he wanted to pamper her and give her all the comforts money could buy. He thought bringing her here would give them time alone to talk, get to the truth of their marriage ... work things out.

A sigh shot from deep in his chest, and he chanced a glance at her preparing their pauper's supper. He swallowed disappointment. In her estimation, he must've moved down a notch or two to the bottom … er … under the barrel. He swatted rain from his lashes. But from here, there was only one way to go, and that was up. He chuckled at the notion, but it came out a dry sound. Surely things couldn't get any worse between them?

"Don't know how he could have forgotten the canned soup," she said, her cool words pulling him from his thoughts.

"Peace offering, perhaps." He glanced around. Sure enough, except for the small round table she 'd cleaned, it was empty. Warmth from the stove and the smell of tomato filled the kitchen, and he could almost believe —he slammed the brakes on his foolishness.

"Doubt it." She glanced up and met his gaze. "You wanna eat, Belen?"

"Yeah." He allowed his hungry gaze to travel the length of her, from the top of her head to the tips of her toes, then back up, until his eyes settled on her breasts, now much fuller since her pregnancy. His gaze encompassed her belly, full with child.

His child.

Emotion rose up inside him, choking. He gulped it down. He wanted to padlock her to him and never let go. "Starved."

"Grab a crate and dig out a couple of mugs from your duffel bag." Sam waved the stir stick at him, spritzing the air with tomato soup. "I assume you came prepared?"

"Sure." He dropped to his haunches and yanking the sack open, rifled through the contents.

The wind had tousled his hair, and he smelled of fresh air, mud…and man. Sam wanted to reach out and smooth the damp hair off his brow, touch her lips to the spot. She sucked in a breath and allowed it to feather out between her lips. Her mother had called him a ne'er-do-well. Had he no roots? No desire to provide better for his family—wife and child? The 'not legally married' summons gave them both an out. Would he take it? She ignored the pounding of her heart. She deplored living on subsistence level and going from place to place like a nomad.

She tightened her grip on the stirring stick, the bark grazing her fingers. How well did she know this man she married— well, thought she'd married? "You can relocate at a drop of a hat, can't you, Belen?"

"I adapt." He was focused searching through the bag and didn't even spare her a glance. "Guess it's the gypsy in my blood. Irish nomad."

"More like your military training."

"That too. Survival. At any cost."

His words were laced with double meaning, and she shook off the feeling of dread. She stirred the soup like her life depended on it. It did. Her future and her child's future. "Well, I'm not of nomadic inclination, nor gypsy mode."

"Guess you're not." He pulled the two mugs from the bag more forcefully than necessary. "Ta, da!" He slammed them onto the table next to the flashlight, and it wobbled under the impact.

"Pretty quick, aren't you?"

"I can be."

"I remember."

"Yeah," Johnny grunted.

Rush courtship … marriage … fight … flight.

Unless he came up with a foolproof plan soon, rush split-up would get tagged on the list. To change the mood, he dragged a couple of wooden crates across the floor to the table and mocked a bow. "For m'lady."

"Thank you, kind sir."

She played along, but how long could he count on that? He straightened up and smoothed back his hair. Was it always going to be a struggle with this woman? A reluctant smile tugged the corner of his mouth. Never a dull moment with her, though.

"What's funny?"

He shrugged, motioning with his head. "This. You and me."

"I find nothing amusing in the circumstances." She turned her back, kicked a small wooden box against the wall and stepped on it.

"Sam!" In two strides, he stood behind her, protecting, yet not touching.

She stretched up on tiptoe, opened the crazy yellow cupboard and rifled across the top shelf. "Looking for crackers." She cast him a cool glance over her shoulder. "Not asking too much, am I?"

"You shouldn't be doing that."

"What?" She lifted a shapely brow, her gaze turning dubious. "Asking for crackers?"

He refrained from responding to her caustic remark and stood firm until she stepped down. "I have some in the duffel bag. I'll get 'em."

She skirted around him, not touching.

He tightened his jaw and turned away.

"Didn't you say exercise was good for pregnant women?"

"Sure thing, Sam. Safe, gentle exercise, like walking, certain moves ..." He shuttered his eyes. Images of her in his arms flashed through his mind ... in bed. Kissing every spot and every inch of her belly and feeling their baby kick life. Hot breath pressured his chest, blood pumped through his veins, arousing. He shifted in discomfort and zeroed in on her tush as she waddled to the table. He wanted to touch, smell, feel her. He always wanted more of her ...

After the wedding, Johnny had taken her for a week-long honeymoon to Hawaii. She thought he'd spent his life's savings on the trip, but it was pocket change compared to his overflowing bank account. He'd wanted to give her the time of her life.

Hot, balmy nights ... a full moon, a million stars and counting. It set the mood. If he could pluck them, he would have offered her a bouquet of radiant lights.

Instead, they'd stood on the balcony and watched them sparkle.

When she turned in his arms, offering him a chocolate dipped strawberry, he'd nipped it from her fingers, and juice trickled from the corner of his mouth. She'd moved to swipe at it with her hand, but he beat her to it. Flame red liquid stained his fingertip and, in slow motion, he outlined her lips and then captured them with his own. He'd tasted strawberry … and her sweetness.

"Mercy, Sam, you feel, taste like heaven," he'd groaned.

"Mmm, good," she'd moaned, her fingers weaving circles in his hair.

Ocean breeze had ruffled the lace curtains behind them, fanning their fervor to combustible levels. He'd scooped her up in his arms and nuzzled her neck, stroding to their bedroom. God help him. She was breathtaking …

Samantha laughed, and the sound penetrated his erotic fantasy, snapping gossamer threads linking him to the not-so-distant past.

"I'm fine."

He took a moment to control his breathing and his gaze brushed over her, settling on her abdomen. "Glad to hear it."

"We're both fine."

Nodding, he tossed several cracker packs on the table and squashed the rest in his fist. He straddled the crate and, glad his loose overalls hid his physical reaction to her, shifted for a more comfortable sitting.

"You're pretty quick yourself, Sam." He grinned. "Swept the floor, cleaned the counter and table, and got supper cooking. All in the time it took me to check the dogs and collect supplies from the truck."

"Yep."

"I'm impressed."

"Don't be. I don't intend to make a habit of it."

"I read you loud and clear."

In the two years they'd lived in the flat in North Hollywood, she'd become more domestic than when he had married her.

She'd had no choice, he supposed. No maids, no gardeners, no cook, no housekeeper, no chauffeur.

Just him. She had him.

Was he enough for her without dollar signs written all over him? He had to know. A deep breath fizzled between his teeth. He skimmed a hand across his eyes, wondering if he'd been too hard on her, on them both.

She grabbed a mug and dipped it in the pot, casting him a closed look. "This is a self-service diner."

"Fine." He hauled himself up and watched while she settled on the apple crate.

Tomato soup dribbled from the side of the mug, and she slid a finger upward to the brim, catching it. She flicked her tongue and licked the warm liquid from her fingertip. His stomach muscles contracted, and he nearly groaned aloud. He'd tasted her sweetness, her soft— Gulping, he glanced around for a distraction. Papers, cartons and empty cans were piled high in the corner by the back door. "I'll take that trash out after we eat."

"Suit yourself." Samantha reached for a package of crackers and crumbled them in her hand. Why did she feel her marriage was like that? Crumbling. "Makes no difference to me." She sprinkled the broken fragments over the soup.

"Why's that?"

"Won't be staying."

"Goin' somewhere?"

Chapter Nine

"Yes."

"Where?"

"Home to mother." Samantha sipped the soup and stared at him over the mug's rim.

"Figures." He scooped soup into his mug and leaned against the counter, sampling the warm liquid.

She ignored his sarcasm. "Until baby comes."

"Then what?" He narrowed his eyes, his jaw rigid.

"Then I-I'll know better what to do."

"You don't know now, Sam?" The gentleness in his voice soothed her ruffled nerves, yet the subtle censure underlining his words challenged her temper.

Samantha lowered her lashes, concealing the confusion she was certain was apparent in her eyes. After she'd married Johnny, she enjoyed 'playing house,' especially with him pitching in and helping turn it into their little home. But by the time she'd gotten pregnant, the novelty had worn off, and now she wanted more. After nearly two years of living the life of a pauper, she began missing the comforts of her previous lifestyle.

When mamma had stopped throwing Michael Scott in her face, finally accepting she'd married Johnny for keeps, Samantha hoped she and Johnny could work out the kinks in their relationship. Make some decisions about their future; like Johnny getting a regular job and moving them into a bigger house and improving their standard of living, especially now with baby on the way.

Crackers floated on the soup, and she took a sip, licking a drop from her lip. She'd been ready to approach him about their future plans, when wham! The notice had arrived claiming their marriage a scam. She'd been mortified, and with her six months pregnant.

Although in these modern times it didn't matter to some that a woman was unmarried and pregnant, to Samantha and her family background it was a scandal. It mattered to her.

Until she learned the truth about the fraudulent marriage license, she'd tread with caution. She wouldn't sell out to appease her mother or the upper-crust snobs in her circle. In the meantime, she expected more from her husband and their life together. Would Johnny meet her expectations, and did he even want to?

Spooning soggy crackers in her mouth, she chewed and tasted tangy tomato. She glanced at him from beneath her lashes. He propped his hip against the counter and drank from the mug in his hands...hands that had held her tenderly, caressed her, touched her in the most intimate of ways ... A blush warmed her skin, and she swerved away from such dangerous memories... dangerous to her peace of mind. As for Johnny, his casual stance, for all intents and purposes, made it seem like he didn't have a care in the world.

Aggravating.

It hadn't seemed things could get worse, but here she was, smack in the middle of nowhere, in a ramshackle house that looked ready to fold at any minute.

"Can this house stand?"

He snapped his head up in surprise, but realizing her query was literal rather than figurative, a blank mask fell on his face. "It's stronger than it looks."

The play on words, the double entendres, seemed apt somehow.

"What's with all this rainfall in the desert?" she asked, her tone irritable.

He shrugged. "In November thunderstorms are common even in the Mojave. High winds—"

"Seems kinda freaky to me."

That made his eyes crinkle with amusement, and her heart melted. And to combat that feeling, she fueled her next words with a sharper edge.

"Next thing you know it'll be a snow blizzard." She toyed with the spoon in the half-filled mug, and then stirred with force. "What with global warming—" A blob of tomato flew up and landed on the tip of her nose. "Oops."

Johnny chuckled, set his mug on the counter and stepped closer, not missing a beat. "Higher altitudes like the Mesquite and Clark Mountains have been known to get snow." He dabbed the splatter from her nose with his shirt cuff. "The Sierra Nevadas."

His eyes held hers.

She felt vulnerable, transparent, nervous. "Thanks," she whispered, raising the mug to her mouth and taking a drink.

"No problem." He sauntered back to the counter and flicked his wrist. "You can use me as your sponge boy anytime."

A hint of a smile on her mouth, but she hid it behind the mug.

"So the weather's not going wacky?" She wished the same could be said for their life, which launched into wacko mode since yesterday.

"Nope."

Their banter simply delayed the inevitable, and they both knew it. As much as it hurt, she had to get away for a little while. To think clearly. Give them both some breathing room to sort things out and see—her lip quivered—if their marriage survived. Or toppled, making them another divorce statistic.

"When you leavin'?" he asked, his words cool, seeming to pick up on her thoughts.

"Tomorrow. The weather should clear by then."

"How you plan on getting there?"

"Joh—"

"Tsk, tsk." He clicked his tongue, downed the soup in two gulps and set the mug in the sink. "I'm not playing chauffeur to you again, so soon."

"I'll get the keys to the truck, Belen."

"Uh, uh." He pulled the keys from his pocket and dangled them from his fingers, out of reach. "You can't go driving a tow truck on the freeway, Sam."

"Why not?" She plopped the near empty mug on the table, liquid sloshing upward but not spilling.

"I'm exchanging it tomorrow for a more practical vehicle."

"Fine. I'll take your new truck rental."

He chuckled, but the sound lacked humor. "Don't think so."

"I'll call and get the Chevy fixed." She tilted her chin, her gaze challenging.

Folding his arms across his broad chest, he met her look and cocked a brow.

"No phone," she said, snapping her fingers and shaking her head, her body language all a bristle.

"That's right."

"I'll walk." She gripped the edge of the table, knots in the wood bumping against her fingers, and pushed herself up. Grabbing the mug from the table, she waddled across the floor and plunked it in the sink.

Mere inches separated them. The tension was a tangible force between them.

She wished she could lay her head on his shoulder and let all their differences wash away. But she couldn't, not until she knew for certain what was on his agenda. She walked back to the table and collected the leftover Saltines.

Johnny straightened to his full six-foot frame and flicked his gaze over her full condition. "Two miles to the main road, Sam."

She glanced around, debating what to do with the cracker packs in her hand. "A little gentle exercise—"

"Not if I can help it."

A package of crackers hurled through the air.

He raised a hand and caught it.

"I will leave here, Belen. I will find a way. I will not live in this pigsty nor bring up my baby in this hovel." Her voice cracked, and she pressed her fingers to her mouth, muzzling sobs.

Her intention from the start had been to make a success of her marriage. She was certain her mother and her bridge partners had taken bets on how long it would last. She'd wanted to prove them wrong. But it looked like she may have made the mistake; the biggest in her life.

Johnny extended his other hand, and she slapped the remaining packets in his palm. At the same moment, he gripped her hand, holding her tight.

A silent tug-o-war ensued.

She resisted.

He tightened his grip.

Just for a second more, Johnny held onto her, and then he let go, turning away and tossing the packs in the duffel bag.

A deep breath hurled from his lungs, the sound undercutting the tension between them. He twisted back and took a pace toward her, but her mutinous expression had his step locking in place. "Is there anything I could say that would change your mind?"

She tossed her head back, eyes blazing. "It would take an act of God to keep me here."

He narrowed his eyes, and flecks of bronze branded her skin. "I'll see if I can arrange it."

She laughed, and the humorless sound vibrated between them. Empty, chilling.

Sam lay inside the sleeping bag by the fireplace in the living room, staring at the ceiling and counting knots in the beams. Earlier Johnny had collected a few dry logs from the shed and kindled a fire in the grate. She nestled her cheek on her hand and glanced at him stretched out in his own sleeping bag several feet from her. His steady breathing was soothing amidst the noise of wind and rain lashing the windowpane.

A flaming log crackled. She pulled the blanket he'd placed over her up to her chin, and a sigh puttered from her mouth. Then she closed her eyes and drifted off to sleep.

After what seemed like minutes, the dogs' barking sounded the wakeup call, and Samantha fluttered her eyelids open. She stretched her limbs and groaned, burrowing deeper inside her cocoon. The fire had gone out during the night, and icy air pierced through the covers and her clothes, chilling her bones.

She folded the blanket back a fraction to peek at Johnny, and frost smacked her face. She rubbed her eyes and yawned. His corner of the room was empty, his bedroll and blankets neatly folded in place.

"Belen, it's like an ice box in here," she called, her teeth chattering.

Just then, he walked in with an armload of logs and a steaming mug in one hand. "I'm going into town to power up the utilities. That should give us hot water, heat and light."

"Telephone?"

"That might take a little longer." He set the mug on the floor beside her and stepped aside, dumping the wood in the grate. "Storm may have knocked the wiring out."

"How convenient." She shoved her tousled hair away from her eyes. "Mobile?"

"Same difference." He crouched before the hearth, his red plaid shirt stretching taut across his back. Faded denim covered his

70

long muscular legs, and scruffy, mud-stained boots reached to his calves. He pulled a matchbook from his shirt's pocket, took out a matchstick, and struck it on the cover. It flared, and the sulfur smell made her twitch her nose. He flicked the match in the grate. A tongue of flame devoured the kindling and clumps of paper, swelling into a miniature inferno.

"The room should heat up soon." He rubbed his hands over the fire.

Warmth drifted to her, and she wiggled her stockinged feet beneath the blankets. She slid a covert glance at him, and her pulse picked up speed. Firelight cast highlights across his features and turned his hair to burnished gold. He'd always worn it long, brushing his collar. According to her mother, another black mark against him. Long hair belonged to the female species or hippies, not men.

Samantha loved it long. She loved running her fingers through it, loved—

A log fell and crackled, sparks spritzing the air and shattering her fantasy. She sighed and curled her fingers on the soft material inside the sleeping bag.

"You all right?" Johnny squinted at her over his shoulder. "That was a sigh from the heart."

Swaddled in blankets, she looked more like seventeen than twenty-seven, with gold curls tangled about her shoulders, her cheeks flushed from sleep, and her eyes blue as an ocean storm. He'd seen them soften with love and shadow with passion for him. He shifted and tossed another log into the fire. Sparks flew and dissipated. Is that what she'd felt for him? An instant spark that'd quickly abated when life's hardships challenged?

"Just thinking," she murmured.

"Of me?" A long shot, but heck, he'd nothing to lose and everything to gain at this point.

"As a matter of fact, yes." She cushioned her head on the crook of her elbow, her fingers fiddling with the bedding. "You mentioned something about amenities of comfort like hot water."

"Yeah."

"Basic needs." She eyed the steaming mug on the floor beside her with zeal.

"That's right."

"Dare I mention television, a radio?" She shook her head. "Of course not." Shuffling up, she reached for the breakfast-in-a-mug he'd brought her and propped her back against the wall. "How about a laptop?" The cup warmed her palms, and she tilted her head, thoughtful. "That'd be an extravagance, wouldn't it?" She dipped a fingertip in the liquid, and then licked it clean. "Mmm, yummy."

Memories of sweet sensations surged through his mind and booted his groin. A low growl built in his throat, and he turned it into a cough, trying to blast away the stirring inside him. "How about a knife and fork to eat with?" She raised the mug to her lips and looked at him over the rim. "And oh yeah, a plate."

"Knock it off, Sam." He shook his hair back from his eyes and stuffed his hands in his pockets. "Didn't want to give you coffee." He inclined his head to the cup in her hand and the mound of blankets hiding her stomach. "The baby. Soup's better."

"That's right, it is." She took several sips then nailed him with her sharp words. "The rest of this" – she waved the mug around – "isn't."

"Thanks for the vote of confidence, Sam."

She set the cup down and burrowed back under the covers. That had been a low blow, but she had to make her point. The stakes were high: her marriage. Would Johnny prove to be the man she thought she married? Or a counterfeit? She only had three months to find out. She had to know whether their marriage was based on love, cash or mamma's defunct schemes.

"Don't mention it," she murmured.

"Oh, he—"

"Watch your mouth, Belen." She smoothed the blanket over

72

her abdomen. "Research shows the developing fetus is sensitive to sound." Of course, she was pushing his buttons big time and he knew it. The maddening thing was that instead of getting annoyed, he shot her his sexiest smile, and her heart went all a flutter.

"Of course, sweetheart." He winked. "Hey, little gopher—"

"No gophers here, Belen."

"Oh, I don't know. All bundled up with your freckled little nose peeking from beneath the bedding, you look like you're testing the weather. Will it be the kiss of spring or the sting of winter?" He paused, creasing his forehead as if in deep thought. "Will you scurry away, or stay snuggled in your shelter, awaiting warmer conditions?"

"Quite a speech that, Johnny," she retorted, not missing the double deal in his words.

Just then, lightning flashed and thunder rumbled.

She jerked beneath the blankets, paling at nature's special effects. A deep breath, and while windswept rain peppered the window, she regrouped. "Seems I'll be stuck in my little nest until the weather changes."

"Good idea." He slammed her with his level gaze. "I'll see you in a couple of hours."

She slapped her hand over her mouth and rolled her eyes. She'd fallen for that fast and quick. More or less, she'd given her word she'd stay put until he got back.

He ambled to the door and glanced over his shoulder, a fickle lock of hair flopping over his brow. "It's a deluge out there, Sam, otherwise I'd take you along."

"You got your act of God, didn't you, Belen?"

A jaunty grin split his mouth. "Guess so." Then, he sobered. "You'll be okay, won't you, Sam?"

"Sure."

He hesitated a second … two … then, without another word, turned and walked out.

Samantha heard the front door open and bang behind him under the force of wind. The rev of the motor blended with the gale and rain pounding the roof. When he drove away, she listened to the roar of the engine until she couldn't hear it anymore.

A tear slid down her cheek, and she bit her lip to stop its trembling. She felt abandoned, isolated, cold, hungry and alone. She covered her face in her hands and allowed the tears to flow unchecked down her cheeks. There was no one to witness her misery; she didn't have to pretend all was well with her and Johnny.

A sound from the door echoed to her, and she swatted wetness from her face. She must be mistaken. No one in their right mind would be out in this cataclysmic storm. Except for Johnny. She smacked that thought aside and listened. A gust of wind rattled the window, and she shivered.

In the split-second lull before nature's fury unleashed another attack upon the land, she heard it again. Someone was banging on the front door.

Chapter Ten

Sam pressed her hands against the wall and struggled to a standing position. The blanket slipped off her, and goosebumps erupted all over her body. Even the flames in the hearth hadn't dispelled the chill from the room yet. She rubbed her hands together to warm them, and then stuffed them in the pockets of Johnny's flannel jacket she'd worn all night over her sweatshirt. Slipping her stocking feet in her mud-stained sneakers, she shuffled out and down the hallway.

The rapping on the door grew more insistent and echoed through the house.

"Just a sec. I'm coming." She withdrew one hand from her pocket, smoothed her hair in place and opened the door. The force of wind propelled her back, and she clutched the doorknob for support, gaping at her unexpected guest.

"Thought you might like a cup of herb tea and warm cherry pie." The woman swathed in a raincoat and with square spectacles propped low on her nose, grinned.

"Why, thank you." Sam crinkled her brow. Something about her unexpected guest teased her mind, but she couldn't quite grasp it. A smile curved her lips, and she discounted the tingling in her memory. "Could anything stay warm in this weather?"

"You'd be surprised." The woman hopped from one booted foot to the other, her gold hoop earrings bouncing.

"Who are you?"

"Mirabella, your next-door neighbor." She pointed behind her with the box in her gloved hand. "I'm about half a mile from here as cupid shoots his arrows."

Samantha's eyebrows shot up, laughter gurgling in her throat. *As cupid*— she thought, bumping the rude noise down her throat. Odd, this. Must be the isolation.

"This is a neighborly welcome."

"How kind." Samantha didn't move, still staring at her.

The woman's features were a mixture of translucent emotion, yet her words held the meaning of experience. When she flashed her radiant smile, her cheeks dimpled, and years fell away. Her bubble of energy and her sparkling blue-green eyes could put her in the age range of twenty-five to fifty-five to forever.

"Yes, well ... brr! It's cold out here."

A gust of wind blew full force in Sam's face, dispelling her befuddled musings and startling her. "Of course. Please come in." She hesitated a moment. "We just got here last night and the place is a mess."

"Not to worry." The woman slipped by her, plopped the pie in her hands, removed her gloves and put them in her coat pockets.

Samantha kicked the door shut with her heel and followed her inside, questions buzzing in her brain. Too early in the a.m., she thought. Yet, she couldn't deny the woman's youthful spirit reflected eons. As for her fashion statement, well— a character from the halls of history wouldn't be too far-fetched.

Amusement tickled her mouth. The woman's choice of wardrobe was out of this world, crossing decades of fashion. From her shabby brown raincoat, to her khaki green galoshes, to her red hair clashing with her hot pink rain-hat, to the metal rings dangling from her ears.

"You came out on a day like this to say hello?" Sam considered giving the woman a few tips on fashion trends, and then thought better of it. As much as she'd enjoyed her fashion seminars, it'd been awhile. She glanced down at her own garments and her mouth twisted. Maybe she should start with her own advice.

"It was nothing."

"You drove here?" Sam asked, eagerness in her voice. Perhaps she might waggle a ride from her to the bus depot, if there was one in this wilderness, before Johnny came home. If he wasn't back on the dot of two hours, she could leave and not have broken her word.

"No." She glided to the kitchen like she knew exactly where it was.

"You walked here in this storm?" Sam lumbered behind her. The woman came only to her shoulder and was clearly a lightweight; she could've been blown away like a feather in the wind.

"Actually, it felt more like flying." She giggled, her penetrating gaze leveled on Sam's quizzical one.

An odd sensation zapped through Sam, then she giggled with her. "In the wind, of course."

"It helped, yes." She shrugged from her raincoat, tossed it at the door, and the coat seemed to glide up and drape over the back of the door.

Samantha blinked, her mouth falling open.

Next, the woman whirled her hat on the counter and a waterfall of curls tumbled down her shoulders. She slipped off her rain-spattered glasses and rubbed them dry on her form-fitting, ultra violet sweater tucked into army fatigues. A gold chain link belt was fastened around her hips.

Samantha shut her lips and swallowed a silly laugh. Fashion 101 definitely wouldn't go amiss.

Her guest had the knock-out body of a twenty-year-old and a dress code a cross between Cosmo hip and Steampunk frump, a direct contrast to her motherly demeanor. The woman grinned, as if levitating coats were the norm.

Thinking she must still be a little dozy from sleep, Samantha rubbed her eyes and remembered her manners. "Won't you sit down?" she invited, pointing to a wooden crate, an embarrassed blush warming her cheeks.

Mirabella straddled the crate like a trooper. "Nice place you've got here."

"Really?" Samantha filled the black pot with water and set it on the wood-burning stove to boil.

"Mmm." Mirabella crossed one leg over the other, one galosh bobbing up and down. "Beats a battlefield fox hole or urban card-box deco." She propped her glasses back on the bridge of her nose. "A quick sweep would turn this pad into a palace."

"It'd take more like a bulldozer—" Samantha bit off the rest of her words before she blurted something she'd cringe at later. "Please excuse me, I'd like to go freshen up." She trudged by Mirabella's coat draped over the door, paused and glanced back at her. "Make yourself at home."

"I will." She grinned.

By the time Samantha waddled back five minutes later, Mirabella had the table set for tea fit for a queen. She sat on the crate opposite her guest and cradled a mug of steaming mint tea between her hands, her gaze fixed on her empty plate.

"Mmm, that was so-o-o good." She licked a drop of cherry syrup off her bottom lip. "I don't know how you managed it, but it was deliciously warm". She chuckled. "In fact, the whole kitchen is comfortably cozy."

Mirabella gazed deep into her eyes. "Did it myself."

An unexplainable peace enveloped Samantha, and she sighed in contentment. It was like the last two days of turmoil propelling her and Johnny to the brink of a break-up never happened.

"Although the cherries were canned." Her guest tapped her hot pink fingernails on the tabletop, then leaped up, collected the dishes and placed them in the sink before Sam could make a move.

"Please, leave them." Sam started to stand. "I'll do them later."

"Done." Mirabella picked up her pink hat off the counter, placed it on her head and tied the still damp ribbon under her chin. That eternally youthful smile brushed across her lips. It was almost cherubic.

"I hear your husb ... er ... *guess* your husband will be home soon." She stepped to the door and pulled on the coat, and when she lifted her arms, it fell in place over her body.

"Ye-es." Sam couldn't take her eyes away. "Ho-o-w did you do that?"

"Do what, dear?" She slipped brass buttons in buttonholes and pulled on her woolen gloves.

"The coat. "I-it ... uh ..."

Mirabella crinkled her eyes in amusement and walked to the front door.

"Uh, nothing, I guess." Samantha lumbered after her.

"Glad to have a new neighbor." Mirabella adjusted her glasses and peered at Sam like she could see into her soul.

That ripple zapped through Sam again, and a memory teased her mind.

"Wish I could return the favor, Mirabella." But she wouldn't be here long enough to do that.

"I'm stationed at the local Pub 'n Grill." Mirabella chuckled. "A.k.a. The Pioneer Saloon & Goodsprings Café circa 1913 fame."

"Stationed?" Sam crinkled her brow, amused. "You mean you work there?"

"You could say that, dearie." She smiled, and her cheek dimpled. "You can always find me flitting about the place."

"Yeah, sure." Sam shook her head to clear it. Was this woman for real or was she hallucinating? The quiet isolation, except for the dogs barking and the drumbeat of rain, might be getting to her. "I could give you a lift. Johnny should be here any minute."

"Lift indeed." Mirabella giggled. "I'll be home in the twinkling of an eye." Her gaze glided across Sam's swollen belly. "I'm good with babies, too." She nodded. "Call if you need anything."

Perhaps in a day or two a phone would be connected, and she wouldn't feel so secluded, like a poodle on a desert island. But by then it wouldn't matter. She'd be long gone.

As if reading her thoughts, Mirabella grinned. "I'll get your message, Samantha." Then she opened the door, waved and disappeared through the curtain of rain.

Dazed, Sam closed the door behind her, the silence of the house buzzing out of proportion in her ears. She started for the kitchen and paused. Mirabella said to call her, but she'd forgotten to give her a telephone number. Sam shrugged, took another step and froze.

Samantha.

The woman had known her name, but in her befuddled state, she'd forgotten to properly introduce herself. How had Mirabella known—

A gust of wind brushed the back of her neck. Slowly she turned, and a sigh of relief burst from her mouth.

"How'd you make out, Sam?" Johnny shoved the front door open with his shoulder and, juggling grocery bags in his arms, booted it shut behind him.

"Miraculously." A secret smile curved her lips. Now why had she said that?

Chapter Eleven

"Glad to hear it." Johnny followed her to the kitchen, set the rain-drenched grocery bags on the table and packages on the counter.

"Did you see her?"

"Who?"

"Mirabella." Samantha peeked into one of the bags and pulled out a package of rice and a milk carton.

"Mira— who?"

"Thought you might give her a lift. She just left. You couldn't have missed her." The words tumbled from her mouth at speed, and she backed away from him to the fridge. She opened the door and put the milk on the shelf, the frigid air fanning her face. "It works," she said below her breath and closed the door. "And it's clean." Shuffling several steps opposite, she opened the cupboard. "The shelves are lined with—" she stumbled back a step— "pink paper."

"Say something, Sam?"

She brushed a hand across her eyes. "N-no." Turning a full three hundred and sixty degrees, she glanced about the room and blinked. And blinked again.

"Nobody out there, Sam. No one in their right mind would

go out on a day like this." He caught her arching a shapely eyebrow. "I had to go."

"Sure you didn't see anyone?"

"Not a soul." He pulled several food items from the bag and set them in the cupboard. "Who's Mari ... who?" He reached for a pack of Cheerios, stopped and did an about face. "Pink shelves, Sam? Come on—" Then realization smacked, and he gaped, spinning around the kitchen. Awestruck.

Of course he would be. The kitchen sparkled. Walls and cupboards painted a glistening white, the stove and fridge were like new, the floor swept and mopped, and the trash in the corner from last night, gone.

"Sam?"

"Bella, Mirabella." Sam took the items from his hands and placed them on the shelves.

"Told you I'd take the garbage out," he grumbled.

"I didn't—"

A sudden clap of thunder drowned out her words.

Spooked, she dropped the rice pack on the counter and swallowed her uneasiness.

"Don't want you to over exert yourself, Sam."

"I'm pregnant, not helpless, Johnny." She snatched up the rice and slammed it on the shelf.

"When did you do all this?" He pointed here and there with the cereal box in his hand.

"I-I didn't."

"No?" he challenged. "Fairy godmother did it for you, Cinderella?"

"No ... yes ... no." She shook her head. "I don't know."

An angel of mercy'd be more like it. She plodded around the kitchen, brushing her hand across the wall, counter, cupboard, refrigerator, and even the window at the back door. She stopped in front of the sink. No sign of the dishes, not even a tea stain, marked the once decrepit sink. Even the chrome tap was shining.

Samantha plodded back to the table and collapsed on the crate. She propped her elbows on the table, chin in hand, and stared into space.

Angels?

Could she be under such emotional strain that she imagined that kind woman? Mirabella. Odd name that.

"Guess the wind whooshed through here full force when I opened the door and swept up all the dust and junk." She didn't believe it for a minute. Sounded less believable than an angel visiting.

Johnny peered at her from beneath his bushy brows and touched his fingers to her forehead. "No fever."

She knocked his hand away. "I'm well, thank you."

He glowered. "Glad to hear it."

"I had a visitor. We had tea and cherry—" She pushed herself up and trudged to the sink to double check. No dishes. She glimpsed the plastic bag from behind several packages Johnny had placed on the counter.

Pink. Bright. Real. Hot pink.

Samantha pushed the packets aside and Mirabella's trademark stared her in the face. She peeked inside and pulled out the cherry pie in the tin plate. "Aha!"

"Cherry pie?" Johnny's eyes nearly popped from his head. "You did all this cleaning" –he inclined his head— "and had time to bake a pie?" He slapped his hand to his forehead. "Am I hallucinating?"

"A possibility," she mumbled, but which one was going bonkers was the guess.

He peered over her shoulder, his face crestfallen. "Aww Sam, you ate half of it." He slapped the box of cereal on the counter.

"I did not."

"Couldn't you have waited for me?" He curved the corner of his mouth in a lopsided grin that had her heart fluttering. "You *are* eating for two." He extended his arms on either side of her and trapped her between the counter and his chest.

A sizzle of energy.

She quivered.

He sucked in a breath.

Wrapping his arms around her swollen middle, he stroked her with his fingers, and exhaled in a grunt, "I understand."

She turned in his embrace and bumped into his hot gaze. Her pulse skittered off course, and her hands became clammy. He smelled rain-fresh, and she wanted to link her arms around his neck and curl into him. Feel his heart beating against hers. His hands ... His lips ... Of course, that would be foolhardy. So, she glared at him and, lifting his arm up, ducked away from him.

"Mind if I have a piece?" He yanked a drawer open and grabbed one of the plastic spoons he'd tossed in there the night before. Dipping it in the pie, he scooped sweet fruit and flaky pastry and placed it in his mouth. "Mmm, unbelievably good."

"You might say that." Sam plopped back on the crate, folded her arms on the table and laid her head upon them.

"Sam, I want you to take it easy," Johnny said between mouthfuls. "Bang on delicious." He dipped the spoon back in the thick syrup and, spooning up cherries, popped them in his mouth. "Hot coffee would hit the spot right about now."

Sam lifted her head and hurled him a look, rivaling the tempestuous elements outdoors. She dropped her head back on her folded arms and bawled.

"What'd I say?" He chewed and swallowed sweet cherry taste. "Don't get upset, okay. I can do without the coffee." He'd learned that pregnant women had a tendency to get overly emotional at times, but Sam? So frequently? Then he licked his mouth in appreciation of the treat. *Be thankful, Belen, that she didn't start throwing things, like the batter missiles she did at the apartment.* He smacked his lips and smiled. She sure had a good eye for a target.

"What're you grinning about, Belen?" Sniffing, she grabbed a package of macaroni and threw it at him. He angled to the left, and it landed in the sink. She pushed herself up and brushed a stray curl off her brow. "And I'm not upset." Her shoulders drooped.

"Okay." He was thankful the canned goods and water bottles were at the bottom of the bag.

The day's events must've caught up with her, leaving her emotionally and physically exhausted. Heck, he was putting on a good show, but he was feeling whacked himself. He wanted nothing more than to haul her into his arms like old times. Dip his head to her bosom and taste ambrosia, rivaling the sweet cherry taste upon his tongue.

He pulverized the pastry in his mouth, knowing that with the baby due, he had to exercise extreme control. The unexpected dessert was a welcome distraction. He heaped another spoonful and put it in his mouth. Slowly he chewed, noting she gripped the tabletop tight. "Something wrong, Sam?"

"No. Yes." She waved her hand around encompassing her surroundings. "Everything."

He swallowed the piece of pie in his mouth. "I'll hire some help."

She took a deep breath and expelled it in a rush. "Fine. At least you'll be doing something constructive."

He narrowed his eyes to laser points. "That's not fair, Sam." He tossed the spoon in the sink.

Quick as she could, she shuffled past him to inspect the sink. It was still there. The spoon he'd thrown in the sink lay next to the macaroni packet she'd hurled at him. It hadn't been miraculously washed and replaced in the drawer. What was going on? She brushed a hand across her eyes smarting with tears and held them in check.

"You're not fair, either." She turned and faced him. "Bringing me to this deserted place. Miles from anywhere."

"I thought we could talk, work out—"

"You thought wrong." She stomped her foot and waddled from the kitchen to the bathroom, tossing over her shoulder. "Talking 's over." Her voice wobbled. "It's time for action."

Chapter Twelve

At the sound of her weeping, Johnny whacked emotion down his throat and, tough as it was, he let her be. She wanted time alone, he'd give it to her. He leaned back against the counter and shoved both hands through his hair, a humorless sound bursting from his mouth. She'd been alone. Obviously, she didn't want to be near him. Once or twice, he'd even caught her glancing at him like he'd sprouted horns and landed in her life from another planet.

Red flag alerts flashed in his mind, signaling their domestic dispute was on the verge of detonating. To diffuse the bomb, he was forced to walk a tightrope from Mount Everest to the Grand Canyon. One wrong move and ... kaboom!

He collected the packages from the counter and stuffed them in the cupboards. If he and Sam survived a week together, never mind three months, it would be a miracle.

"Johnny, get in here," she called from the living room.

"In a minute." Heck, he could play hard to get a little, couldn't he?

"Now, please."

Please. Well, that was an improvement. Worth an investigation.

He marched from the kitchen and down the hall way to the living room. "What is—huh?" He skidded to a stop, stunned.

"This is what's the matter." She stood in the middle of the floor, swiping her damp face with one hand and waving around the room with the other.

The room nearly sparkled it was so clean. Johnny gaped at the moth-eaten sofa, now like new. Lace curtains hanging from the window had replaced the torn bed-sheet. The carpet had been vacuumed and reflected the original dusty rose hue. Not a sign of paper or box anywhere. Several chocolate-colored cushions with pink tassels sat in the rocker, and a fire in the grate blazed a welcome.

Perplexed, he scrubbed his chin with his fist. He'd stacked the fireplace with enough logs before he'd left for town to ensure the fire lasted until he returned. By now it should 've turned to embers. Someone had refueled it. He furrowed his brow. In her condition, Sam shouldn't be traipsing out in that rainstorm and carrying logs back to the house. She could have slipped in the mud and ... he checked that thought slam fast. "Sam, I don't like you going out in that rain."

"What?"

"I would've stocked more logs and started the fire in a few minutes."

She slipped him a bemused glance. "I haven't stepped out of this house since you brought me here last night."

"Now, Sam ..."

"Yes?" She gave him such an innocent look that he chuckled.

"What's going on?"

"That's what I'd like to know."

"You did a great job with this room, Sam."

"Mmm." She plunked down on the rocking chair and rocked. "The whole house." And rocked.

"You're a super whiz for sure." He raised a hand and rubbed the crick from his neck. "I want you to take it easy. Don't do too much."

"I didn't lift a finger." Adjusting the cushions, Samantha leaned back and stretched her legs out in front of her, her thickening ankles a sore spot. A hint of a smile, and she hugged her swollen middle. Her baby'd be worth it.

"You didn't do this?"

"Nope." She rocked.

Johnny guffawed and hooked his thumbs in the waistband of his jeans. That had her pulse tripping and her eyes focusing on the snap. Slowly she raised her eyes, and he shuttered his. He took a step closer, and she stopped rocking. He brushed a finger down her cheek and curved his mouth in a rakish smile that fueled her heartbeat to a nonsensical speed. She reached out and grabbed his wrist, his strong bones and sinew hard beneath her fingers.

Hot.

She'd touched him. Big, big mistake.

She felt his heat ... him.

At once, she rerouted his hand to the arm of the chair and gave it a pat. Avoiding his baffled look, she made to get up and fell back on the cushions. A nervous giggle glided from her mouth.

"Let me help you," he offered, extending his hand to her.

"I'm not helpless."

He stepped aside, watching her struggle through his narrowed focus.

Samantha gritted her teeth and managed to push herself to an upright stance.

"Well done, Mrs. Belen." He clapped his hands in slow motion.

Ignoring his mocking words, she stepped to the fireplace and fanned her hands over the flames.

"Next time you decide to clean house in one go, let me know." He strode to the door. "I don't want you endangering yourself or our child."

She turned and glared at his rigid back. "How dare you make such a ridiculous assumption."

He eyed her over his shoulder. "What's ridiculous about it?"

"I would never do anything to endanger—"

"You don't think cleaning a seventeen hundred square foot house from top to bottom in under two hours is rather reckless?"

"Less than five minutes."

He shot her an odd look.

"In the twinkling of an eye."

"Really?" He stroked his unshaven jaw with the back of his hand.

"Yes, really." She released an exasperated breath and flailed her hands about. "I didn't do it."

For a space, she'd thought the hyper sensitive emotions during her pregnancy and the shocking news about the legality of their marriage might have sent her off the deep end. But she hadn't conjured things up. She was not 'seeing' things. She was definitely in her right mind.

"If not you, then who?" He hiked a burnished brow. "Tinkerbell?"

She ignored his verbal hit and murmured, "Mirabella."

"Mira ... who?"

"The lady who visited me when you were in town."

"Ah huh." He drilled her with his gaze and her heart skipped a beat. "Well, next time she comes by, you be sure to let me know." He winked. "I'd like to meet this superwoman." Chuckling, he made his exit.

Samantha stomped her foot. The man was aggravating. She shuffled to the window and stared at the rain battering the land. Groaning, she massaged her temples. Whatever happened to living happily ever after? A mirthless sound burst from her, and she clamped her hand over her mouth, smothering it. She straightened her shoulders, determined to rethink her next move in unraveling this fiasco that had become her life. It was evolved into a comedy of manners like Noel Coward's *How the Other Half Loves*, but, unlike the play, it lagged in humor big time.

Slowly she twisted around and surveyed the room. For the first time in two days, the house was warm, clean and in order, the pantry stocked. It should have felt like home, but something niggled at her. So much so that when she heard Johnny whistling from the kitchen she waddled out and down the hall, whooshing through the kitchen doorway as dignified as her pregnant state allowed.

The whistling came to an abrupt stop.

"What're you so happy about, Belen?" She opened and slammed shut cupboards and drawers, wanting to rattle him. In her condition, she figured she was entitled.

"Being here with you?" Johnny treaded thin ice, pushing her buttons like that but, sheesh, man. She'd patted, actually patted his hand on the arm of the rocking chair like he was some fool needing comfort, instead of her husband wanting to—a jab of sexual awareness hit him. Savagely, he thrust it away. Far and away, because it made him vulnerable.

Vulnerable to her. That was something he couldn't afford ... to feel for her.

It was time to take a firm hand here and put a spoke in the super diva's wheel, or he'd get squashed beneath. He stepped aside, propped a shoulder against the wall and watched her shuffle about. Dang it! Emotion surged inside him, and he mocked a cough. If he was really honest, he'd admit that what lay beneath his provocation was that he wanted to get a sexual reaction from her.

For him. Only him.

Instead, she avoided looking at him, tossed a golden strand over her shoulder and rummaged through a drawer.

"Looking for something?"

"Tea."

Johnny slapped his open palm to his forehead. "Sorry Sam, I forgot. Of all things not to buy. I'll get us some next time."

"No need." She turned and held a package in her hand, a triumphant smile on her mouth.

"Where'd that come from? I didn't buy—"

"Yes, well, Mirabella kindly—"

"Enough." Now, who was pushing whose pressure points? Who the heck was Mirabella? "If I didn't know you better, I'd think—"

He'd done it again and stepped on a land mine.

"What?" she challenged, placing her hands on her hips.

He flashed her his sexiest smile. "You do have an imagination."

She smirked. "Hmm."

"An asset, of course."

She bared her dainty white teeth. "Think what you like."

Okay, that didn't work. He straddled the crate, propped his elbows on the table and resting his chin in one palm, watched her beneath his heavy lids. "Willie's side kick must've forgotten it."

"No, he didn't." She tossed the teabag in the air, opened her hand and it landed in her palm. "By the shambles he left behind, I doubt he could afford even that simple luxury."

Johnny set his mouth in a grim line. "He got a good salary."

"How would you know?" She yanked the clear plastic wrap off the teabag and blinked at it. "A pink hue. Hmm." She grabbed the mug from the dish rack. "You pay him?"

"I did," he said, refraining from rebutting the color tinting the clear plastic in her hand.

Samantha laughed and plopped the teabag in the mug. "That explains it."

A muscle rammed his jaw. "What?"

She slanted him an impish gaze from beneath her golden lashes. "The reason he didn't have enough to live decently."

"As a matter of fact, he had plenty because I—"

"A matter of opinion." She turned on the stove and set the pot of water on the element.

Samantha was provoking *him*—how had she turned that around? And she was doing it like a pro—major league. Steam expanded in his chest, and it was all he could do to prevent the pressure detonating from him. He ground his teeth together and gulped down his discontent.

"It's obvious the man gambled his salary in Vegas."

She turned off the stove, poured hot water in the mug and replaced the pot. A few jiggles of the teabag to extract full flavor, then she picked up the mug, nestling it between her palms. "You knew him that well, did you, Johnny?"

Score for her. "Never met the man."

"Then how—"

Point for him. "I know the guy who hired him."

"Willie."

"Yep."

"And what does that make Willie?"

He elevated his brow and allowed her to draw her own deductions.

"Primary gambler." Sounded very much like mamma's vice, she thought, sipping the tea.

"Bingo."

The delicate chamomile flavor warmed her throat, soothing. Mamma's penchant for gambling had been behind the inception of her wedding woes. She chanced a glance at Johnny. Would she ever have control of her life? Or would someone else always be grabbing the reins? Mamma. Michael Scott. Johnny.

Breath rustled from her lungs. For the time being, she'd best keep that profound thought to herself and avoid doing anything rash, which she might later regret.

"Want some tea?"

"No thanks"—he pushed himself off the crate— "unless this Mirabe ... whatever her name is left something to spike it with." He gave her a hopeful glance.

She lowered her lashes a fraction and shook her head.

"Ah huh." Johnny grabbed a huge bag of dog chow with the CRK logo emblazoned in red from the corner of the room and hoisted it over his shoulder. "Going to feed the dogs." At least he knew where he stood with them.

"How many did you say there are?" she asked, veering the conversation away from Mirabella.

"Half a dozen." He tilted his head, considering her a moment and then clicked his tongue, dismissing this whiz woman as a figment of her imagination; and relieved they were back to more practical matters.

"Pedigree?"

"All kinds. Dobermans, Great Danes, Chihuahuas."

"Who do they belong to? Clients?"

"Previous owner's pets." Johnny didn't expound that Willie's wife had left because he'd given more attention to the dogs than to her. His gambling addiction hadn't helped either. Blackjack, roulette, slot machines; you name it, Willie was on the frontlines calling the bets. Unfortunately, most missed the mark, and he'd run into a serious losing streak. Strapped for cash, he always looked for his next break to make a comeback.

When Johnny made him an offer on the Kennels, he'd jumped at it. Grabbed the money and relocated to L.A. to be closer to his ex in hopes of a reconciliation. He wanted to show her he was the man in charge.

Johnny pursed his lips. Were he and Sam heading down that same road? Their turbulent life whipped through his mind. A deep sigh erupted from his chest. Were men destined to always strive to show their women their better side? Couldn't they take them as they were?

To distance himself from the temptation of Vegas, Willie had opened a dog grooming salon cum limo service in Los Angeles, which had been pivotal in Johnny's pursuit of Sam on that fateful wedding day two years ago. After Johnny had picked up an unsuspecting Michael in the limo, he dropped him off at the Salon. While Willie kept him busy filling forms, thinking they were required for the marriage ceremony, Johnny had zipped off to church and to Sam.

When the dogs gatecrashed the nuptials, it had been a shocking surprise as much as it had been a rollicking stunt. Willie had been about to deliver them to the owners when

94

Michael confiscated the truck's keys and drove like a maniac to church.

The whole incident still brought an amused twitch to his mouth, and a flip to his heart. He'd put everything on the line that day to get to Samantha and make her his.

Johnny swerved a glance in her direction. Something about her rolly- polly condition had his insides turning to mush. He took a tentative step toward her, itching to haul her into his arms and devour her with kisses, satiating this hunger fueling his gut, never mind another part of his anatomy. Shifting his hand from the load on his shoulder, he adjusted his belt, easing tension. He groaned. After that fiasco they'd gone through to get hitched, he couldn't believe they weren't legal.

Yeah, he could empathize with Willie's predicament. Wasn't Johnny in a similar situation, except in reverse? He'd given Sam too much attention. Apparently she didn't want it, or him. While she planned ways to bolt, he plotted ways to keep her, at least 'til the baby arrived.

"There are no accounts?" She stared at him in disbelief. "No clients?" Plopping the empty teacup in the sink, she turned on the faucet full blast. "No paying customers?"

Johnny curbed his recollections. "Not yet." Adjusting the heavy load on his shoulder, he reluctantly tuned in to her tirade. "But we're okay with money. In fact, I have a surpri—"

She laughed, a brittle sound. "How you figure?"

"All's not always as it seems," he said, and then clamped his mouth shut.

"Best remember that, Johnny." Realizing the faucet was still running and the cup overflowing, she picked it up and rinsed it.

"Don't start with Mirabe ... bebe, again."

"She's not a figment of my imagination."

He pretended to be taken aback. "Did I say—"

"No." She plunked the mug on the dish rack. "But you thought it."

"So, now I can't think?"

She twisted the tap shut with force. "If it hadn't been for her, this place would still be a dump." She wiped her hands on the towel hanging from a nail on the wall. "Now, it's a clean dump."

"Samantha."

She cast him a wide-eyed gaze and smirky smile, but the sting of her words grazed him anyway. "What kind of biz sense is it to buy a business without product and without clients?"

A sudden gust of wind whirled against the window and the whole house rattled, intercepting his reply. Samantha shivered and rubbed her palms together to chase away the chill.

"That's going to change." He flexed his shoulder blades. Definitely a north wind blowing through their home, he thought.

"When?"

When you learn to trust me. Unconditionally, Samantha Belen.

"Soon."

"Sure, Johnny."

He raised his other hand and supported the weight on his shoulders. "Soon as I get that ad in the paper—"

"For the 'hired help wanted' you mentioned earlier?"

"Yeah." Finally, he heaved the satchel off his shoulder and plunked it on the floor at his feet. "Catch two birds—"

"Catch nothing, Belen," she bit back, her stance challenging even in her condition. "How'll you pay wages when you don't have enough—"

"Is that what you think, Sam?" Pain wrestled with anger inside him. Could he blame her? He thrust his fingers through his hair and down the back of his neck, easing a muscle knotting there. Would the stigma of his origin never leave him? Must he feel like a second-class citizen compared to Michael Scott and, worse still, Sam?

He glanced at his callused hands. Heck, he was proud of his heritage. He'd worked hard helping his folks till the land. After he'd saved enough cash, he flew overseas to good ol' USA and studied even harder, claiming his chance at a better life. Although he'd gotten a late start, he determined to make good at the bank, climb the ladder of success and help care for his folks and six siblings.

"That's not all I think, Johnny," Samantha said, softening her words.

"Dare I ask?" He squinted, studying her from head to toe.

She shrugged.

"I guess not," he muttered below his breath. Either she didn't hear him or didn't want to respond, for she grew quiet, scuffing the toe of her sneaker on the floor.

It hadn't been easy. He'd gone to school, worked at the bank and supplemented his meager salary by moonlighting as caddie for the rich and famous at the Bel Air Country Club. While he lugged their golf clubs around, they often peered down their socialite noses at him. With his pride trampled, but needing the cash, he tried to ignore that aspect of his job.

Then, one fateful day, he'd met Sam. She'd smiled, and he'd been lost. Everything and everyone else had taken a back seat. And now, it looked like he'd come full circle, knowing he had to seriously rethink his life.

"You think I can't provide adequately for you, Sam?"

"Yes, no ... uh ..." She scrubbed her hands on her hips. "Have I known any different, Johnny?" she asked, so quietly, he nearly missed it.

Yes, he wanted to shout. The first six months of their marriage he'd showered her with gifts, outings and dining with the social elite. Whatever she'd wanted, he'd given her. He'd wanted to show her a good time. Make her happy. Guess she'd forgotten.

He propped his hip against the windowsill and folded his arms across his chest. He'd waited for the perfect opportunity to tell her of his good fortune ... their golden ticket. Somehow, it hadn't arrived.

"You will," he murmured, his words so quiet, she had to strain to hear.

"Sure, Johnny." Samantha studied him from his tousled head to the mud-caked toes of his boots and avoided his searching gaze. Her shoulders sagged. How she wanted to believe him – believe in him – and prove her mother wrong.

During the first few months of their marriage, Johnny 'd given her the 'red carpet' treatment like he was king of the castle and she his queen; but soon after, things deteriorated financially for them. She hadn't seen any significant change in their life in almost two years. Her mother had noticed, too.

Sam thought he'd recklessly spent all his savings those first few months, leaving them with nothing for the future. Nevertheless, she'd wanted to stand by him no matter what until he made something of himself, of their life together. She sighed, the sound so deep, so intense it seemed to vibrate around her. Until now, he'd proved unable to sustain a regular job, and his pipe dreams seemed just that: puffs of air.

"What happened to your grand schemes of making good and helping your folks in Ireland?" Sam blurted, an accusatory tone in her voice.

"I was just thinking that very same thing." He chuckled, nearly flabbergasted. "Talk about mental telepathy."

That fueled her ire even more, and she rolled her eyes at the extra sensory perception notion.

"How're you going to do that when we're almost a family of three" –she stroked a hand across her swollen stomach— "and barely making ends meet?"

"And are we, Sam?" His voice soft, tender.

"What?"

"A family."

He brushed his gaze over her like a caress. Confused for a moment, she avoided giving him a straight answer. "Your folks, Johnny?"

"I've taken care of it." He'd been sending them a generous allowance since his windfall win two years ago, but he hadn't mentioned it to her. If he did now, she'd more than likely laugh in his face, not believing him, and accuse him of pipe dreaming again.

She slanted him a skeptical glance. "And how're we going to afford paying hired help?"

His heart lifted a fraction. She said *we*, so subconsciously she still thought of them as a unit. Johnny was clutching at straws. He wasn't ready to call it quits on his marriage, although at the back of his mind the possibility pestered him. He tightened his jaw. He might lose Sam, but he wasn't about to forfeit his child into the bargain.

"I'll come to some arrangement." He allowed his gaze to roam over her, top to toe, tripping over her big tummy. A nerve tapped his temple, and his heart cracked.

Curls that'd escaped the confines of her ponytail brushed her flushed cheeks, and Johnny wanted to cup her face in his hands. Swipe at the smudge on the tip of her nose with his thumb, and touch the spot with his mouth, working his way to her lips, tasting their moist softness … touching, caressing, loving her …

She licked her lips.

He drew in a sharp breath. She'd never looked more beautiful to him. Heat pulsed through his blood. He unfolded his arms, let them drop to his sides and flexed his fingers.

"A hired hand wouldn't much matter." He pushed away from the window ledge. "Would be manageable."

She tucked a golden wisp behind her ear and remained silent.

"Live in. Room and board. Work out something."

Her look of utter consternation cut him to the raw.

Faith.

He wanted her to believe in him. No matter the odds, they'd make it. He hoisted the bag of dog food back onto his shoulder, welcoming the heavy hit; kinda shook him from his melancholy mood.

"That's always your answer."

99

"No, it's not." He paused, debated, then, what the heck. "Maybe you don't listen, Sam."

"If I had listened—"

"To mamma?"

"I wouldn't have—"

"Married me?" His eyes darkened, his words ice.

"If you had to do over, would you have married me, Johnny?" She held her breath, her gaze clashing with his, her pulse stuttering.

"I ..." He stomped to the backdoor. "Gotta get those dogs fed."

Her heart squeezed blood, and perspiration oozed from her every pore. The 'illegally married' summons allowed him an easy exit. A wet drop slid between her breasts. Had he married her to cash in? She giggled, an empty sound.

"What's funny?" he tossed over his shoulder, pausing in stride.

Sam shook her head. That would explain his lack of motivation in holding down a job. Perhaps he imagined she'd tap into her bank account and bail them out. Her giggle turned into a strained sound. If he but knew the true state of her financial affairs, he'd think again.

"Samantha, there's something I've got to tell—"

"Sure, Johnny." She clenched her fists by her sides, bracing herself, thinking he was about to say he wanted out of the marriage.

"Soon 's I feed the dogs, we'll clear—" The sudden ringing of the doorbell eclipsed the rest of his words.

"That must be Mirabella," Sam murmured, thankful for the interruption.

Shaking his head, Johnny heavy stepped it to the front door and yanked it open. "Is Mirabella six feet two, about a hundred and seventy pounds and driving a banged pick-up?"

"No." Sam waddled after him.

"Special delivery for the lady of the house." The gangly teenager, his blond hair plastered to his forehead, leaped over puddles to the first step. In one bound, he took the remaining three steps and landed at her feet with a thud. "Pete at your service." He offered her a gift box.

Sam fluttered her lashes at Johnny. "Who?"

Johnny shrugged and set his mouth in a firm line.

"Secret admirer?" the boy suggested. At Johnny's scowl, he grabbed the tip he shoved at him and vaulted off the stairs.

"What a surprise." She untied the gold ribbon and opened the box. A dozen long-stemmed red roses nestled in the tissue paper. She peeked at her husband from beneath her lashes. "Johnny, you shouldn't ... we can't afford—"

"I didn't." He must be a dolt. He should've gotten her not only flowers but candy. Chocolate. Jewelry. Isn't that what women liked as peace offerings? A muscle pulsed near his jaw. Once, Sam had told him talking—communication between the sexes—was something women appreciated much more than presents.

Disappointment flitted across her features. "If you didn't, then who?"

He unclenched his teeth and a rush of air exploded from his lungs. Another black mark against him. He just couldn't win with her.

She held the blooms to her bosom and opened the card. "Michael Scott." She laughed.

Johnny's feet seemed set in cement, his neck muscles cording. "Couldn't wait to tell him your whereabouts, could you?"

"That's nonsense, and you know it." However, she didn't enlighten him. Annoyed with him, she let him steam a little. He'd soon figure out their present living quarters allowed for no communication with anyone.

She smelled the flowers. "Mmm, nice." Ignoring his dour look, she walked into the house, searching for a vase. "Wonder how he found me?"

Chapter Thirteen

Johnny slammed the door shut, nearly pulling it from its hinges, and marched through the onslaught of rain to the kennels. He'd like nothing better than to get his hands around that buffoon's neck. For that reason, he welcomed the icy pellets smacking his face. They cooled him down.

Of course, Sam couldn't have notified Michael. Had no phone and no time to do it. But someone had, and he'd like to get his hands on that person.

That unleashed a blue streak of blarney from his mouth, but the dogs barking and the rain pinging on the tin roof of their shelter made them inaudible. Amazing how these animals sensed his conflicting emotions and looked up at him with doleful faces.

"What d'you think I should do?" He sank down on his haunches and ruffled their ears.

The six dogs leaped at him, nearly knocking him into the mud.

"Whoa!" He laughed, a deep hearty sound that diffused tension from his body. A gust of wind snatched the sound from him, leaving him to suck in a mouthful of air.

Woof! Woof!

"You telling me I should play along?" He swayed, trying to maintain his balance while they slurped at him and brushed against his legs. "I'm not good at that, especially when it comes to that caffler." A deep frown folded his forehead, and he set his mouth in a tight line.

A chihuahua snarled. It was so comical, it made him chuckle.

"Go along with the gag until I'm ready to make my move. Think that might work?" His troupe yelped enthusiastic agreement. "Could backfire though." He patted a cocker spaniel on the head. "Just about everything I've tried has turned out a disaster." The canine mentors panted, tongues lolling and tails wagging. "That means you're on my side, fellas." He jumped up, grabbed the feedbag and filled another container. "Yeah. Us outcasts gotta stick together."

Rain fell through the gouges in the roof and filled the water bowls, the spray misting his face. "Mmm, fresh." He glanced at the dogs wolfing down their lunch. Outcasts, right on target. These friendly brutes had been abandoned by Willie's hired hand, and the coward fled to avoid a confrontation with Johnny. And what consequences followed.

In town earlier that morning, Johnny 'd learned someone from the local tavern had fed them until he arrived. Then, it hit his noggin. He felt like the dogs. His skin bristled. An outsider in his own home, his own marriage, with his own wife. "Hang in there, pups. Things are so far down, they can only go up." The big question … when?

Did Michael Scott have another slick trick up his sleeve to woo his wife? Johnny 'd be a puppet on a string if he rolled over and played dead. A resounding bark made him smile. He patted their backs and they returned to crunching canine chow. "You wouldn't either, I take it."

He pushed a wet lock off his brow and rubbed his nape. "How much could a man take seeing another guy make a play for his wife, virtually under his nose?" He inhaled, filling his lungs with the rain fresh air. On the exhale, the air pressure exploded from him like a grenade.

Until the baby came, he'd have to walk a fine line. He'd do nothing to jeopardize either of them. And that included having his nose rubbed in Michael's preening antics. On the other hand, he could cut him a right hook on the jaw and be done with it. But Samantha was a cream puff when it came to the underdog, and that 'd only pave the way for her sympathies to veer toward Scott.

If pushed to his limit, Johnny could seek refuge in isolation. Walk out, and Sam could make her choice. He tightened his belly, his muscles steel. Could he accept her decision?

The answer eluded him as he trudged through the muck to the house. He stomped his feet on the porch mat, shoved the door open, and let it slam behind him. Pulling off his boots, he set them in the corner by the door. Thick woolen socks covered his feet. He shrugged from his raingear and hung it on the hook on the wall beside the walnut framed mirror.

He walked down the hall, shaking excess water off his hair like a shaggy dog and chuckled. When he glanced up, he slammed into Samantha standing in the kitchen doorway with a dented paint can in her hands, red roses spilling over the rim.

So much for his good intentions.

Scarlet petals brushed her chin, and she breathed in their scent. Amusement twitched her bottom lip.

Johnny grinned. A fragile thread of sweet memories passed between them. His heart maneuvered a triple leap in his chest, but bitterness sheathed his tongue. "Need help with those?"

She lowered her lashes, camouflaging the fleeting memories mirrored in her eyes. "No, thank you."

"Where you going with them?"

"Bedroom."

Astounded, he plunged a hand through his wet hair, lifting it off his forehead—a preventive measure so as not to smash his fist into the wall. She was actually going to put those—he swallowed the X-rated adjectives stinging his tongue—flowers in their bedroom.

Breath sizzled between his teeth. He counted to three. Another approach, a smarter way; a little psychology might do the trick. That had been his best subject in college. He twisted his lips in a humorless line. How'd he ended up a bank teller, and now running dog kennels? It's not like he had to do this. Like he had to pretend to be a poor man. He was a wealthy man. Beyond everyday dreams. All he had to do was mention that to Sam. He brushed a hand across his eyes. And what?

She'd fall into his arms because he could provide her the life she'd been accustomed to or because he was the love of her life? A rough sound grazed his tight lips.

She gave him an odd look.

He was playing a long shot. His marriage, his life, his future. "You're actually going to put them in our bedroom?"

"Sure. Why not?" She flicked the blooms with her fingers. "It isn't really a bedroom. More a storage area to stash our sleeping bags and your camp gear."

His gaze skipped to the bed, then at her. Although revamped with a granny quilt and matching pillows … at least it wasn't pink, he thought in a black mood … it was doubtful they'd be sharing it any time soon.

"Well then, I know the perfect spot for it."

Showtime.

Johnny was about to put on the performance of his life.

"You do?" she asked, a note of surprise in her voice.

"Sure thing."

"Sure thing, indeed." She buried her face in the petals and peeked at him from between them. "Is the phone working, yet?"

"Yeah. Why?"

She seemed to slide past him, even with her roly-poly frame, her head held high. "I'd like to thank Michael for being so thoughtful."

A myriad of emotions rough-housed through him. Anger, disbelief, disappointment, pain and back to anger. When pigs fly ... when hell freezes over ... when— Abruptly, he banished the combative words from his mind. *Psychology, remember, Belen*. A grin split his lips. "Good idea."

"What?" Her head shot up.

"Good idea," he repeated in a nonchalant manner. "I'll even dial the number for you if you want." Stomping two steps closer, he took the can from her hands. "I'll put these in that special spot for you." A heavy beat. "In our bedroom."

Johnny strode past her into the bedroom and made a beeline for the window. Raising it, he tossed the bouquet with can, out. The force of the wind swallowed them up.

"No." Samantha stood in the doorway.

"Yes." He swiped his palms together. End of that story. Just blew his psychology theory to smithereens. He shrugged, satisfied. There was something to be said for quick action and instant gratification. "So long, bimbo man." He began to push the window closed, but a fierce undercurrent hurled one scarlet bloom back into the room. He felt a little sheepish, but enough was enough. Psychology just didn't go well with emotion. His temper had been on the climb since that morning, although it had abated some now. The knot in his gut loosened, and he breathed easier.

"That was a mean thing to do, Johnny."

"Wasn't it," he said, voice unflinching.

Sam shoved past him and squinted through rivulets of rain rolling down the windowpane at the flowers massacred by the storm. When she turned, she spied the abandoned rose at her feet. Her eyes blazed a warning, but Johnny swept it up with one motion, ready to squash it in his fist. She snatched it from his hand and trailed the smooth petals along her cheek.

He felt like she'd slugged him in the solar plexus. "Means that much to you?"

"Yes." But her gaze didn't quite meet the fury in his.

"Sleep with it under your pillow for all I care." He stalked past her to the living room, doubts plaguing his mind and turning his heart to mincemeat.

"I intend to," she bit back, but her voice wobbled.

Chapter Fourteen

Johnny crouched before the hearth and stirred the embers with a stick. Unlike his marriage to Sam, they came to life, bursting into flame. A sobering thought smacked him. Maybe he'd made a mistake marrying Sam. Maybe she'd married him to get back at her mother for pushing her at Scott. Maybe she now realized she'd married the wrong man. The thoughts bombarded his brain, lacerating his innards.

Maybe.

Maybe isn't bang on, Belen. Get facts. Face facts.

Sam still saw him as an ordinary guy from the wrong side of town. When Michael Scott, with mamma's blessing, rode up in his white charger ... er ... Lotus, would she fly the coop?

His heart sank.

Definitely. In three months he intended to get the facts. All of them.

Samantha held the limp rose in her hand and trudged from the bedroom to the hallway. A pause, and she took several more steps to the living room, the warmth from the blaze in the hearth inviting.

Johnny sat on his haunches, adding more fuel to the fire, his shirt stretching taut across his back. Emotion flared inside her.

She imagined feeling the firmness of his muscles beneath her fingers, his heat, sweat... caressing him. She used to do that. A lifetime ago.

She blinked against the sting of tears in her eyes. *What happened Johnny? What happened to us?*

Maybe he'd only married her to get one over on Michael Scott. And if that were true, maybe she'd made a big blunder in marrying Johnny. Maybe it had to do with her money. Maybe Johnny was a counterfeit masquerading as a sweet-talking bank teller turned kennel keeper. She couldn't stomach that. Maybe there was no chance for them. Why else did he look like he was ready to split in three months? He'd admitted as much.

She placed a fist to her mouth, swallowing a whimper. Maybe there was someone else not so pregnant, not so fat and not so grumpy that he had his eye on. *He's here with you, isn't he?* The thought flashed through her brain. Yeah, but was it for her or for his baby? She placed a protective hand over her belly.

Doubts tormented her mind. She needed assurance. Reassurance. No maybes. In three months, the uncertainties would be gone. She'd be sure then. If forced to, she'd fight like a tigress for her child. A moan skimmed her lips, and she swiped a tear slipping from the corner of her eye.

"Anything wrong?" Johnny hauled himself up and studied her beneath his furrowed brow. He'd felt her presence in the room even before he turned to look at her. Smelled her delicate rose scent. And he'd also sensed her turmoil. Because it matched his own.

She shook her head.

The flames in the grate cast a gleam of light on the curve of her cheek and highlights in her hair.

She looked so forlorn, he wanted to take her in his arms and bury his face in the nape of her neck. Feel her, touch her, taste ... He slammed the brakes on the direction of his thoughts. She was probably missing rich boy Scott. He snapped the stick in his hand in half and tossed it in the fire.

"The baby kicked." A tremulous smile touched her lips, and she spanned her fingers across her abdomen.

"No kiddin'." He stepped beside her and covered her hand with his.

"Feel her?"

"Yeah." A lump lodged in his throat, and he squeezed her fingers. "Sure it's a her?"

"A feeling. A hunch."

"Boy, girl. Doesn't matter."

"Sure?" she whispered.

"Yeah." There was that lump again, constricting his breathing. He feigned a cough to cover the awkward moment. "Yeah."

Samantha focused on his hand warming hers, and shyness swept over her. "Me, too."

Seconds ticked by.

Finally, Samantha glanced up and caught his shadowed gaze. High voltage charged between them. She lowered her lashes, concealing her own rising heat. He brushed her hand with his thumb. The gentle motion soothed; she wanted to curve into him. Have him hold her closer, caress ... the erotic images sensitized her nerves.

He tightened his fingers over hers, raised his other hand and cupped her cheek. "Look at me, Sam."

Slowly, she lifted her lashes. The hunger in his gaze took her breath away, and her heart leaped.

"Sam ..." He drew her closer and lowered his head.

The sudden ringing of the telephone shattered the intimate moment between them.

Johnny paused a feather breadth from her mouth.

Samantha licked her lips, and a tremor rippled through her. And it had nothing to do with the desire that'd flamed between them a sec ago.

110

"Bad timing." He attempted a joke, brushing her lips with his thumb.

She nodded and remained spot on while he grabbed the cellular from the mantel above the fireplace. He placed it to his ear and his face clouded. A nerve assaulted his jaw.

Taciturn, he plopped the phone in her hand and stepped away, staring out the window.

"Johnny?" Cold air slammed them apart, and she shivered, rubbing her arms to calm the chills. "Who is it?"

Chapter Fifteen

"Your mother."

Sam held the phone slightly away from her ear; her mother's excited voice crackled over the airwaves and irritated her eardrum.

"What?!" She glanced at Johnny's rigid back. "Mother, you didn't—" She rolled her eyes heavenward. "How?" A silent beat. "Impossible."

Samantha gripped the receiver between her fingers like she wanted to snap it in half. "You're telling me the kennel man, Willie, was at the bank and blabbed?"

While her mother chattered away, she lumbered across the living room and sank on the rocker. "It's not his business where Johnny and I—"

Johnny turned around, tuning in.

"He was just making conversation." She switched the phone to her other ear. "You happened to be there and overheard—"

Johnny cocked an eyebrow.

"Yes, I got the flowers." This almost a reluctant whisper but Johnny heard her.

"Oh, mother, you didn't." Sam watched Johnny stalk from the room and her heart sank. "All right, good-bye, mother."

The echo of the disconnected line reverberated in her ear, and she pressed the mobile to her forehead. "What have you done, mother?" She sighed, the sound fluttering from deep inside her. Her mother meant well, but she definitely had her own agenda, which had caused enough damage to the family all ready. Especially to her and Johnny.

The thread holding them together was fraying, but with mamma's butting in, it could snap any minute. Three months from now, Samantha doubted she'd still be Mrs. J. Belen. Despair welled up inside her, and she hiccuped on a sob. A deep breath to gain control, and she pushed herself up from the chair and set the phone back on the mantelshelf.

She squared her shoulders and, like an oversized duck, marched into the kitchen. "Mother said hi."

"No, she didn't." Johnny turned from the sink, a potato in one hand and a peeler in the other.

"Okay." Sam tapped her foot on the floor. "She was so excited, she forgot."

"Excited about what?"

She mocked a cough. "A visitor."

"Let me guess."

"No, don't."

"I'm right."

Sam's foot tapping turned to a stomp. "You're being unreasonable."

"No." He shook his head and attacked another potato with the peeler.

"Yes."

"Is it unreasonable for a man to want privacy with his wife?" He tossed the spud in the sink and drilled her with a rock brown gaze. "Even if it's a temporary arrangement?"

"This is not privacy." She held his gaze. "This is in the middle of nowhere, an isolated—"

"It's on the map."

"Seen with a magnifying glass."

"Thought the small-town setting would be good for us," he said, half- heartedly.

A sound, not quite a chortle, bounced from her mouth. "I feel locked up, especially with the storm raging outside."

"How was I to know we'd be caught in it?"

"You're supposed to," she said, a quiver in her voice.

He elevated both eyebrows heavenward. "So, now I'm supposed to have super powers and predict—"

"Oh, Johnny." She waddled over and wrapped her arms around his waist, resting her head on his shoulder.

"Where did we get our wires crossed?" He rubbed the top of her head with his chin.

"I don't know." She turned in his embrace and peeked at him from beneath her lashes. "Maybe we should go dancing?"

"Dancing?" He chuckled, and waltzed her once around the kitchen still clutching the peeler between his fingers. "That's as much boogieing I've got time for, not with trying to make a go of this place and—"

"Make time, Johnny," she whispered.

He stroked her arms with the back of his fingers. "I will Sam, soon as the kennels start turning a profit."

"Shouldn't they already be doing that?"

"A set-back's all, Sam."

"You mean another one in a series of—"

"Enough." He scowled, and dropped his hands to his sides.

"Huh!" She stepped back, considered him, and softened her words. "Afterward we can go for pizza ... have some fun." She wrinkled her nose. "There must be some entertainment nearby, especially so close to Vegas."

"You want more action? City lights, city glitz?"

"What's wrong with that?" A chill frosted her skin and it had nothing to do with the weather.

"Not a thing, Sam." He was quiet for a moment, and then added, "Action on the home front is ... er ... fun too."

114

"You saying I haven't been a good wife to you, Belen?"

"Stop shoving words down my throat, Samantha."

She pinched the bridge of her nose, and then lifted her head, pinning him with a clear gaze. "Going out on the town is also part of the deal."

"Don't I know it," he muttered the words below his breath.

"Okay, then you'll go?"

"Where?"

"Boogie-woogying." She grinned, and wiggling her fingers, tickled him.

"Hey," he chuckled and stepped back, scratching his head with the butt of the peeler. "Sure thing, Sam. Soon as this place starts—"

"You've got your priorities screwed around," she blurted.

"You complaining? You think I haven't been a good husband to you, Samantha?"

She sighed. "Must you always twist what I say, Johnny?"

"*Moi?*" He pointed to himself in mock innocence. "I read you loud and clear." He took a bow, sweeping his arm upward. "Gallivanting around the city is what the lady ordered. And what the lady wants, she gets."

"From the right man," she murmured without thinking, resentment bubbling inside her. She tossed her head back. And he could make of that what he wanted. Gosh, but he got her riled, he did.

Riled?

Did she actually think that? She definitely had to get to the city soon.

"Let me guess," he bit out. "Michael Scott."

A telling moment crackled between them.

Samantha gaped at him and then flounced from the room as best as she could. You're wrong, Johnny, she wanted to shout, but bit her tongue to stay the words. Perhaps these verbal hits were his way of signaling he wanted out of the marriage.

Waddling to the bedroom window, she pressed her forehead against the pane, cold seeping into her skin. "What happened to

115

forever, Johnny?" Her breath clouded the pane, and she lifted her head, drawing a love heart through the mist with a shaky finger. She scribbled S and J in the center. When it blurred before her eyes, she swiped at it with her fist.

A deep sigh, and she walked to the bed and sank on the edge, the mattress depressing beneath her weight. She kicked off her running shoes. After she fluffed the pillows, she lay down and pulled the granny quilt up to her chin. She stared up at the ceiling and covered her eyes with her arm.

Rain hip-hopped on the roof.

Sleep. Oblivion was what she wanted, at least for a little while.

Chapter Sixteen

Samantha was ready to holler at the insistent pounding prodding her awake just moments later. The rapping on the door echoed through the house, and then stopped.

She struggled out of bed, slipped her feet into her sneakers and shuffled from the room. In the hallway, she paused to listen. The wind's ferocity had slowed down. The house was so quiet.

Eerie.

Where was Johnny?

She took a deep breath, exhaled and plodded to the front door. When she opened it, a smile lit her heart. "Mirabella." Samantha giggled. "Hey, you weren't a figment of my imagination." Then, she realized how rude that might sound. "Oh, I'm sorry, I didn't mean it like that."

"It's all right, dearie." Mirabella grinned, blinking her ocean green eyes. "People tend to think that of us ... er ... *me* for some reason." She juggled the parcel in her arms, her grin widening, her teeth sparkling white. "I assure you we ... er ... *I* am real."

Enraptured by her dazzling smile, Sam stood speechless for a sec, and then remembered her manners. "Would you like to come in?"

"Thank you. Can't. On my way to work." She adjusted the

square spectacles on her nose. "But I did want to drop off this housewarming gift." Mirabella pushed the pink parcel in her hands.

She opened the box. "Oh my, a pink teapot."

"Glad you like it," Mirabella said, her lips lifting at the corners. "Shouldn't clash with your furnishings."

"No indeed." Samantha chuckled her thank you and stared at her. A fleeting memory teased her mind, and she wrinkled her brow. The woman reminded her of someone, something but she couldn't quite grasp it.

Frustrating.

"Don't mention it. 'Tis a pleasure. I have plenty." Mirabella stomped her galoshes on the mat and curved her mouth into that knock-out smile. "Have to fly, now." She winked. "Duty calls."

Before Samantha uttered another word, Mirabella glided down the steps and along the path. Samantha gaped after her.

A moment of mesmerized silence, then she refocused and called,

"Where do you work, Mirabella?" Just as the query left her lips, she remembered Mirabella had previously mentioned the local Tavern…

"Everywhere dear." She giggled as a gust of wind twirled her around. "Right now, at the Tavern. Bring that husband of yours by sometime." In a twinkling, she disappeared in the mist.

Sam squinted, but she was gone. Pensive, she closed the door and hugged the teapot to her breast. She doubted she and Johnny would be on good speaking terms, let alone go on a date to the local tavern.

A fresh cup of tea would do wonders for her melancholy mood though. She walked to the kitchen, and an unbidden chuckle bobbled from her mouth. At this rate, she'd be the best tea brewer in town. She set the teapot on the counter, filled the kettle with water from the faucet and placed it on the stove to boil. They really must get more bottled water, she thought as she turned on the element. She kicked the crate against the wall and sat, stretching her legs out in front of her.

Quietness vibrated around her. She leaned her head against the wall, closed her eyes and stroked her full stomach with her fingers. "Baby mine, any words of wisdom for your mamma?" She curved her lips in a tender smile. A moment later, her mouth drooped at the corners. "And your poppa?" She felt the child move inside her and her heart lifted. Come what may, she'd do right by her baby.

Quiet moments ticked by.

When steam rose from the kettle, she shuffled to the stove and turned it off. She poured hot water in the teapot, opened the drawer by the sink, took a teabag and plunked it in the liquid. Scent of apple blossoms with a hint of cinnamon permeated the room. She breathed in deeply. Mmm, bliss. She grabbed a mug from the cupboard, filled it with brew and carried it to the table. As she set the teapot beside it, she glimpsed a note propped against the salt and peppershakers.

She unfolded the scrap of paper and read, "Gone to town to place the ad. Back before sundown. Johnny."

His curt words shimmied up her spine and nicked a nerve. She waggled her shoulders, squared her chin and crumpled the note in her hand. Picking up the mug, she marched to the living room and tossed the wad of paper in the fireplace. "I'll not let you ruin another moment of my life, Johnny Belen."

She sank in the rocker and, cradling the mug in her hands, rocked, finding the gentle rhythm comforting.

What of his life? A still small voice penetrated her thoughts.

She rocked faster and blew on the steaming tea to cool it. She was entitled to ask for better, wasn't she? After all, she worked hard to make the marriage work.

Oh? the voice prodded.

It did get tiresome waiting and waiting for things to be better, she thought.

Maybe Johnny's tired too, the voice persisted. *His desire is to keep you in the style you've been accustomed.*

"Well, nobody asked him to," she murmured to no one in particular.

Nobody asked, the voice whispered, *but someone expected, Samantha. Mamma. Must I continue?*

"No." Samantha surprised herself by answering back aloud.

It wasn't like she had to eat from gold plates and drink from matching goblets. Just to live a more comfortable … mmm … exciting life. It wasn't only for herself, it was for her baby too. Their baby.

Don't you think Johnny would like some comforts too? the quiet voice flashed through her mind, nicking her heart.

"Fine." she said, surprised at the sudden prickling all over her body.

After a moment, she realized how ridiculous she must appear, rocking in the chair with a mug of tea in her hands and talking to herself. She raised the cup to her mouth and sipped the warm brew. Sweet herbal taste slid down her throat, soothing her ruffled nerves. Johnny could live the life he wanted. So could she. She took two more mouthfuls, swallowed and shut her eyes. Perhaps their lives could no longer connect.

Tsk! Tsk! the voice tickled her thoughts … her heart.

"Okay, point taken." She set the half-filled mug on the window ledge, pulled the elastic from her ponytail and wove her fingers through her hair. "Help please, Lord," she whispered, leaning her head back against the cushions.

I just did.

Samantha missed that, too busy thinking of what else she could do to inspire Johnny to change. "I don't know what to do."

You will.

The sudden pounding on the door had her nearly jumping from the chair. "Mirabella." She took a calming breath. "To the rescue, again."

Chapter Seventeen

Samantha trudged to the front door feeling like leaden weights were clamped around her ankles. When she clicked it open, she stumbled back a pace, her hand fluttering to her throat.

"Hello, gorgeous!"

"Mi-Michael, what are you doing he-here?"

He handed her a gold box of chocolates, a saucy grin on his mouth. "I was in the neighborhood and thought I'd come by to say hello."

She raised her eyebrows. "Hardly your hangout."

"Actually," –he brushed imaginary lint off the breast pocket of his sports jacket— "I was at a bankers convention in Vegas and took a detour to check the countryside." He seemed immune to the wind buffeting him and billowing his blazer.

"Your idea of course?"

He avoided her gaze. "Your mother wanted to know how you were, so I decided to whip by here."

"Michael, I just talked with mother this morning," she said. "As you can see, I'm fine. Anything else?"

He stroked a washed-out blonde brow with his manicured index finger and glanced about, his face mirroring his distaste.

"I'm well, Michael." She repeated as if to convince more herself than him.

"I can see." He kept looking down at her, a smile stretching his lips in a thin line. "I'm staying a few extra days to rest up and look around."

"Would you like to start with the house?" She stepped aside and gripped the doorknob. "Then, you'd really have something to report to mamma." But she didn't care. She'd come through this if it was the last thing she did.

"Oh yeah." He leaped through the front door. In his haste, he missed his footing and would've fallen flat on his face if she hadn't grabbed him by his lapels.

"Oops!" He chuckled and leaned into her to regain his balance. "Mmm, you smell nice."

She pushed at him.

"I could get used to this, Samantha." Instead of taking the hint and letting go, he wrapped his arms around her.

"You mean living in this place?" She pretended not to understand his innuendo.

He paled at the possibility.

She laughed and smartly disengaged herself from his hold.

"And neither should you," he murmured, stroking her shoulder. "I could provide so much more—"

"Brr," she said, nixing his train of thought. "It's cold here." She hurried away, and he trotted after her.

"The battle's not over 'til I get what I want."

"By fair means or foul?" She tossed him a curious glance over her shoulder. "But what war are we talking about?"

Michael had the grace to blush.

She wouldn't leave well enough alone. "Yours, mother's or both?"

Michael raised his hand in a peaceful gesture. "I'll never tell." He clucked his tongue and drew closer. "But you'd be better off—"

"Michael." Her tone alone stopped him in his tracks.

She may be going through marital problems with Johnny, but she'd not have Michael butting his nose in it. A niggle pestered her mind. What if he was right? What if mother was right? What if she was fooling herself with Johnny? Well, she had three months to find out, and she'd put them to good use. Until then, she'd play hostess — she hadn't forgotten the social graces yet, even in this dismal place — to Michael Scott ... an old family friend ... her childhood ballet partner ... an ex-fiancé — and to whoever else entered this house. Temporary home, she reminded herself.

"Okay, Samantha." He was smart enough to know when to change the subject. "Show me this monstrosity."

She frowned, about to blast him again, then broke out laughing. "Very well. Come along, then."

Michael examined the house in his upper crust way like he gutted a loan application at the bank. She couldn't help grinning.

When the tour took them to the kitchen, she invited him to sit on the apple crate. His look of utter dismay had her breaking up in a fit of giggles. "If it can carry my weight, it can carry yours." She placed the box of chocolates on the table and unraveled the ribbon.

"You don't actually sit on that piece of wood in your condition?"

"More of a squat—"

"You deserve soft velvet ... ahem ... for your posterior and cushions to prop up your feet," he rambled on, missing her attempt at a joke.

"Sounds very nice," she agreed. "Now sit, Michael."

"Okay, Samantha." Gingerly, he lowered himself until his behind brushed the wood, then he jumped up like a toad.

Laughter bubbled inside her, but she pressed her mouth closed, containing her mirth. She folded her arms across her bosom, trying to ignore the amused twitch at the corner of her lip.

He lowered himself back down and shifted for a better sitting, and the box wobbled. Grabbing onto the table to prevent himself from falling, his abrupt movement almost tipped the crate over. When it stayed upright, he breathed a sigh of relief. "I don't want to upset you or your furniture."

She did laugh then. "Nice of you." Opening his gift, she sampled a chocolate truffle. "Mmm, this is good." She rolled her eyes in appreciation and offered him the box. When he declined, she popped the remainder of the sweet in her mouth, chewed and swallowed. "You want some tea?"

"Only if you go with it?"

"Michael," she said, her tone stern, although there was an underlining lilt in her voice. What woman didn't like flattery? *Hmm,* she thought, then dismissed the foolishness.

"Okay," he mouthed, careful to avoid any unnecessary movement.

"You don't mind roughing it a bit, do you?" She nipped the amusement teasing her bottom lip, handed him a mug of brew and sat on the crate opposite him.

"Not if I can be near you." He looked at her over the mug's rim with his pallid gaze, gulped a mouthful, and then coughed, spewing tea.

As fast as she could, she got to her feet and pounded his back. "You, okay?"

"Y-y-yes, he stammered, his eyes watering. "S-s-stop h-h-hitting me."

She snatched a paper towel from the stack on the table, blotted the spray from her clothes and the table.

"So-orry about that, Sam. Went down the wrong way." He swept up a napkin to help her and bumped his mug with his elbow, nearly tipping it.

"No, don't … help." She grabbed for the cup and Michael pulled his arm back, his fingers brushing her hand. At the same instant, she jerked her hand away and placed the cup on the table several inches from him.

Not missing her maneuver, his eyes darkened for a fleeting second, then he flashed her his even toothed smile. "Thanks."

She refilled his mug and took her seat, waving her hand about the room. "Not your style this, mmm?"

Affronted, he blurted, "It certainly is not." Methodically, he lifted the cup, sipped and gulped. "And it certainly is not yours, either." He set the mug down with the utmost care as not to jostle the contents. "However, it'll be an unexpected distraction for what I have in mind."

"What's that?"

"I don't want to bore you with details." He walked his fingers toward hers, and surreptitiously she dropped her hand to her lap. "A beautiful woman like you should not be concerned with business matters." He peered at her from beneath his ashen lashes. "You should be draped on a man's arm, enhancing his home, warming his b—"

At her frown, he amended, "Decorating his—"

Samantha burst out laughing. He was serious.

"What's funny?"

"You."

"I'll take that as a compliment."

"Okay." He would, she thought.

He reversed his fingers and slid his index finger down the side of the mug. "I've a few weeks off and I'm going to research human habitats and habits."

She swallowed the mirth bubbling to burst from her again.

"See how some can actually stand living in a hove—" Abruptly he stopped, thinking better of his choice of words.

Hovel, she finished for him, but didn't voice it.

"You be sure to have a good time jetting around the globe."

"I've done that for the last two years." He paused to let his words sink in. "This time 'round I'm thinking of somewhere closer to home."

"How close?" She squinted at him, a sliver of suspicion stabbing.

"I'd like to see more of the Las Vegas territory … Henderson, Green Valley … Paradise …" He crossed one leg over the other and leaned back, but remembering he was balancing precariously on a box, quickly righted himself. A sigh of relief blew from his mouth.

Samantha hid a smile behind her hand.

"We're thinking of expanding, maybe building," he announced, his chest puffing with self-importance. "In fact, I've heard the city of Henderson's got its eye on this area for future development."

"You want to bulldoze ahead, don't you?" She chuckled. "With any potential high profit investments."

"Any and all … among other things." His gaze steady on her face.

"Better get started," she advised. "It'll be nightfall soon."

"Do you know where I might book a room for the night?" he asked. "I'm low on gas. Won't even make it to the I-15 Primm Valley casino pumps before heading back to Vegas."

She popped a chocolate caramel in her mouth and shook her head.

"I'd even work for my room and board," he joked. "Hardly."

"Part of the adventure you had in mind, Michael?" she asked, her words muffled by the chewy sweet in her mouth.

"Now that you mention it, might be worth the toil and trouble."

"Really?"

"Pays to know those I might do business with. Gives me the edge … inside info."

"Oh Michael, there's more to life than money."

It was his turn to look dumbfounded.

"Love, a family."

"Like yours?"

Samantha could feel the red hot-heat spiraling inside her but checked it just in time. "What's wrong with my life? I like it just fine." She did, didn't she?

126

"You mean you like going from riches to rags right after saying, 'I do?'"

"We're hardly that." But her heart twisted. Day by day they seemed to be getting closer to the penury Michael described. And yet, she sensed Johnny'd been trying to tell her something. She didn't know what, and doubted it would even matter to them as a couple. Fiddling with the candy box ribbon, she belted back a sob together with the caramel.

"Of course not." He rapped his knuckles on the crate beneath him. "Worse."

"That's enough, Michael." She slid the gift box away from her and pushed herself up from the crate. "Well, say hello to mother when you see her."

"Why don't you come back with me and say hi yourself?"

"No can do."

"You're shackled to this wretched place and it's barely habitable."

And just to prove his point, a gust of wind slammed against the house, rattling the windows.

Michael choked the mug between his fingers, his features hinting a grey pallor.

"Glad to be inside this crude shelter, mmm?" Samantha lifted her shapely brow, raised her cup and took a sip of tea.

Michael inclined his head, sitting ramrod straight and not moving.

Mirth teased her mouth, but she bit it away. Although Mirabella's sweep cleaned the place, repaired the furniture and revamped the stove, Michael's words hit bull's-eye. The place needed a major overhaul. And that took money. Plenty of it.

Sighing, she set the cup on the table and flicked a loose curl off her forehead. "Johnny's gone to town to advertise for a hired hand."

"Good luck."

"What's that supposed to mean?" she asked, pressing her hand to the small of her back.

"Seems everyone prefers work in Vegas." He uncrossed his legs and the sudden motion made him totter on the crate. "Oops!" He let go of the mug and slammed his hands on the table. "More tips 'n thrills in glitz city."

She chuckled. "Steady there, Michael."

"I had to wait for hours for this car rental," he grumbled as if she hadn't spoken. "Some rodeo event going on … hotels booked … and—"

"This is not Las Vegas. This is Goodsprings, Nevada."

"Near enough on the outskirts" –he picked up the mug and sniffed the peach-flavored tea— "for a good investment, even with a start-up population of only two hundred and thirty-two … thirty-four with you two."

"Why Michael, you surprise me."

He nodded, preening.

"You've jumped-started your research on how the other half lives."

He laughed and nearly spilled the brew over himself. Samantha handed him another napkin and he dabbed liquid from the table.

"Always like to be a step ahead of my competition." He took several small sips, emptied the cup and held it out to her. "A surer bet that way." A nerve ticked at the corner of his mouth. "Smarter … safer too."

"Sure." She sidestepped him and set the cup in the sink.

"Mind if I use your phone?" He stood up, stretched and wiggled his shoulders. "Left my cell in the car." He rotated his neck. "I'd like to engage the rental company to find me lodging for the night."

While Michael talked on the telephone, Samantha washed the mugs, her imagination on the move. For all his apparent naiveté, Michael had an endearing quality about him. And his klutziness hid a keen business mind. She wiped the counter with a damp rag, opened the cupboard beneath the sink and tossed it in the plastic tray.

Could she make use of his business skills in some way in exchange for— She got stumped on that one; she'd think of something. She shut the cupboard door with the toe of her sneaker and stared out the window. For certain the kennels had to start paying, or they'd be out on their ear.

Although, Johnny had assured her all was well ... she crinkled her brow ... she couldn't see how. The struggle to meet monthly payments had maxed out. She'd better take a hand in improving their meager income, especially now with baby on the way. Johnny wouldn't like it, but she eased her conscience by telling herself it would only be for a short while. By then, she'd have a better idea how things stood between them. She licked her lips, possibilities whirling through her mind.

"How'd it go?" she asked when Michael ambled back to the kitchen. "Got something?"

"Nope." He plunked down on the crate and slouched across the table.

"Money can't buy what's unavailable." She rubbed her hands together, and then, realizing what she was doing, stopped. "Cheer up."

"I thought it 'd be fun to 'rough it' with the rest of them for a while."

"Them?"

"The local yokels—" he bit the rest of his words off, thinking he may have put his foot in the mix. "Not you of course, Samantha." A scowl folded his forehead. "But the Irishman would certainly fit—"

At the warning of her uplifted brow, he was quick to add, "I'd have something to tell dad. Something to make him think more of m—" He shrugged, slamming his mouth shut and breaking off his confession.

Samantha tilted her head and considered him for a moment.

129

"Uh, there might be a place where you can start." She smoothed creases from the front of her sweatshirt with her fingertips.

"Where?" He straightened like an eager teenager about to get the car keys. "Hope it's near here. I'd want to keep an eye on you."

"It's closer than you think and … uh … rougher living too."

He waited in a half questioning, half hopeful mode.

She took a deep breath and expelled it in a rush. "Right here."

"W-w-with that red-haired Irishman you married?" he sputtered.

"Of course." She gave him a bright smile. "If what you say is true, then you're the only one available for hire."

"I'd do it for you, Samantha."

"Don't you want to know what your duties are?"

"So long as I can be near you, I can tackle anything."

"I wouldn't be too sure, Michael. However, if it's information about the locals you want, you've aced it from here."

He pushed himself up, took a step closer and placed his hands on her shoulders. "Then will you come home, Samantha?"

Samantha glanced down at her mud stained sneakers, wondering where her home truly was. Just then, a footstep sounded from behind Michael, and her head shot up.

"She is home."

Chapter Eighteen

Johnny burst into the kitchen and tossed a box of candy on the table. "Out." His peace offering looked pint-sized next to Michael's gargantuan box of chocolates.

Hoping to initiate a softer mood for that talk with Samantha, Johnny had leaped from the Chevy Silverado eager to surprise her. But then, he'd spied the white Lotus parked outside. His heart sank. His worst nightmare.

In a flash, he'd bounded up the stairs and through the door, stumbling to a halt at the cozy kitchen scene. How dare that jerk put his paws on his wife. And Samantha just stood there and let him. His blood began to boil, his muscles coiling his gut.

Danger signals detonated in his brain.

"He's got to go, Sam."

"Can't."

"Why not?"

She stepped away from Michael, and rubbed her hands on her thighs, her expression wary. "Meet the new hand, Johnny."

"What?" A storm began brewing inside Johnny, far worse than the tempest wreaking havoc across the desert.

"I hired him," she explained, the words tumbling from her mouth. "Seems there's a shortage of help in this area and he kindly agreed to help out" —she sucked in a quick breath— "in exchange for room and board for the next few weeks"—she exhaled a resounding puff of air— "while he conducts his studies on the desert dwellers."

"Over my dead bod—"

Michael came to attention. "That could be arranged."

"You know nothing about running a kennel."

"I know business."

"You don't even like dogs."

"For Samantha, I'll learn."

"It won't be here," Johnny took a menacing step, bridging the gap between Michael and himself.

"It will too." Michael plunked back down on the crate, his words almost a whine.

"Stop it, the both of you." Samantha placed the back of one hand across her brow, staggered back and grabbed the counter with the other.

Immediately, Johnny relented and placed his arm around her shoulders. "Honey, why don't you go sit down."

At the endearment, Samantha blinked, and Michael shot up straight, darting his eyes from one to the other.

There was more than one way to chase a skunk out before he left his foul odor behind. Johnny grinned. "Michael will cook our dinner." Taking her elbow, he escorted her to the crate, but when he tried to help her sit down, she deftly slid from his hold and sat down by herself.

"Brr." Johnny shook off his slicker and with it the scowl about to break across his face. Psychology, he reminded himself.

"Now, wait a minute," Michael sputtered.

"Your duties include indoor/outdoor work."

"Samantha?"

She nodded, slanting him a gaze from beneath her lashes. What had she done? Added fuel to ignite an inferno, that's what. Time would tell whether it fizzled out or exploded. It would certainly reveal Johnny's, and, for that matter, Michael's true character. She rapped her fingers on the table, and her lip quivered a smile. She might even enjoy the show. For the first time in the last two days, she felt hopeful.

"You want the job or not?" Johnny barked, hanging his raingear behind the door.

"I'll do this for Samantha."

"Don't do my wife any favors." He unbuttoned his shirt cuffs and, rolling up his sleeves, stomped a step closer to the other man, his intent if pushed unmistakable.

"She's not legally yours, remember?" Michael said, jutting his chin.

A split-second pause, and Johnny lowered his lids, studying the other man through the slit of his lashes. "What makes you say that?"

"No reason," Michael sputtered, leaping up from the crate and knocking it over.

Johnny frowned. "You damage the furniture and it'll come out of your wages."

"Huh!" Michael snorted, and tossing his head back, retreated several steps.

"Make sure it's a hearty meal," Johnny said. "After you've served us, eat up a good portion. You'll need it." He perused him from head to toe, dressed in his city slicker threads. "Your day starts at five a.m."

Michael's eyes nearly popped from his head. "Rather an uncivilized hour, isn't it?"

"To soft-bellied city folk, maybe." Johnny hooked his thumbs beneath his armpits and rocked on his heels. "To us country bumpkins that's the middle of the mornin'."

"Figures." Michael sniffed, his nose in the air, and straightened the cuff of his jacket sleeve.

"If it's too much for you" – Johnny tipped his head toward the door – "You know the way out."

Michael took a pose, his eyes slitting. "Can't get rid of me so easily."

A grin split Johnny's lips. "Too bad." Sidestepping Michael, he took the pot off the stove and set it on the counter. Then he yanked the refrigerator door open, grabbed tomatoes and carrots and tossed them in the sink. After booting it shut, he opened the pantry, took potatoes and onions from the burlap sack and basketballed them in the sink. "Veg stew. On a night like this, should hit the spot." He smacked his belly with his hand, his eyes granite hard. "Think you can manage that?"

"Uh ... uh ..." Michael's mouth fell open.

Samantha shuffled up from the crate, walked to the pantry and picked up a bottle of olive oil. When she lumbered past him, Johnny reached out to stop her, thought better of it and shrugged. Miffed, she slammed the bottle on the counter beside the pot.

"I'll help you, Michael," she offered, turning the faucet on full force.

"Rip roarin' dandy," Johnny muttered, stroking his chin, but the running water smothered his words. A second later, he snapped his fingers. "Since Samantha is preparing the basics, you might as well go and feed the dogs." At least he could maneuver him out of the house and away from her.

Michael held up both hands and backed away until he bumped into the wall. "Do-o-ogs?"

"Friendly brutes."

"Only six of them," Samantha added, scrubbing vegetables.

"You met their cousins at the wedding, remember?" Johnny said, a wicked grin playing on his mouth.

Michael dropped his hands and waggled his shoulders. "You are such a crass creature." His face contorted, and he looked at Johnny like some rodent that'd crawled from the woodwork. He turned to Samantha and smiled. "I don't know how sweet Sam ever got stuck with you."

"Why don't you ask her?" Johnny drilled her eye to eye, an air pocket jamming in his throat.

In that highly charged moment, they could've been alone in the room or anywhere on the planet.

"That won't get dinner cooked, will it?" She averted her gaze, hurled the carrots in the pot and grabbed a tomato.

"See, you've gone and upset her," Michael needled. "You are such a peasant."

"Aww, you don't like me," Johnny goaded, but the other man's words nicked.

"Loathe." Michael glanced at his fingernails and buffed them against the lapel of his jacket. "Don't worry, Samantha. I shan't leave you alone with this ape for another minute."

A string of choice words singed Johnny's tongue, and he tightened his jaw, not wanting to replay the scene in their apartment of two days ago. But, the more he tried to shake the man, the more he stuck like crazy glue.

"I'm sure you'll be a big help." She gave Michael a saccharine smile and him a dour one.

It made Michael preen.

It made Johnny nearly puke.

A lonesome howl pierced the momentary lull in their verbal battle.

"Critters are hungry." Johnny grabbed the dog chow he'd put in the corner after the morning feed and slammed it into Michael's chest. From reflex, Michael flung his arms out and hugged the bag, noting the Canine Kennel Resort logo, CKR.

Johnny caught his unusual interest in the lettering and smirked, ignoring the check in his gut. "We're building a reputable biz here, Michael."

"Never happen." Michael juggled the feedbag in his arms and staggered several steps forward.

"You could help make it happen, Michael." Samantha shot a wary glance at Johnny. "Your business sense—"

Johnny guffawed.

"Mikey," Samantha said, ignoring her husband's uncouth behavior. "You're so sweet, the dogs'll love you."

Like you, Samantha? The silent query knifed through Johnny, magnifying his doubts. He flexed his hand, then stuffed it in the back pocket of his jeans.

"Hrumph." Michael found his balance. "Only six, you say?"

"Six pack." Johnny leaned against the window ledge, folded his arms across his chest and watched the by-play between his wife and this dizzler. Only thing, Samantha didn't see him a jerk. She seemed to like him just fine and even complimented his business savvy. Huh! If she but knew the half of it: who really carried whom, and who was the brains behind his success.

Johnny hadn't worked at the bank for three years without being in the loop about the Scotts. Especially daddy-o and son. Of course, he could beep not a word because Sam would accuse him of badmouthing their guest ... er ... help. So, he did the next best thing. He ground his teeth together, unable to stomach the idea.

"M-manageable, I'd say." Michael peeked from behind the bag in his arms, still hesitating.

"Of course it is, Michael." Samantha cast him her sweetest smile. "You're so capable."

Bitterness scoured Johnny's tongue. He'd come into this with a huge handicap. Not only was he from the wrong side of the tracks, but Sam and this bimbo had a history. Mamma had relished turning the screw and reminding him that not only had they attended the same co-ed boarding school, but Michael had been Sam's ballet partner. He chortled at the image of Michael Scott in that sissy outfit and then scowled at the thought of him holding Sam in a *pas de deux*. A rude noise sounded from his mouth.

Samantha and Michael shot him a puzzled glance. Johnny shook his head as if to say never mind, but an unbidden grin wavered on his mouth. A sliver of hope pestered his insides. Although Sam and he didn't go as far back as she and Michael, dare he believe they went deeper, much deeper?

It must've been a twist of fate – or a divine appointment, as Sam often said – that had him bumping into her that blustery winter day nearly three and a half years ago ....

He'd been jogging in the rain across the Los Angeles City College campus to register for a finance class before the registrar's office closed at four-thirty. Almost there, he skidded to a halt under the canopy above the doorway to avoid the impact, but it was too late.

Seeking shelter from the Santa Ana windstorm, she'd run smack into him, the parcels in her arms flying every which way.

"Oops, sorry," she said.

"Ah, sorry," he said.

For a moment of profound silence, they gazed at each other.

She smiled, and her cheek dimpled.

He grinned, and his heart lurched.

To ease the awkward moment, he bent to retrieve the packages, and she did the same, her head bumping his.

She giggled.

He chuckled.

Hearing the door open and shut behind him, Johnny glanced over his shoulder through the glass doors to the clock in the office. He came to his senses. He had three minutes. In record time, he'd swept up her shopping bags and shoved them in her arms.

"Thank you," she said, her blue eyes wide with surprise.

A curt nod, and he slid through the panels just as the doorman jiggled his keys in readiness to lock up.

Twenty minutes later, the doorman let him out. He pulled the collar of his overcoat up, rounded the corner on his way to the bus stop and skidded to a halt.

She stood sheltering against the wall of the building, her light jacket flapping in the wind. Shivering like a lost puppy, she juggled the sodden parcels in her arms and glanced about.

"You look stranded." He flicked damp hair off his forehead and walked nearer.

"Loo-ooks like it." Her teeth chattered. "M-my limo is late."

He cocked an eyebrow. Limo indeed. If he'd heard one tale, he'd heard them all. "I see. Well, good lu ..." He turned to go, but something about her forlorn appearance made him blurt, "I'm catching the bus to North Hollywood. You ... uh ... wanna come aboard?"

A nervous giggle. "No, thank ..." She squinted through the screen of rain, then down at her squelching sandals. "Yes, that would be nice. I'll call from the depot for a ride." She ventured from her spot. "I don't know what happened ... the chauffeur was to pick me up at four, right after my guest lecture in Fashion 101. My mother must be using the limo and late get ..." She allowed her words to trail off.

Sure sweetheart, he thought, but said nothing. Instead, he scooped up her shopping bags with one hand, draped an arm around her shoulders, drawing her into the shelter of his coat, and made a dash for it.

A moment later, the bus pulled up, wheels sloshing on the pavement and spraying muddied water in their direction. He swerved in front of her and got the brunt of the splatter.

"Oh, my, thank you!"

He grinned and shook his head, droplets spraying her. She laughed, and his gut hitched.

All too soon, the bus ride ended. She waved good-bye and hurried to the telephone booth in the station. He walked away, but a satisfied smile settled on his mouth. Samantha Carroll had agreed to have coffee with him on that Saturday, which was two days away.

Whistling a jaunty Irish tune, he trudged up the hill to his small pad and paused on the rise. He squinted through the fine drizzle and caught sight of her standing inside the phone booth. Soon, a cab drove up, but no limo. The auto moved, and she was gone.

He climbed the front steps to his building, thinking she'd just splurged half a day's wage on the cab fare. He shrugged. If she wanted to play princess, he'd go along, but the joke had turned on him ...

"I'll be right back Samantha." Michael's ingratiating words to his wife jolted him from his reverie.

A muscle twitched in his jaw.

"I'll have the stew ready to go on when you get back." Samantha curved her lips in a soft smile.

Johnny narrowed his gaze and wanted to spit.

"Get some firewood on your way back, *Mikey*," he ground out instead. He rolled his eyes and caught her disapproving glance. "We'll need it for the night."

Michael tossed his head at an obtuse angle and edged his way to the door, a worried wrinkle on his forehead. He looked like he was venturing into the lion's den rather than the dog pen.

When the door shut behind him, Johnny burst out laughing, and then gulped down the sound, thinking perhaps the joke was still on him. He rubbed the bridge of his nose and sobered. He was behaving like a teenager. Is this what love did to a grown man?

He glanced at Samantha from beneath his lids. A hint of a smile still on her lips, she hummed while peeling the potatoes.

Johnny punched his fist in his hand. Humming. Can that beat all? She was actually pleased with that nerd.

What do you see in him, Sam? Money, looks, what? He scratched his head and bolted upright away from the wall. There was a slim chance this fiasco might turn in his favor. Sam would see Michael for what he was, a shallow fluff ball, and turn to her husband. *And elephants fly, Belen.* A laugh ripped through him, but amusement didn't touch his heart. More likely, he'd lose his cool and blow it all.

"What's funny, Belen?"

"The hired help." He grabbed her wrist and pulled her to his side, her head tilting back to look at him. "Who you kidding? He'll be falling flat on his fanny before you peel that spud." Her eyes darkened with uncertainty. Johnny wanted to find another message in her gaze. For him alone.

The moment she lowered her lashes, concealing her feelings, he dipped his head. A fleeting brush of his mouth upon hers, a gentle touch that demanded more, and he deepened the kiss. Just as quickly, he lifted his head, his breath fanning her mouth. "Don't you think?"

She shoved him back. "No."

He stumbled over the crate and grabbed onto the table to keep from falling flat on his face. So much for Michael being the klutz.

Ten minutes later, a shell-shocked Michael covered in mud and reeking of dog stumbled into the kitchen

"Point." Johnny winked at Samantha.

She ignored him and turned to Michael. "Anything wrong?"

"I'd like to wash, and, uh … where do I sleep?"

"In the shed," Johnny bit out. "With the dogs."

Michael's face turned ashen.

"Johnny." Samantha grilled him with a stern look. "Bathroom's down the hall from the bedroom."

Johnny wondered what kind of sleeping arrangements she'd come up with. Gall rose in his throat, and he shoved it down. Air like the hissing of a flat tire seethed from his between his teeth.

Samantha curved a shapely brow.

Pulling his mouth into a stiff smile, Johnny shrugged like he hadn't a care in the world. But what got his pumps fueled was that bank boy had scored one thing right. Vegas drew most of the work force, thus depleting the local resource. Vacationers and retirees were left, and most passed through on tour buses, definitely not interested in scooping dog poop.

To recoup the losses, Willie and his sidekick had stacked up, and to get back into Sam's good graces, he was forced to accept the dolt's presence here for a time. A very brief time if he had anything to do with it, and of course he intended to have everything to do with it.

Johnny flexed his fingers, and then folded them into a fist. He didn't like him being anywhere near his home, his wife, him. He detested it. The man would be more a hindrance than help. But he consoled himself with the thought that it might be a good thing for Samantha to witness the man's ineptitude at domestic *and* business matters.

Until the holiday rush in glitz city was over, workers here would be nil. For the time being, he couldn't be choosey. However, he'd keep Scott in sight, especially when he was anywhere near Samantha. Any tomfoolery and he'd toss him out on his backside, the six pack chasing him outta town.

"If you need anything else, Michael," Samantha said, "just call."

A bowlegged Michael shuffled from the room, the heavy-duty odor wafting behind him.

Johnny chuckled, but it lacked humor. Deflated, like he felt. He'd just played his long shot with that kiss and lost.

"Tell golden boy that I want my dinner in thirty minutes."

She glared at him. "I bet Michael'll deliver gourmet fare, something you're not accustomed to."

A hit, that.

He shuttered his gaze, concealing the sting of her words he was sure glinted in his pupils. If she'd called him a peon, she couldn't have done it better. "Us peasants, Sam, have been known to taste of the good life now and then."

"Johnny, I didn't mean—"

"Enough said. Thirty minutes, or he'll be up at four thirty."

"Stop acting like a caveman."

"From peasant to caveman?" He brushed his knuckles across his jaw. "I don't know if that's a notch up or a peg down in your estimation."

"Oh, you're one aggravating Irishman."

"Is that good?" he asked with a straight face.

She ignored him, and vented her ire by banging the cupboards open and shut.

"Looking for something?"

"Salt."

"To pour on my wounds?"

She swept up the towel from the counter and hurled it at him.

He ducked, and it flew over his head, landing in the trashcan.

At least he'd gotten a reaction. Whistling, he backtracked from the kitchen and turned, nearly catapulting into Michael patting his hair in place and smelling like a cologne factory.

"I'd lighten up on that stuff if I were you." He waved his hand to and fro beneath his nose. No sir-ee. He wasn't about to throw in the towel yet and concede to poster boy here. But the thorn raked his insides.

Michael slid past him into the kitchen, and Johnny ambled to the living room. Once there, he slouched on the rocking chair and stared into the flames devouring the logs in the grate. His mind drifted to the kitchen, and he wondered what was cooking between Michael and his wife. His glance strayed in that direction, but tempted as he was to barge in he resisted. *Psychology*. But he did prick up his ears.

Whispered words sailed out to him, but he couldn't decipher them.

Aggravating.

The banging of the pot then silence.

Infuriating.

A giggle, a squeal and a tinkle of laughter.

Annihilating.

Get a grip, Belen. He'd be a basket case if he let his mind wander along that twisted path. He leaned back and closed his eyes. Where had he and Samantha gone wrong?

Chapter Nineteen

Minutes slogged by.

Johnny tightened his hands over the arms of the rocker, imagining someone's neck. When his stomach growled, he paced the time on his Swiss wristwatch. Two minutes ... one ... and counting ....

"Dinner is served." Michael stepped in the living room doorway and clicked his heels, a towel over his forearm.

"'Bout time," Johnny grumbled and pried his fingers loose from his chokehold on the chair.

A moment later, he stomped into the kitchen and skidded to a halt.

The table looked ready for a dining extravaganza rivaling the finest restaurant. Two red towels covered the scratched surface, and white napkins with plastic cutlery marked each of three place settings. The two mugs and an empty jar became drinking vessels. Flanked by salt and pepper shakers, a candle on the jar's lid flared at center table. A paint can and the two apple crates morphed into chairs.

"Not bad," Johnny said. "However, it's dinner for two."

Samantha slid him a dour look.

"The hired help doesn't dine with the family."

"You are a snob, Johnny Belen," she snapped.

Was there something wrong with wanting to spend some quiet time with his wife?

"Michael eats with us or you eat alone." She gave her ultimatum, stamping her foot in frustration.

Johnny shrugged his shoulders and straddled one of the boxes. He'd tried. Then, he pounded his fists on the table. "Where's my dinner?"

"Good heavens, I've created a monster," she murmured, blinking rapidly. "Michael, honey, would you get this uncouth man his food?"

"Certainly, Samantha dear."

Johnny narrowed his eyes at them both, doubting he could keep said food down. Just too sugary all of a sudden. Too sickening sweet.

After about twenty minutes of enduring the syrupy looks and giggly conversation between Sam and her 'butler', he'd had enough. Nursing his grilled emotions and shredded ego, he stalked out to keep company with the dogs, the welcoming woofs a direct contrast to Sam's cold shoulder and icy blue glare. Brr! There was definitely a blizzard from the North Pole on the rise.

****

Samantha stood at the window, squeezing the towel in her hands, and gazed at her husband trudging to the kennels. Apparently he didn't mind venturing out on this cold wet night, with shoulders slouched and head bent against the onslaught of windswept rain. It seemed he preferred to face the elements rather than her, to spend time with the dogs rather than with his wife.

A tear slipped down her cheek, and she swiped at it with the back of her hand. Twisting away from the window, she folded the towel and set it on the counter. Johnny was a hard taskmaster. Often, he was harder on himself than others. Would she ever understand this man she married? She hiccupped. Thought she married. Would she ever know the real Johnny Belen?

A burst of a breath, and she pulled her sleeves up and plunged elbow-deep in the soapsuds filling the sink. No dishwasher appliance on the premises yet.

Since it was Michael's first day on the job, she'd given him a break from washing the dishes. He'd looked ready to drop on his feet, so she'd handed him a couple of blankets, suggesting he get some sleep.

After she placed the last dish on the draining board to dry, she tidied the table and returned the food items to the refrigerator. She stifled a yawn, turned off the light switch and paused, her fingers stilling upon her mouth. Even the memory of Johnny brushing her mouth with his when Michael had been out in the kennels made her pulse leap and heat radiate inside her, jumbling her emotions.

A sigh from the heart, and she plodded down the hall to the bedroom. Bypassing the living room, she glanced at Michael crashed out on the sofa near the blazing fire. The two spare rooms lacked furnishings and were ice cold without a wall heater. In lieu of better sleeping accommodations, blankets tossed over the couch turned it into a bed for the night. He was cocooned in the covers, snoring like old man winter.

A fleeting grin feathered her lips. At least Johnny didn't snore. She squirmed, wondering if she'd overdone the flirting with Michael. Probably not. Not if Johnny preferred canine company to her. Hammers nailed her brain to her skull, and a moan tumbled from her mouth. What was a woman to do? Not with one man, but two to contend with. One her husband, the other claiming he'd be better husband material. Massaging her temples with her fingertips, she slogged into the bedroom and turned on the light. Then, she screamed.

And screamed and screamed.

Startled, Michael jumped up and the blankets pooled at his feet. Disoriented for a moment, he thought he'd had a nightmare. Cool air had him crossing his legs and yanking down his undershirt over purple satin boxer shorts. When he heard Samantha scream a second time, he rushed to the front door, fumbling to open it.

"Jonathan Belen, come quick. Samantha is screaming!" He pressed himself against the wall and the door slammed shut behind him. His imagination stampeded through his brain. Shaking from the top of his head to the soles of his stocking feet, he inched his way to the bedroom, his teeth chattering.

"Samantha, what's the matter?" He peeked around the doorway at the precise moment Johnny careened into him and bumped him inside.

"Not a thing, big boy." Samantha sat on a mound of bedding on the floor, back propped against the wall, filing her fingernails.

"Sam, what happened?" Johnny swiped wet hair from his eyes and blinked, taking in the serene scene before him. Then, he turned a dark look on Michael. "You called me in here on false pretenses, nearly giving me a heart atta—"

"She really did scream." Agitated, Michael shrank in the corner and waved his hands in front of him. "Real loud."

Johnny noticed Michael's state of undress and scowled. "Cover yourself, man, when you're in the presence of my wife."

"She's not really your wife."

"You're deluded."

"If you two he-men are going to have another fist fight, kindly do it outside." Samantha blew on her nails. "The rain'll cool your tempers."

"You did scream, didn't you, Samantha?" Michael took a tentative step away from his corner and looked at her for confirmation. "Real loud."

146

"I did." She buffed her nails across her sweatshirt. "Real loud."

Michael sagged down the wall and hit the floor, breath fizzing from his tense mouth.

"What'd you scream for, Sam?" Johnny asked, annoyed.

"A minor inconvenience." She waved the nail file about. "One of many since we got here."

"What?" Johnny asked in exasperation.

She raised her brow at the impatience in his voice and because of that, she waited a beat before answering him. "I went to get in my cozy bed and" –she glanced up at the drippy ceiling— "it was soaked." Seemingly unconcerned, she scratched her cheek with a well-manicured fingernail. "Guess it was the last straw." She looked at both men with her wide-open baby blues and blinked. "However, I'm over my hysterics, now."

"Glad to hear it," Johnny muttered.

"I took the sleeping bags, Belen." She smoothed her nails with her thumb. "You may sleep in the bed, between wet, clammy sheets."

He lurched a step closer to her makeshift nest and pinned her with his hard gaze. "I think not, Mrs. Belen."

"What do you mean?"

A wicked grin split his mouth.

A chortle from Samantha.

"I'm bedding down where it's warm." A saucy glint lit his eyes.

"Only room for one here, Belen." She belted him with her words, then ignoring both men, burrowed beneath the blankets.

Johnny clicked his tongue against the inside of his cheek. "I intend to get a good night's sleep."

A sound from behind him, and he glanced over his shoulder.

Michael clutched the wall for support, slithered up and tottered out.

"I suggest you do the same, Mikey," he bit out. "Five o'clock comes mighty early."

Chapter Twenty

Samantha stirred beneath the warm covers and listened to the pitter- patter of rain on the roof. A smile curved her lips. She shifted, brushing against Johnny's leg, the rhythm of his breathing soothing. Her heart pulsed with joy. As nature serenaded outside, she slid her foot along the muscles of his calf, and his hair tickled her instep. He growled in her ear and pulled her closer to his side, his arm possessively around her.

Lifting her gaze, she glanced through the slit in the drapes Mirabella had revamped. Still pitch-black outside. She lowered her lashes and cuddled closer to her husband, relishing the thought of a couple of more hours' sleep.

A sudden bang, then a clatter had her nearly leaping from the bed, and only her weight kept her from flying off the mattress.

"What the ..." Rattled awake, Johnny slid from the bedding and landed with a thump on the floor. "Oomph!"

Samantha bent her elbow and propped her chin in her hand, watching her husband sprawled on the carpet, bare-chested and barefoot, his brief shorts his only covering. Heat infused her body, and nerve endings on her extremities tingled. She flopped her head back on the pillow and shut her eyes tight, recalling the conditions existing between them.

A moment of angst, and she opened her eyes, staring at the ceiling. She lifted her arms up high and slammed them back down at her sides, a groan bursting from her mouth. "Belen, it's not even the crack of dawn. Can't a woman sleep?" She reached over and clicked on the bedside lamp. "Let alone a pregnant one?"

"I'm with you there, Mrs. Belen."

Another resounding crash echoed through the house.

"Are we being invaded, Johnny?"

He sprang up, rubbed a hand across his eyes and scratched his head. "Only by your secret admirer."

"Oh, gosh, Michael." She yawned and pushed hair away from her eyes. "Do you think he's all right?

"I hope not."

"John—"

"Save it, Samantha." The moment he leaped up, she fixed her eyes on his briefs and the strong evidence of his reaction to her proximity. A flush warmed his skin. Man, what was happening to him? She was his wife for heaven's sake, seen him in less many a time, yet here he was, blushing from every follicle like a schoolboy. "The cold."

"Ah huh." She wiggled upward and leaned back against the cushioned headboard, her gaze teasing. A knowing smile curved her mouth, and his heart stirred with feelings he didn't want to deal with just yet. Too vulnerable, especially with the buffoon not two yards away.

He lowered his lids a fraction and decided to take the bull by the horns. "See something you like, Mrs. Belen?" A step took him closer, and he stood over her like a warrior in all his splendor.

"Possibly."

"Hmm." He pressed one knee on the bed and the mattress pressed beneath his weight. "What'll it be?" His hot gaze met her shadowed eyes. A breathless moment, and he straddled her over the covers, pressing his palms against the headboard, capturing her between them. "A quickie, or long and leisurely?"

149

"Can I have both?"

"I'll see what I can do." He shuffled in bed beside her and pulled the blankets over them both. He nuzzled her throat. The warmth of her skin invited, and the erratic beat of her pulse signaled. Well, good. He wasn't the only one affected. He touched and tasted. Sweetness. He nibbled upward along her jaw, the curve of her cheek to her mouth. A feather's breadth from her sweet surrender, then a loud bang from the hall had her warding him off with both hands.

He bit an epithet off his tongue and tightened his jaw against the frustration. "Rain check, Mrs. Belen?" He brushed her mouth with his in a quick kiss and grinned at the pun, listening to the rain upon the roof.

Considering the uncertainty of their marriage, Samantha should've been glad of Michael's untimely interruption. But the wild beating of her heart told another story ... and her breathlessness told its own tale.

Reluctantly, Johnny yanked his clothes off the chair by the dresser and slid his arms through his shirt. Pulling on his jeans, he hopped to the door and paused to wiggle his feet into socks and boots. "Keep warm, Sam. No need to get up."

He turned her bones to mush with those caring, tender words. And yet, he could get her so riled, she could spit and hit bulls-eye. She pulled the covers under her chin, glad he'd had the foresight last night to move the bed away from the leak. A tin can caught the drips from the ceiling. After he'd stripped the wet linen off the mattress, he'd scooped her up in the bundle of bedding from the floor and plopped her on the bed.

She sighed. Once, it could have been called their love nest. Yearning tugged at her heart. She shoved it aside and, difficult as it was, determined to focus on the new circumstances of her marriage. The road ahead seemed bumpy, and without a compass she was sure to swerve off course. Then a quiet small voice signaled that her heart pointed her to true love.

She laughed, wondering if she'd heard right. She'd followed her heart, and look where she'd landed: in a cold room with a leaky roof and confusion in her life.

"Scott, show yourself," Johnny bellowed.

Realizing she'd get no more sleep, she shuffled off the bed, and goosebumps popped up all over her skin. She was glad she'd showered last night, right after Johnny; a smart move, for by the time the house warmed up, her teeth would be chattering a broken melody. Not long ago, she and Johnny would've frolicked beneath the spray and—emotion welled up inside her, abruptly curbing her erotic thoughts.

She pulled off her wrinkled sweatshirt and slipped into a creme-colored pullover sweater and billowy skirt. She pulled socks on her feet, then sneakers, shaking her head at the ingenious way Johnny had her clothes delivered and hanging in the closet. She'd have to ask him about that. Yet, all his intelligence didn't translate into a steady job and income; a necessity for any normal and decent living conditions. The man she married, or thought she married, was certainly turning out to be an enigma.

"Speak up, man."

She heard Johnny stomp down the hall, his irritable words mingling with the rumble of water pipes in the decrepit little bathroom. When he pounded on the bathroom door, she plodded across the bedroom and peeked around the doorjamb.

"Yes?" Michael opened the bathroom door an inch and peered through the crack.

"Has the army landed, Michael, or what?"

"What do you mean?" he blubbered, a toothbrush hanging from his mouth, toothpaste fizzing at the corner of his lip.

"Must you be so inhumanely insensitive and abrasive at the crack of dawn?"

"It is five o'clock." Michael tilted back inside, spit and gargled. A moment later, he showed his face and opened the door a little wider. "I didn't want to be late for my first official day on the job."

"Conscientious son of a gun."

"I wanted to impress Samantha."

"Of course." Johnny scratched his tousled head. "You will put the coffee on, start the fire, stock firewood, clean kennels, feed and water the dogs." He ticked off each chore on his fingers. "Hurry it up before the storm picks up. "When you get back, I like bacon and eggs for my breakfast. Bacon crisp, eggs over easy. Got that?"

Michael shut the door, but his groan filtered through.

Johnny nearly knocked the door down.

Michael pulled it open. "What now?"

"Make the brew strong." Johnny scrubbed his unshaven jaw with his knuckles. "And laundry's on the list."

Michael's eyes nearly popped from his head. "Where do I do—"

"Figure it out."

Michael slitted his gaze and gave him a look that would've seared another mortal to ashes.

It didn't faze Johnny though. He yawned and, scratching his scalp, sauntered off.

"Michael, did you sleep well?" Samantha asked, venturing a step into the hallway.

"Mmm, so-so."

Johnny paused in stride and turned, his forehead creasing. "Michael, you're up to the task, aren't you? You'll have quite a progress report to give ... er ... daddy. Good marks beyond his wildest expectations."

Michael's head shot up in surprise. "Mmm, yes." His lashes veiled his eyes, his words sharp. "Totally unexpected, it will be."

Johnny rubbed his nape, tried to decipher any hidden meaning in his cutting response, and then shrugged. "Move a leg, man."

Michael stalked out, hair spruced back, shirt and pants immaculate. The man was a walking mannequin. He made him feel like a bum. And for that, Johnny pushed a little more. "And if you

152

can manage it, fresh baked bread is my favorite." At Michael's mutinous look, he hollered, "It's Samantha's, too."

Michael slapped his hands over his ears. "You don't have to shout, leprechaun."

"Uh, uh, no name calling, Mikey Tikey." Johnny guffawed.

A glower from over his shoulder, then Michael tossed his head and marched to the kitchen.

"I don't want your stuff cluttering the living room, either."

Michael stopped and turned a perfect pirouette. "Where will I put it? It's a designer original and only one suitcase."

"I've seen it. Size of a tank." Johnny yanked up his shirt collar and stuffed the shirttails in the waistband of his jeans. "If you can't keep your junk from spilling all over the place, I'm going to trash it."

"You can't do that," Michael wailed. "I've spent thousands of dollars on imported suits and ties and shoes ..."

"Better get 'em outta there, then."

He stomped for the living room, and then stumbled to a halt at Johnny's next command.

"That's personal biz, man. Do it on your own time."

"Oh, sure." He spun around, a haughty tilt to his chin. "Don't think you're fooling me, peasant man." He shook his finger at Johnny. "By the time I get back, I'll have no clothes left."

Johnny grinned, then sobered. The last thing he needed was for a half-dressed dodo-man parading around the premises and playing upon Sam's sympathies. "You will. Relocated to the outside garbage heap."

"You are the most vulgar, uncivilized—"

"Such compliments first thing in the morning," Johnny said, voice silky smooth, his jaw hard.

Samantha stepped between the two men. "Michael, I'll have your things moved to our bedroom."

Johnny balked.

"Until one of the guestrooms is made suitable for you."

A look of triumph pinched Michael's features. "Thank you, Samantha." He leaned closer and whispered in her ear. "I can't wait to get you away from this beast."

But Johnny heard. And Johnny growled at Michael from behind.

Michael jumped and stepped forward.

"Breakfast at six sharp. Bacon crisp, eggs over easy." He watched as Michael, with head held high, rerouted his steps to the front door. "Toast better not be burned."

Michael slammed the door behind him.

"We don't have a toaster," Samantha said.

"A minor inconvenience." Johnny slid around her, his hand brushing her hip and resting a moment on the curve of her buttock. Then he strolled into the bathroom and vaulted back out.

"What's the matter?"

"Smells like a perfumery in there."

Samantha chuckled. "Open the window."

****

Precisely at six a.m., Johnny straddled the crate and wolfed down his breakfast. "You're getting better by the hour, man." He chomped, swallowed and took a gulp of coffee. "Gotta work on the brew, though."

Michael rolled his eyes and offered Samantha more toast, but she declined.

"There'll be some furniture delivered today," Johnny said, between mouthfuls. "Before it arrives, make sure the house is clean."

"But Mirabella—" Samantha interjected.

"Mira—whoever didn't do it all, however much you keep insisting." He picked up his mug and waved it at Michael for a refill. "Sweep floors, make beds, clean bathroom, toilet included,

154

trash out, dishes done. Afterward, be ready to help move furniture inside. By then, it'll be lunch." He turned to Samantha. "What would you like for lunch, my sweet?"

"I'll let Michael surprise me."

"Well, I won't." He took another gulp of coffee, and then slammed the cup on the table, liquid sloshing on the sides. "Got insurance, Michael?"

"I don't know what—"

"If you're determined to burn my tongue with your brew, then you might pay up."

"You swine. You lowlife. You ... you ..."

Johnny inclined his head at Samantha. "Don't think Sam would approve of your choice of words."

"Sorry, Samantha." Michael set a second plate of toast on the counter, picked up a slice and ripped off a piece with his teeth. "I don't like him trying to extort money—"

"What?" Johnny leaped for him.

Michael stepped aside, swallowed the chunk of toast and put up his dukes.

"Watch your mouth, you dandied up mannequin."

Michael spurted, "You're so financially strapped, you'll—"

About to blast him with a series of verbal bullets, Johnny changed his mind; instead, he tossed back his head and laughed, the sound burst from deep in his chest and ricocheted off the kitchen walls.

"You have a boorish sense of humor." Michael skirted around him to Samantha's side.

Samantha studied the two men above the brim of her teacup. Things were unraveling faster than she realized. She patted her extended stomach, blinked and set her mouth in a firm line. She wanted her baby to come into the world in a warm and loving home. Not in a battle zone.

"As I was saying ..." Johnny scratched the stubble on his cheek with his callused hand.

"You've said enough, Johnny."

"I've just started, my sweet." He gave her a knowing glance, and focused on Michael hovering behind her. "After lunch, the yard needs tending. Seed the lawn, weed the garden—"

"Of what?" Michael grunted. "Cactus?"

"I'll overlook that interruption, Mikey, as I'm feeling rather lenient with a full stomach," he said. "However, don't push it." He scratched the bridge of his nose. "Rose bushes need trimming. Fence and shed need mending. Painting. Then, bathe the dogs."

"What?" Michael gasped, his jaw nearly dropping to his chest. "I-I-I canno—"

"You're interrupting the boss again, man." He shook his head in disapproval, pushed back the crate and stood. "After those chores are done, dinner. Nothing fancy. Palatable. Then, wash up for the night. By eight o'clock, you're on your own."

He caught Samantha's appalled expression from the corner of his eye. "Oh, and in case I forget to mention it. Guest rooms need refurbishing. Paint, carpeting, draperies, heater. Hope you're equipped for that." And on an afterthought, he added, "Don't forget to scoop up dog poop from the yard when you take out the trash."

"What will I do for entertainment?" Michael picked up the teapot to refill Samantha's cup but she shook her head, her gaze fixed on Johnny.

"Use your imagination. Just stay outta my way." If the man thought he'd have time to dally around and get more ideas about Sam, he was greatly mistaken. But the next moment, said woman burst his bubble big time.

"I'll entertain you, Michael."

Like heck, you will.

"I've got a pack of cards. We can play gin rummy." Samantha raised her teacup, took a sip and set it down beside her plate.

Johnny pursed his lips and waited.

"Sure thing, Samantha," Michael said, an eager lilt to his words.

Johnny glowered, feeling like an iron bar had been shoved down his throat. He'd walked right into that, he did. Best he kept moving to the doorway.

"When do I get my day off?"

Johnny swerved around, his words dangerously soft. "The man's not even started and he wants time off."

"With pay." Michael jutted his chin.

"And Dumbo flew," Johnny said, his brows meeting at the bridge of his nose. "If you can't handle it, just say so, Scott."

Michael brushed his hands against the makeshift towel apron he'd tucked around his waist and glanced at Samantha. "Won't chase me from what's rightfully mine, Jonathan."

"Nothing here belongs to you, Scott." A wary look at Samantha.

"I beg to differ." Michael's gaze skittered to Samantha as well.

"Beg all you want." Johnny sized him up and down. "You ain't gettin' it."

Michael gurgled. His neck muscles bulged, his face turned beet red, and he wrung the towel between his fingers.

Splaying her hands over the weave of material covering the table, Samantha propped herself up. "Your day off is Sunday." Lumbering two steps closer, she stood between the two men. "You can drive me to town, Michael. On the way, you can tell me what my mother and you are up—"

"Plotting," Johnny interjected. "Let's not mince words, shall we?"

A lethal glance at Johnny, then Michael turned his pale blues on Sam. "What an idea, Samantha." He chuckled, but it came out a gurgle. "You have such an imagination."

"I know." Sam glanced from one to the other, catching her bottom lip between her teeth. "Afterward you can take me to lunch."

"No, he won't," Johnny bit out. "He'll be far too busy working."

"No, I won't," Michael spouted back.

Samantha glanced at her husband. He was being an uncouth

bear. What was he trying to prove? Men! If she only understood them. At least one. Johnny Belen.

A grin lit Michael's face. "It's a date, Samantha."

"Sam won't be comfortable in that go-cart of yours."

"I'll call a cab," Michael said, looking dopy-eyed at her.

Johnny flexed his abs. "Not with your meager wages here."

"I have some cash on me." He wiggled his brows. "Paper and plastic."

Of course. Can't do Vegas without a little dough in the pocket. Johnny looped his thumb at the waistband of his jeans and folded his fingers in a fist. "You play craps?"

"Black Jack." Michael stacked dishes from the table to take them to the sink. "In fact, Samantha's mother and I have shared many a game at the Lucky Lou."

"You don't say?"

"Oh, but I do, Irishman."

"That explains it."

"What?"

Johnny favored his wife with a deep gaze. "I'll let Samantha do the honors." A pause when his life seemed to be suspended. "If she cares to."

Samantha averted her gaze, her fingers pleating the hem of her sweater.

A curt nod, and Johnny strode from the room.

"Excuse me, Michael. I'd like to freshen up," she said, slodging from the kitchen. "Then I think I'll lie down for a bit."

Once in the bathroom, she turned the faucet on, scooped up cold water with her palms and splashed her face. Her skin tingled. Her life was becoming fuzzier with each passing day.

Johnny's innuendos didn't help.

Her mother's butting in was worse.

And Michael's strutting his feathers, although comical, fueled the fire.

Of course, her stalling for time didn't help. She turned off the tap, reached for a white towel off the rack and blotted her face. A glimpse of her reflection in the stained mirror above the sink, and she collapsed on the toilet lid, the towel slipping onto her lap.

Two years ago, her mother had threatened to stop her allowance and more besides if she refused to marry Michael. Sam had played along for a time until she figured out how to extricate herself from mamma's machinations. She refused to succumb to mamma's claims that one day she'd thank her. A sound, not quite a snort, burst from her mouth. The tables had turned, big time. And in a way mamma couldn't have controlled and certainly hadn't expected.

With memories pummeling her brain, Sam pushed her hair off her face and stood, draping the towel over the rack. A moment later, she waddled to the bedroom and lay on the bed, a dejected sound slipping from her mouth. Pulling the sleeping bag over her shoulders, she stared up at the ceiling and counted knots in the pinewood.

Unlike Michael, her mother was a piranha at the gaming tables. Playing high stakes, she won big and lost bigger. The last few years she'd been on a losing streak, putting her Casino on the brink of bankruptcy.

A wistful smile skimmed her lips and then vanished. She'd nearly become a gaming chip in her mother's hand. The family's financial tanking had almost duped her into succumbing to mamma's coercion to marry Michael. An only child, she'd felt responsible for her parents' future happiness, but she hadn't been so foolish as to have it be at the cost of her own.

Samantha stretched her legs beneath the sleeping bag and nestled her cheek in her palm. The argument she'd had with her mother had been a doozy, until she'd agreed to have coffee with Michael. A latte or two later and she ended up in church two years ago, almost marrying mamma's choice.

But her heart had led her back to Johnny.

Pressing her fist against her quivering lip, she blinked away the sting of tears. Did she now know what she was doing? Or had she come full circle, once again a pawn in mamma's schemes?

With the family fortune dwindling to pocket change, her mother had become desperate. Add to that the gossip circulating that a drifter busted the house for five million on the very day she married Johnny, and the already-lean Lucky Lou continued on a downhill spiral. If her mother had been close to bankruptcy two years ago, she was certainly within a hair of it today.

Samantha brushed wisps of hair from her eyes and clenched her hand, fingernails digging into her palm. Economically struggling, and with her marriage to Johnny on a crash course, she had to think of herself and her baby's future. She twisted her wedding ring around her finger. She had to be sure about the man she'd married. If she was wrong about Johnny, God help her, she'd have to make another heart-wrenching decision.

Chapter Twenty-One

A floorboard creaked. Samantha stirred from her semi-doze and blinked.

"Just checking to see if you're alright," Michael said, standing in the doorway.

"She is." Johnny had returned to get a screwdriver from the kitchen and caught Michael heavy-stepping it to the bedroom. Instinct prompted him to follow. Good thing, too. "I'll take over. The dogs await you in the shed."

Samantha peered at the two of them through the screen of her lashes. "Michael, how kind of you to be so concerned. But I'm fine." Not a word to Johnny.

"Well, if you think you'll be alright" – Michael slithered a scathing glance over Johnny – "I'll go finish up."

"Good idea." Johnny stood in the doorway, pointing the way out.

Michael grinned at Samantha. "Sooner I get done, the sooner we can have that card game."

"I'll look forward to it." A pixie smile brushed her lips, and she waved him from the room.

Johnny allowed his pent-up breath to shoot from his mouth, then ambled to her bedside. He settled down on the mattress, the springs squeaking beneath him, and took her hand. "Something I can get you, sweetheart?"

She pulled her hand away. "Johnny, you are the most boorish man."

"Now what have I done?" He leaped up from the bed and plowed his fingers through his hair.

"How could you prattle—"

"I don't prattle."

She wiggled up to a sitting position and wrapped her arms around her protruding middle. "You do, Belen."

"Nah."

"Yes, you do." She slapped her hand on the bedding, but the sound came out muffled. "What was that nonsense about fresh baked bread, furniture delivery and all that work it'd take a team of men a month to get done? You nearly scared the man off."

Johnny grinned and sank back down on the bed. "That was the idea."

"But he didn't."

"Too bad."

Samantha fiddled with the edge of the blanket and veiled her eyes with her down-swept lashes. "And I'm not ready to have him go yet."

"Why's that?" His heart dipped, but his eyes turned rock hard.

"I like the idea of a home-cooked meal?"

I'm no fool, Samantha. Aloud he said, "Try again."

"I don't know." She smoothed the bedding around her. "He's helping get this place in order. He's a family friend."

Johnny elevated a bronzed brow.

"In this isolated existence, it's nice to know there's a friend nearby."

"Your husband isn't good enough?"

"Didn't say that."

"Didn't have to." He set his mouth in a hard line and hauled himself from the bed, his thigh brushing her hand on the bedding.

A zap of heat penetrated through the denim and into his leg. He clamped down on the feelings stirring inside him. "I'll go and see how your ... er ... pal is doing." The words left a bitter taste in his mouth.

"He could be your friend too, Johnny."

"No." He shot her a level gaze. "Scott's no friend of mine."

She sighed. "What're you going to do?"

"Why Sam, I'm going to test the mettle of that man." He inclined his head toward the kennels, thinking, and see what he's got that captured your interest. "See if he's got what it takes to work with us bumpkins."

"I already know it." Sam smiled.

He gulped down a growl.

"Michael might seem a little odd—"

"Seem?"

"—at times and fare better on the city scene, but he's sweet and does try."

He rubbed his chest with his fist, diminishing the pressure there. "Not good enough in my book." Patting her hand, he turned and stalked to the door.

"Determined, too."

A pause in stride, and he hurled over his shoulder. "I bet."

"You won't bulldoze him into leaving, will you, Johnny?"

He shot her a blank look, but a grin tugged the corner of his mouth.

"He won't, you know."

"And if he does skedaddle back to daddy?" he asked.

A myriad of emotions flittered across her face until doubt settled in.

"Sweet can turn sour mighty fast."

She pulled the bedding under her chin like a protective covering. "As I know from experience."

"Care to expand on that?" he challenged.

"You ... I ... we ..." She waved her hands about the room,

somehow a reflection of their relationship. Dismal. How did that happen?

Johnny's gaze drilled deeper. "As I said, that can easily be remedied." Okay, he'd just backed her into a corner for an answer. His heart vaulted in his throat, waiting for her reply.

"In a variety of ways."

His pulse stuttered. He'd have to be hit over the head to miss that one. She was contemplating a way out. One, he'd wager, that kept publicity at a low hubbub. "You be sure to let me know which way you're aimin' for, Mrs. Belen." A hard line marked his mouth, and he delivered his own shot. "And I'll be sure to let you know mine."

She sat bolt upright, sparks shooting from her eyes and singeing his skin. "What's that supposed to mean?"

"Whatever you want it to."

"Was I so wrong about you, Johnny?"

"I don't know. Were you, Sam?" If she had doubts about his caliber, he wanted it out in the open; wanted to know where he stood with her once and for all. A level playing field was more to his liking, giving him clearer options to devise his strategy.

"I'll know soon enough, won't I?" She tugged at a stray strand and wound it around her finger.

He queried with his brow.

"In three months, I'll be sure of your mettle, too, Johnny."

"If you don't know it by now, Sam, you won't get it after three months." Steam built in his chest, and he sucked it down. So, she was playing a game. A test. If he didn't pass her criteria for husband the second time around, Michael lurked, ready to catch her. He grimaced, and a harsh sound ripped through him. *Isn't that what you've been doing? Testing? To see if she'd stick around for you, and not your mega bucks?* Shut up, brain.

He was playing for keeps. His life and his child's future. A deep frown carved his forehead. He couldn't afford to be blindsided by Sam, her mother or pal Mikey. Knowing she'd be around for the next three months eased the pressure in his lungs and the ache in his gut. It also made it easier to keep an eye on her and his child. "I take it you'll be hanging around for a while yet?"

"Michael would find it uncomfortable without me," she murmured, casting him a covert glance. "His research."

"Of course. We must think of … uh … Mikey." He gripped the doorknob behind him and squeezed, the metal imprinting on his fingertips. "Mamma's golden boy." His gaze shuttered, and a nerve battered his cheek. "And possibly yours?"

She gaped at him aghast. "That's a rotten thing to say."

"Seems to me you want it that way." He just burned his bridges for sure. He shrugged. They were ablaze as soon as he'd read that special delivery letter with bank-boy hot on its trail. He didn't know how to snuff out the flames and salvage his life with her. How to rebuild now the baby was coming.

"I-I," She leaned her head against the headboard and lowered her lashes.

Johnny unhooked his hand from the doorknob and took a step closer to make sure she was all right. At that moment, she lifted her lashes, and her cool gaze iced over him. "I have to use the bathroom."

"Need any help?"

"No, thank you."

She pushed his buttons big time, this woman he married. An indifferent mask settled on his features. What he wanted was to haul her into his arms and smother smooches all over her face. A savage grunt, and he thrust the feeling aside, his abs rigid and his heart pulsing a staccato.

"Okay, be my guest." He marched to the door but couldn't help tossing over his shoulder, "call if you need anything."

Samantha heard his footsteps echoing down the hall and out the front door. A quiet moment passed, and she folded her hands into fists, pressing them against her eyes to stem the tears. She hiccupped. Things seemed to be going from bad to worse between them. She didn't know what to do nor how to fix it. Or if it could be salvaged. She took a deep breath, exhaled and brushed hair off her forehead. Well, she wouldn't sit here and let circumstances dictate how her life would turn out. No, sir-ee!

Once again, she determined to take a hand in her life. A whimper sounded from her mouth. She'd done that on her wedding day, and look where it had landed her. Sitting here, six months pregnant, penniless and supposedly not legally married to the father of her child. Could that be possible?

She sniffed at the near-empty room. She'd begin by checking up on the furniture Johnny mentioned earlier. If it wasn't up to standard, she'd make some demands of her own. She'd throw out the challenge and see what Johnny, the provider of the family, could do in the next three months.

And what Michael, the hired hand, could stand.

Samantha shuffled off the bed and, after a quick visit to the bathroom, waddled to the front door. A second later she pulled it open, wind smacking her face. Resolute, she walked out to the porch, her sights on the kennels. "Johnny. Michael," she called, competing with the wind for audibility. "I want to talk to the both of you. Now."

Chapter Twenty-Two

While waiting for the men to come into the house, Samantha took pad and pencil and strolled from room to room, jotting down notes and doodling designs. By the time she'd finished her tour, they still hadn't shown up, and she stood by the living room window contemplating the outdoors. After a while, she turned and sat on the rocker and flipped through a Showtime magazine spouting Vegas glitz and glam. Finally, she tossed the trade onto one of the crates, but it slid to the floor. Too much for her to bend down and pick up, she left it there and plodded to the kitchen.

Fresh brewed coffee aroma filled the room, indicating the men had been in for lunch. She glanced at the note taped on the refrigerator and opened the door, finding the toasted cheese and lettuce sandwich they'd left her. She took a bite and peeked in the pot on the stove still half-filled with simmering water. Swiping a dribble of mayonnaise from the corner of her mouth with her tongue, she grabbed a mug from the dish rack.

At least Michael had washed the dishes. She filled it to the brim with hot liquid, disregarding the crumbs scattered across the cooker's surface. Improvisation in any situation was one of Johnny's talents. In this instance, without a toaster, he'd tutored

Michael on the art of 'roughing it' by grilling bread over the gas element, cookout style.

A half smile played on her mouth thinking of the tough yet tender Irishman she married. Her smile dissolved, food in her mouth turned tasteless, and she gulped it down. He was so different now.

She took an orange spice-flavored teabag from the box on the counter and, dipping it in the mug, stepped to the table and plopped on the crate. Fruity scent sailed around her. She wrapped her hands around the mug, the warmth soothing her ruffled feelings. She'd called them nearly two hours ago and they still hadn't answered. If they didn't show up after she finished eating, she'd go and find out why.

After a bite or two of the sandwich, she screwed up her face at a soggy section. She forced herself to chew and swallow, then opened the bread slices and picked out the cheese and lettuce. A couple of nibbles on them, and she discarded the remains in the trash bin, determined to ask for better meals. And real dishes to eat from. She lifted the mug and sipped the flavored liquid.

Done with her snack, she grabbed her coat from the hall closet, slipped her feet into sneakers and ventured outdoors. She paused on the bottom step. Clouds billowed overhead, but the wind had abated some. Resolute, she held her coat in place around her big belly and sloshed through the yard to the kennels, peering through the torn wire fence.

Dog dishes with remnants of dried food and half opened feedbags were strewn about. A couple of mud-stained animals lolled about in need of a bath, while the rest barked from the shed. The smell was unbearable, and she covered her mouth with her hand.

She walked a few more steps and peeked into the shed. No wonder the dogs woofed and wagged their tails. They had two exceptional specimens of man for company, strong and attractive. Johnny leaned negligently against one termite-bitten wall, chewing

168

on a dry blade of grass, while Michael shoveled soil to level the ground, sweat pouring down his face.

"Hose down the concrete border. If we're not hit by another storm, it should hold until you fix the roof." Johnny spit the grass from his mouth. "Otherwise, you'll have to scramble and pour in that cement."

At the look of dismay on Michael's face, Sam nearly burst out laughing. "Hello, boys."

"Sam, what the dickens are you doing out in this weather?" Johnny asked.

"Storm's about run out of steam." She glanced up at the rain-drenched sky. "It's just spitting."

"Deceptive."

There seemed to be an underlining meaning to his words, and she inclined her head. "Time will tell; don't you think?"

"Betcha, Sam."

Michael darted his eyes between them. "Can the hired hand get in on the rap?"

"No." Johnny scowled.

"Yes." Samantha nodded.

"Oh, goody," Michael gushed.

"I called you both a couple of hours ago," she said. "Guess you didn't hear me in the wind."

"Something wrong, Sam?" Johnny pushed away from the wall and walked to her side.

"Were you hungry?" Michael shoved the shovel in the dirt and brushed his hair from his eyes, smearing dirt across his cheek. "I left a sandwich for you." A quick glance at Johnny, signaling he was to blame. "I didn't call you for lunch because he thought you should rest."

"I had a taste of … uh … lunch." She pushed her hands in the pockets of her coat, and her gaze skipped between the two men. "I want to talk to you."

"Sure," both men said in unison.

"Good." She turned and started to walk away. "I'll see you inside."

"Don't forget to pad behind the door," Johnny said, and Michael started, his eyes shifty. "Looks like that dirt's been flipped over recently."

When Samantha reached the sagging wire-link gate, she paused and turned, hands on hips. "Now."

"Sure Sam, soon as we finish this," Johnny called, pointing with his boot. "Missed a spot, Scott."

Michael pounded the ground behind the door with more vigor using the back of the shovel.

"Easy there." Johnny waved his hand in front of his face. "You're stirring up dust, man."

Michael curled his lip in contempt.

"I don't think this should wait," Samantha called back, tapping her foot against the fence.

"Sam, is something wrong?" Johnny slopped through the mud to her side, Michael at his heels.

"Not yet." She lowered her lashes. "But there might be."

"What d'ya mean?"

"Something must be wrong." Michael fluttered his hands and stamped his feet. "And you're not telling, Samantha."

"The baby is fine."

Air whooshed from both men in utter relief.

"Okay, Michael, get to work." Johnny made to turn away and resume his supervisory position. "Sam, I'll see you in fifteen."

"No, boys," she said, emphasizing her words. "You'll see me, now."

"Aww, Sam, Michael's almost finished this. What's the rush?"

"You'll not only have a pregnant woman on your hands but a hysterical one." She slammed the gate shut, but it swung back open, bumping her posterior. "Ooo!"

"What're you talking about, woman?" Johnny scratched his head. "We gotta finish this before dusk."

170

"Yep, gotta do it," Michael murmured beneath his breath.

Johnny nodded, surprised at the other man's agreement.

Samantha lifted a hand and pointed the two men to the house.

"I-I-I mean," Michael stuttered, shoveling dirt. "Gotta do what Samantha says."

"Dig," Johnny ordered. "Five minutes, Sam."

She trudged several steps to the house, her head held high, her sneakers sinking in the moist earth. A second later, she did an about face and looked straight at the workhand. "Michael."

Michael dropped the spade, smirked at Johnny and sprinted to her. After wiping his hand on his pant leg, he took her arm and pitched a jubilant glance over his shoulder at an astounded Johnny. "Since Samantha officially hired me, I guess her orders override yours." He turned back to her, dazzling her with his smile. "I'm all yours."

Two beats later, taciturn, Johnny stalked after them into the house.

"Leave your dirty boots on the porch both of you," Samantha called from the hallway. "And come into the living room, please."

Several minutes later, both men skidded to the living room doorway at precisely the same instant and bumped each other aside to gain entrance. Finally, Johnny stepped aside. "Be my guest, Scott."

"Pull up a crate and sit by the fire so you'll be warm," Samantha invited, rocking in the chair.

Michael marched to the beat of her words and dragged the box beside her.

Johnny pulled an old paint can from the corner and plopped his rear on it. Next instant, he leaped up. "What's this rap session about Sam? We got work to do before sundown."

"You just can't imagine how much, husband." She motioned him to sit.

Of course, he stood. Propping a shoulder against the wall, he folded his arms and paced her every move beneath his bunched brows, noting every nuance.

Samantha shrugged and turned a bright smile on Michael. He dragged his crate closer to the rocker and she shrank back in the chair, waving her hand beneath her nose. She caught Johnny's amused expression and dropped her hand to her lap.

"While you men were out, I took an inventory of the house and found it wanting." She patted the pleat on her skirt and then the hem of her sweater. "If this is going to be my home ... er ... our home" –she smoothed her hand over her abdomen— "for the next three months, then there's going to be some changes. Fast."

She licked her lips and chanced a glimpse at Johnny. If anything, his gaze had narrowed even more. Razor sharp. She exhaled a puff of air in her throat, willing her pulse to regulate. "Although Mirabella did her part—"

"Who's Mirabella?" Michael asked.

Samantha smiled sweetly, and Johnny swished his hand in dismissal, as if to say *don't even ask.*

"—the premises have to be maintained at a certain level of comfort and style." She took out the pad and pencil she'd placed in her skirt's pocket earlier. "Inside, the house needs a major overhaul. Plumbing, painting, new carpets—"

"What's wrong with the carpets?" Johnny asked. "Your ... er ... Mirabella spiffed them up."

"Who is Mirabella?" Michael asked in a squeaky voice.

Both Johnny and Samantha ignored his question.

"Yes, she did." She tapped the pencil on the pad. "The color scheme may not match the furniture you're having delivered. And I do so like a coordinated decor."

Johnny looked dumbfounded.

Probably he was wondering why she started throwing her weight around; she smiled at the pun and patted her tummy. Samantha decided to make the most of her position as lady of the manor, especially with two men at her beck and call. Although she wasn't sure about Johnny in that respect, Michael she could count on. A sliver of uncertainty zapped through her, and she shook it off.

"I hope a television, iPad, and iPod are part of the items you're having delivered, Johnny." She checked each off on her notepad. "A laptop. Kitchen appliances." She glanced at Michael. "They'll make it easier for Michael to perform his duties."

"Duties?" The word blasted from Johnny like a bullet, his features stern.

"In the kitchen." She fluttered her lashes at him, then turned her attention back to Michael, who looked at her with puppy dog eyes.

"I'm partial to self-cleaning appliances," Michael spouted.

"Oh, me too, Michael," Samantha gushed.

Johnny lifted his eyes heavenward. *Patience Belen, patience.*

"And," she continued, checking off her list of demands. "A laundry room equipped with washer and dryer with the latest tech gadgets." She patted Michael's arm. "A newborn needs frequent changes, laundry piles up ..."

Michael nodded.

Johnny said nothing.

But a magnetic current sizzled between her and Johnny, making fine down on her skin stand on end. She brushed the writing pad across her arms to settle the goose-bumps.

"The most comfy furniture will be for the bedroom and, of course, the guest room." She directed this last sweetly to the help. "Michael deserves a decent place to sleep and relax after a hard day's work."

"You about done?" Johnny asked, his words clipped.

"Not quite." She glanced at her list. "Bathroom needs a cosmetic facelift and ..." She flipped a page on her writing pad. "When the inside is done, there's the outside to do. But we'll leave that for another time."

"Imagine that," Johnny muttered.

"That shouldn't be a problem, Samantha," Michael said. "I'd be glad to do that for you."

"Not your job," Johnny said. "It's mine."

"You can't afford it, Jonathan." His gaze fawned over Samantha. "I can."

"You have no idea of what I can or cannot afford," Johnny ground out, muscles in his neck tightening.

Michael turned his haughty nose up at him. "The condition of your pocketbook is quite obvious." He gave Samantha a sympathetic look. "You've kept poor Samantha in that tiny apartment for two years."

"You been keeping tabs?"

"Of course."

"Together with mamma."

"Y-yes." Michael stammered, thinking maybe he'd said too much.

"Figures."

"I don't care what you think, Jonathan. I may not have had the relations—" he settled his bottom on the crate and blushed— "with Samantha that you've had—"

Johnny came to rapt attention, the skin taut across his cheekbones. "Don't even go there."

But Michael saw his chance and blindly ventured in. "But that was an oversight. I'll help her out now, and as for th-th-the rest, we'll work something out."

"You're a sick man, Scott."

Michael leaped up, his hands in fists. "I've had enough of your insults."

"Oh, really." Johnny toughened his jaw, ready for a fight.

Samantha rapped the pencil on the rocker's arm. "You think you can get your act together and make this—" she waved her hand around "—a home fit for a newborn before he or she arrives? I'll not have my baby exposed to these barbaric conditions." She

174

shot Johnny a knowing glance. "While I'm in limbo, I might as well be in limbo in style."

Michael snickered.

Johnny growled.

"When will the kennels open for business" –she directed this specifically to her husband— "and generate cash flow to pay for these renovations?"

A smirky grin played on Johnny's mouth. "Since Michael wants to put in his two cents—"

"Two million ... three—" Michael piped in.

"Well, excuse me," Johnny drawled. "He won't mind working overtime to get the kennels ready for you, Sam. And that should speed up the remodeling indoors." The grin turned into a satisfied smile. Michael would be up to his elbows in dogs, and his extended work schedule would allow for no extracurricular activities here or in town with Sam. "That work for you, Scott?"

"I'm going to show Samantha who's the best man."

"You do that," Johnny said, his voice cool. Hard.

Samantha figured that with the two of them pitching in, the house should improve in no time. The money was an issue, but she'd cross that barrier when she came to it. No way would she have Michael finance any of it; for sure it would get back to mamma. She could do without mamma's gloating and complicating things further. A sigh sailed from her mouth. She hoped Johnny had some credit to begin the repairs.

"Now, I'm hungry," she said to change the subject. "That soggy sandwich was not to standard."

"Hear that, Scott?" Johnny couldn't help ribbing. "Your culinary skills are slipping. Better shape up or she might hire another hand."

"Or marry another man," Michael countered, twisting his lip in derision.

Johnny flexed his hand, itching to floor the dancing boy. Instead, he slid his palm across his face and deflected his rising temperature. The jerk's words hit too close for comfort, especially with the rocky state of affairs between Samantha and himself. But the last person he wanted to voice it was Michael Scott, who saw himself as the best contender for her hand.

"Surely you jest?" Johnny mocked, and his eyes veered to Samantha, holding her gaze for a heartbeat.

Samantha glanced away to avoid that delicate subject, her pulse thudding so loud it echoed in her ears. "I'm really looking forward to the remodeling—" Her voice cracked, and she clapped her hands to conceal the revealing moment. "Should be fun."

But would it?

Even with Johnny looking a disgruntled bear, there was no contest where her affections lay—with her husband. But what if she was wrong? Could she have been fooled for two years? Could Johnny be a phony? She had to be sure. She would use every moment of the three months to unearth the truth. She couldn't be wrong on this one.

"Michael, do you think you can whip up a couple of burgers and some fries?" she asked, smiling. "A salad?"

"For you, anything."

She rubbed the eraser point of the pencil across her chin. "You deserve a new title, Michael." An idea hit, and she snapped her fingers. "You are now foreman of our desert estate."

"Wow, a promotion so soon."

She nodded. "Sure, all this work—"

"Yeah, man. Toughing it out with us country folk—"

"—isn't too much for you?" she asked, concern in her voice. "You're not used to all this physical activity."

"Oh, but I am, pretty lady." Michael took her hand and lifting her from the chair, twirled her around the room in a pirouette. "Remember how we danced in ballet class for years?" He wiggled his brows. "I'm accustomed to a variety of physical maneuvers."

She laughed and paused for breath.

"Well, maneuver yourself out to the worksite, Scott," Johnny bit out, his countenance rivaling the storm brewing on the horizon. "Reminiscing time is over."

"Thanks for the dance, my lovely," he murmured, bowing with a flourish.

Johnny rolled his shoulders to work out the crick from his neck.

"Dad'll be impressed," Michael said. "This city boy's getting in the trenches with the locals." His eyes glazed over. "Our future banking clients."

"Always got your eye on fleecing some fool," Johnny fired.

"Sure, why not." Michael snubbed his aristocratic nose at Johnny. "Natch."

"You agree, don't you, Samantha?" Michael asked, a hopeful look on his face.

On alert, Johnny unfolded his arms and waited for the shell to drop.

But Samantha sidestepped the issue. "After dinner, I'd like to show you some designs, Michael."

"Do I get a look-see?" Johnny asked, his eyes shadowed.

"If you can tear yourself away from your pet project."

Michael guffawed. "Quite a pun that. Pet project. Dogs. Kennels."

Johnny cast him an odd look, then turned to Sam. "I'll see what I can do."

"After the house is finished" –Samantha warmed to her cause— "you can start on the grounds. Desert landscaping should make for easy maintenance." She sighed. "I'm especially partial to roses but—"

"Sure thing, Mrs. Belen. Your every wish is my command," Johnny muttered, his words a subtle reminder of their early morning romp gone awry in their bedroom.

A blush burned her skin.

Michael missed the friction sizzling beneath their banter, and made the mistake of mumbling, "As it should be."

"Shut up!"

Affronted, Michael sidled to the doorway. "Well, I've never—"

"Keep outta my way." Johnny stomped to the window and stared morosely at the approaching dusk.

"Samantha, your meal will be ready shortly."

"Thank you, Michael."

Their syrupy interchange had Johnny's gut in knots. He'd do it. He'd renovate the house for the baby. And Sam didn't have to know how he funded it at this stage. His pulse boomed in his chest. He'd spend the whole blasted five million bucks on her if he knew for sure her love was true; that she wasn't looking out for number one in the guise of looking after the baby.

Tightlipped he turned, flickered a glance at her then on Michael, still hovering in the hallway. "After you've prepped gourmet fare for princess, show your face in the kennels."

"Aren't you going to eat, Johnny?" Samantha studied him beneath her lashes, wondering if she'd pushed his hand too far.

"Later." He shoved past Michael, traipsed into the foyer and out the front door. The sound of his footsteps across the porch and down the stairs echoed back to her.

"That settles that." Michael peeked back around the doorway, swiping his hands together. "Finally, you and I can be alone."

By this time, her head buzzed, her eyes dazed.

"Samantha, I want you to know—"

"Michael I'm really hungry." She patted her big tummy. "For the baby."

"Sure. Right away." He backpedaled to the kitchen. "Just give me twenty minutes."

Left alone, she wondered if she'd gone overboard with her plan. What had seemed like a good idea might very well backfire. Johnny left the house in a huff, and an indignant Michael banged the only pot they had around in the kitchen. Then again, her requests were reasonable. If Johnny wanted to behave like a bear with a sore head, fine by her. She wasn't asking for a palace, just

178

comfy living quarters. A giggle skimmed her mouth. As for Michael, he was just a big pussycat.

With or without claws?

In a quandary, she paced the floor in the foyer.

Shortly after, mouth-watering smells floated to her, and she made her way to the kitchen. It was surprising how fast Michael got the hang of cooking a decent meal. A hidden aptitude, perhaps.

"Michael, that smells delicious," she said, a silly grin playing on her mouth. He looked in his element, flipping burgers and toasting buns. "Didn't know you liked cooking."

"There's much you don't know about me." He wiggled his brows, grabbed a paper plate and stacked the buns. "One of my pet hobbies, although I haven't put it to use in a while." He picked up the patties with a plastic fork and placed them atop the buns. The fork melted, and chuckling, he tossed it in the sink. "That's why I was a little rusty with the stew last night."

"You certainly gave us a surprise."

"Please don't tell dad. He thinks I dine out at all the fine restaurants."

She sat on the crate, and Michael served her a hamburger with all the trimmings and condiments fit for a queen. She bit into the burger with gusto and rolled her eyes in satisfaction. "Yummy. Real yummy."

A flush began to rise on his neck, staining his cheeks, and she realized he was rather shy. A side to him she hadn't known. She'd bet all that haughty posturing was a cover up. "Michael, come and join me."

"The kennels—"

"You're entitled to a dinner break."

"If you insist." He piled a plate of food and pulled the crate up to the table.

"I'm beginning to realize you're not what people made you out to be."

"What's that?" he asked, chomping on the burger.

"Playboy of Beverly Hills."

"Well, I won't deny I do the Hollywood club scene sometimes … get some of my best clients there."

Samantha raised both her eyebrows, wondering exactly what he was referring to, but she continued munching.

"But yes, I'd prefer a wife" – he stopped chewing and swallowed – "and home." He placed the half-eaten hamburger on the plate, wiped his fingers on the napkin and reached for her hand.

She diverted her fingers from any contact with his by reaching for the saltshaker. "I bet you could open a restaurant, Michael. Or a chain."

"Or invest in mamma's near-collapsed casino."

Samantha laughed, slightly embarrassed. "You'd caught onto that?"

"Mmm, hasn't everyone?" Then, his voice turned serious, his tone confidential. "I'd do it in a second, if you came with the package."

"You do flatter a girl, Michael." But she was not for sale. Not for mamma. Not for Michael. Not for anyone.

"Not just any girl," he whispered, his gaze earnest.

Samantha gulped down the food in her mouth. He was dangling a dangerous temptation before her eyes, for the success of the family business would ultimately be her baby's legacy. A flash of the serpent tempting Eve with the apple in the Garden flashed through her mind. She blinked, and shook her head at her own foolish musings.

"Such compliments, Mich—"

"I meant them."

"Thank you." She picked up a fry and nibbled. "These are good."

"I cooked them just for you." He cleared his throat. "It would solve all your problems, Samanth—"

"What? French fries?"

"No, me."

"Got ketchup?" she asked.

He leaped up to go to the refrigerator.

Would it solve her problems or create new ones? She picked up her glass and took a sip of water. Did Michael really want her? More likely he'd strut and preen, placing her on display with the rest of his family trophies. Her stomach churned, reminding her she'd had a chance to marry this man and she'd run. Samantha pushed her plate of food away.

Underneath the lighthearted chatter, she felt not an ounce of emotion ripple between Michael and herself. He didn't move her. His conversation didn't excite her. His life didn't intrigue her like her Irishman. Her feelings hadn't changed where Michael Scott was concerned. And neither did the situation between Johnny and herself.

"Just give me the nod, Samantha." Michael set the bottle of ketchup on the table, plunked down on the crate, his pale blues glued on her face.

To avoid the awkward moment, she sprinkled a few grains of salt on her abandoned food, and returned the shaker to its spot. But Michael was quicker on the draw this time and grabbed her hand. Before she could yank her hand away, the kitchen door swung open.

Johnny filled the doorway, his face a thundercloud.

"Cozy," he bit out, his eyes zeroing in on her. "Fraternizing with the hired help?"

Chapter Twenty-Three

Samantha stood, the force of her movement toppling the crate and surprising both men. "Do you want to eat or not?" Her eyes flashed at Johnny.

"No thanks," he said, his features taut.

She grabbed her plate and marched to the sink. She'd had it with his innuendoes, veiled suggestions, hints. If he didn't trust her, she'd just as soon have him spit it out.

"Don't upset yourself, Samantha." Michael jumped up and followed her, plate in hand. "I'll take care of Jonathan." He placed a concerned hand on her shoulder.

A low growl from Johnny.

Michael dropped his hand to his side. "I mean; I'll fetch his meal." He took the plate from her hand and put it in the sink, together with his. "Why don't you go lie down and put your feet up."

Samantha gripped the counter top, took a deep breath and exhaled a pool of sound. "Perhaps you're right, Michael." She patted his hand and stepped away.

"Don't let me interrupt you," Johnny said, his voice low, lethal.

Without another word, she made to brush past him, and the air crackled between them, forcing her to take a step back. She skirted around him and kept moving. But where could she go? She felt claustrophobic in the house. There was a storm brewing inside to rival the intensity of the one on the brink outside. With another cold night approaching, and with her choices minimal, she trudged to the living room. Once again, she sank into the rocking chair by the fireplace.

And rocked … rocked … rocked.

A moment later, she caught a glimpse of Johnny stalking to the bathroom, which left Michael clearing up in the kitchen. She sighed and leaned back in the soft padding of the recliner. A sound, not quite a laugh, bubbled from her mouth. She'd spent so much time in this one room and in this rocker; they'd become her security blanket.

She stared at the miniature inferno blazing in the grate and tried to make sense of her life. How had she gotten herself in this predicament? And, more importantly, how was she going to get herself out? Facing Johnny was like confronting a cold front. She closed her eyes. The rocking and warmth of the fire were a balm to her frayed nerves.

She was almost asleep when she sensed someone near. Felt the tickle of a blanket, a gentle hand brushing hair off her forehead, his lips on her brow. She stirred. Her lashes felt heavy, and by the time she lifted them, he'd gone. She smelled him though, and his scent was unmistakable.

Johnny.

Her husband.

She hadn't imagined it. And that just added to her confusion. How could he be so gentle and tender when she wasn't looking and be such a brute when she challenged him?

****

In the bathroom, Johnny turned on the tap full force, scooped cold water in his palms and splashed his face and nape. Turning

183

the water off, he grabbed a towel off the rack and scrubbed his face nearly raw. That domestic scene he'd stumbled across between Michael and Samantha in the kitchen replayed in his mind, stoking his irritation. If he didn't leave now, get some fresh air and cool down, he'd be dragging Michael out on his back.

He seemed to be losing ground fast where his marriage was concerned. If only Samantha would have faith in him, want him and love him for himself. *She married you, didn't she?* A voice battered his brain. Yeah, but the burning question was, why? For his own peace of mind, he had to find out and pronto in order to make a smart decision about his future. After all, he had a baby to think about. He wanted a better home life for his child than what he'd experienced the last few days.

A sigh blasted from his chest, and he gripped the sink tight. Just moments ago, on his way to the bathroom, he'd glimpsed Samantha dozing in the rocker, and his pulse throbbed. He'd backtracked to the bedroom, grabbed a blanket and walked back to her in the living room, each step reserved. Her arms were wrapped protectively around her abdomen, her breasts rising and falling to the rhythm of her breathing. His muscles tensed, his blood stirred, and he wanted to enfold her in his arms and take her to bed.

But he did neither. Instead, he watched her.

Firelight glinted off her hair. Curls framed her face, and gold tipped lashes cushioned her eyes … eyes that could be gentle as a mountain stream one moment and turbulent as an ocean storm the next. He'd kissed and counted each freckle on her pert nose so many times before; the curve of her cheek was smooth as satin in his callused palm. Her lips were cherry-red, soft, sweet. He'd yearned to taste, to play, to mate … he licked his dry mouth and slammed it shut. Another step took him closer, and about to cover her hands with his, he veered away. Then back again. He'd brushed his lips upon her brow, and then walked out and into the bathroom and shut the door.

A growl built in his throat, and hurling the towel on the counter

– the bimbo-boy could clean it up – he stalked from the bathroom and down the hall. He paused in step when he passed the living room … good, she was still dozing … and then he stormed out the front door.

Against the force of wind, he kept on walking until he reached the kennels.

"Come on gang, time for exercise." He snapped leashes on the dogs' collars, seized the straps and led them out. The rain had stopped, but the bite of wind warned another stormy round was imminent.

A reflection of his life? A dry sound burst from his mouth.

After hiking about a mile, he found himself on the dirt road flanked by fields dotted with Mojave Prickly Pear and Barrel Cactus. A handful of desert flowers – wooly sunflowers, lilac sunbonnets and parish larkspur – swayed amidst the Joshua Trees and dry thistle.

The year he'd worked the kennels for Willie had stocked his knowledge of desert flora and fauna. He squinted at the miles of open scrubland in the twilight.

If he kept on trekking, he'd eventually come to a neighboring homestead and the saddle in the road that led to town.

"What do you say, group?" He paused, allowing the dogs to sniff and explore the ground. Sure as heck, he was messing things up. He glanced up at the sky … he needed all the help he could get. A heavy sigh came from deep in his heart, and he bashed it down his throat.

Suddenly, a banged-up truck with blinding headlights barreled by, and he leaped onto the shoulder of the road.

"What the—?" He thought crazy drivers were in California.

Wrong again.

He glanced up at the gathering clouds. If that had been a sign from above, he'd do better slogging through and getting his own answers. A heaviness settled on his shoulders, and he reined in the growling six pack, straining to chase after the vehicle.

His four-footed buddies trotted beside him and, sensing his turbulent mood, rubbed their muzzles against his thigh.

"Telling me to calm down, aren't you?" He patted their backs and rubbed behind their ears. "Tough doing, but you could be right." A frown dug into his forehead, and an unsettling feeling stirred inside him, but he ignored it.

"Come on, troupe," he muttered, traipsing for the open acreage.

Wind whipped through his clothing like an ice shower. He hunched his shoulders and pulled up the collar of his overcoat. "Let's grab a handful of those wild daisies as a peace offering and head for home."

Yelping, the dogs dashed ahead, and he stumbled after them.

Thirty minutes later, Johnny had settled the animals in for the night and bounded up the stairs to the front porch. "Nothing like fresh air to clear a man's head," he murmured to himself. With a smile on his mouth and a bouquet in his hand, he marched through the front door and to Samantha.

And braked in his tracks.

Roses. The scent of roses was everywhere. Nauseating.

"What's going on?" He dropped his hand to his side, and the daisy spray drooped behind his thigh unnoticed.

A myriad of vases overflowing with flowers flanked Sam's chair. She juggled the bouquets of blooms in her arms and shuffled from the chair, the blanket … his blanket … pooling at her feet. "Michael surprised me with dozens of red roses."

"And dozens," Johnny muttered beneath his breath.

"Samantha said she was partial to roses." Michael beamed like a schoolboy. "So, I ordered them when she was snoozing. Nice surprise, eh?"

Not nice. Johnny snarled in his throat, but didn't voice the combative words.

"That young man from town delivered them." Samantha sneezed an explanation, holding the blooms slightly away from her nose.

"Got a hefty tip for it, too." Michael waggled his brows, pleased with himself.

"Yeah." The kid had nearly plowed into him and the dogs, busting the speedometer to get here on record time. Johnny curled his lip. Bet that had something to do with the super-size tip.

"Where should I put this bunch?" Samantha glanced about. "There aren't enough vases." She giggled. "I mean tin cans."

"I'll get you some tomorrow," Michael offered.

"What, tin cans?" Johnny couldn't help jabbing.

"That's your department," he said, his features folding in distaste. "From me Samantha shall have crystal."

While Samantha chattered to Michael about roses and vases, Johnny withdrew from the room. Trudging down the hall, he flexed and unflexed his hand. He'd been about to blast the joker but then checked himself. It would backfire, and he'd appear the jerk. Copy that if he refused to allow Samantha to accept the bimbo's gifts.

Johnny stormed out the front door and banged it behind him. It was beyond him how she could like that goofball. A groan staggered from deep inside him. It was time he faced the truth. He just didn't measure up. He didn't when he was poor, and didn't now, even with his millions.

Samantha and Michael had lived the life of the rich and famous all their lives. He'd lived the life of a pauper since the day he was born almost thirty-five years ago. The five million didn't suddenly morph him into a new man. He was still the same guy Samantha married. If that wasn't good enough for her, then too bad. She was free to choose again.

After the baby arrived.

Brave words, but the sinking feeling in his heart told a different story.

Plunking down on the top step, he held the wildflowers loosely in his hands and contemplated the sky. It reflected his mood. A second later, the heavens opened, and rain gushed to earth. A myriad of emotions welled up inside him, and he was ready to explode. Ruthlessly he shoved them aside, except for one.

Anger.

Anger was safe.

It masked his true feelings from a discerning eye. Vulnerable. Gutted emotionally.

A sudden gust smacked him in the face, and whipped the daisies from his hand. He threw back his head and laughed, the sound sucked from him by nature's fury. And just like that, it seemed his life was being stolen from him too.

His marriage to Samantha was on a downhill spiral, and he didn't know how to break the momentum. Every time he tried to get close to her, Michael butted in. If he protested too much about the goon's helping out, she'd dig in her heels and insist the man stay. Of course, he could demand he pack his belongings and get out, but he'd probably incur her wrath. Another mark against him. He rubbed his hands together to warm them. Somehow, he had to keep a cool head and gain an advantage.

How to do it was his dilemma.

He clicked his tongue, baffled. Was it him? The strain of approaching fatherhood? Matrimonial uncertainty? Or was it Sam? The stress of approaching motherhood? He doubted if the condition of their marriage affected her much. Whenever he turned his back, Michael seemed to be fawning over her and making her laugh with his antics.

Johnny couldn't remember the last time he'd made her laugh.

Going with the flow and biding his time until the baby arrived was his best bet. He grunted. Otherwise, if she flew the coop to mamma with that simpleton, he'd be left out in the cold. A wry smile brushed his mouth at his choice of words. Another blast of wind wiped the smile from his face and stung his cheeks.

He'd make his presence known but keep a low profile for the next few weeks. It'd be hard to do in his own house, especially while watching that moron make a play for his wife. His insides eroded. But he had no other recourse.

The psychology thing again possibly. He'd sleep on it and come up with a definite strategy by morning.

He swung his fist in the air. Still in the game. And he'd play to win.

He'd chase Michael out of his life for good. Johnny grimaced at his thoughts. Mercenary. But then he tightened his jaw, resolute. No more mercenary than Michael, who threatened his family and his future.

If you really believed it was yours, Johnny, no one could take it. Not even Michael, the little voice in his head jabbed. He scrubbed his chin with his hand. "Yeah! Yeah!" *I heard you.* "Now buzz off!" A groan, and he glanced about. Man, he must be losing it, talking to himself like that.

He vaulted off the steps, stuffed his hands in his coat's pockets and slogged away from the house. He got as far as the gate and booted a stone into cyberspace.

"Wait a minute." He glanced back at the house, his words vibrating around him.

A light shone from the living room window. A welcome beacon, but as things stood not for him. He rolled his shoulders, working out the kinks. That was his house and his wife in there. No way would he allow bank-boy to push him out. With that thought uppermost in his mind, he marched back to the home front ready to battle.

Chapter Twenty-Four

Over the next several weeks, Johnny kept to his strategy to regain ground on his marriage. He'd also managed to keep Michael so busy fetching and carrying outside during the renovations, he'd kept his distance from both Samantha and him for most of the day. The late evenings had been more of a challenge, but none-theless, unobtrusively as possible, Johnny kept watch over what was his.

Samantha and the baby.

Once again, having finished settling the dogs for the night, Johnny stomped his boots on the doormat, dusting the air, and sauntered to the living room. Beneath his veiled gaze, he caught the two of them sitting side by side on the sofa, seemingly engrossed in a game of cards. Innocent enough, but he wouldn't put anything past the diddler. As had become his custom, Johnny crossed the floor and took residence on the crate by the fireside to wait it out until Michael had had enough and turned in.

Samantha peered at Johnny from above the fan of cards in her hands, noting his wind-bitten face, tousled hair and set jaw. "Your move, Michael," she said concealing the whoosh of air leaving her lips.

"It certainly is." Michael rubbed the bridge of his nose and slapped a card on the table. "Gotcha."

She squinted at him. Why did she get this unsettling feeling in her stomach that his words held a hidden meaning?

"Heh, heh." Michael jabbed her elbow with his and breathed over her shoulder through the leer on his mouth.

That sounded creepy to her, and she shoved him back. "I think not." Flipping a card over, she grinned. "Gin. I win."

"I'll get you next time." He swept the cards from her hand, brushing his fingers against hers in a distinct signal. Snatching her hand away, Samantha felt a queasy feeling in her stomach again.

With a blank look on his face, Michael shuffled the deck for the next game.

She must stop reading double meanings into his words and actions. Michael looked innocent enough, and so thoughtful to hang out here in the sticks to help them. If that wasn't friendship, she didn't know what was.

"We'll see." She flashed him an extra bright smile to show she appreciated his loyalty and peered at Johnny from beneath her lashes.

He had his ankle propped on one knee and his face hidden behind a magazine. She wondered why he insisted on plunking down on the wooden crate instead of the armchair beside her and Michael on the sofa. The furniture from their apartment had been delivered, and although just a few pieces, they offered a semblance of comfort. Was it another hint he didn't want to be near her?

"Johnny?"

"Mmm." He didn't even peek over the publication in his hands.

"Michael has offered to drive me to town tomorrow to look at remodeling catalogues for the final touches on the house," she said. "You don't mind if he uses the truck, do you?"

"Over my—" Johnny bit off the combative words and lowered

191

the tabloid a fraction, his eyes straying to his wife. Then, recalling his newfound wisdom, he snapped it back in place. "Be my guest, Scott."

Samantha was so big now, and getting more beautiful each day. He wanted to take her in his arms and show her once again how good it could be between them. But, of course, he didn't. The timing was off. A grunt erupted from his chest, and he muffled the sound by flipping pages.

Yawning, Michael rubbed his eyes. Good. With all the extra work he had to do, by nightfall he was ready to crash out on his bunk in the attic.

At first he'd fussed at the idea of his attic quarters, until Johnny explained it'd be furthest from the yelping dogs. Of course, it was the furthest from their bedroom, too, but he didn't go into that minor detail.

All in all, that only allowed him a brief visit with Sam in the evenings, which suited Johnny just fine.

But slicker-boy found ways to corner Sam whenever he could with some trick, some joke. Whenever Johnny heard her laughter, he put in an appearance and nixed his crafty plans to usurp her attention. Michael slinked out but would always return with some gift or bauble for her. That, of course, did not suit Johnny at all.

On his one day off, by the time Michael dragged himself from the sack, groaning about his aching body, it was often mid-afternoon. Johnny grinned. That had taken care of his anticipated Sunday outings with Sam. His grin vanished. Except for today's unexpected announcement.

"That's very decent of you, Jonathan." Michael slapped his cards on the table and got to his feet.

Johnny shot him a closed look beneath his brows, like, *who you kiddin', bimbo-man?*

"Y-you don't mind?" Samantha stacked the cards and slid them in the package, a slight wobble in her voice.

"'Bout what?" Johnny said in an off-hand way, pretending not to understand what she referred to.

"Michael taking me into town tomorrow."

Johnny rustled pages, feigning interest in a magazine article. "Nah."

****

The next morning, Johnny, barefoot and dressed in low-riding pajama bottoms, strolled into the kitchen, rubbing his damp hair with a towel. He viewed the scene before him with distaste and slung the towel around his neck. His wife and the bimbo were sharing another cozy meal. Forcing a smile on his mouth, he walked to the cupboard and flipped a cup from the shelf into the palm of his hand. He grabbed the jar of Nescafe, shook a teaspoon worth of granules into the mug and filled it with steaming water from the pot.

A cup of coffee first thing in the morning did a man good. Then he shuttered his eyes, watching her lean into Michael to better hear what he said. He could think of a more entertaining activity in the a.m. which got a man a heck of a lot more excited than a cup of brew. Oxygen filled his lungs, blood traveling fast and hot through his veins. He didn't know how Sam had managed it, but he'd found himself on the floor in the sleeping bag last night, while she snoozed on the freshly made bed. Something about not wanting to cause him discomfort during the night when she got up to go to the bathroom.

Lame excuse.

She'd never been that considerate of his feelings before when it came to that. But he'd gone along. Playing. Testing. Waiting. There'd be a showdown soon enough.

Since all he had warming him now was the black brew, he propped his hip against the counter and took a long sip. "What time you headin' out?" he asked in a casual voice.

Michael glanced at Samantha for word.

She sent Michael a smile that rivaled the sunshine that'd sizzled since those couple of freaky thunderstorms. "Right after breakfast would be nice."

Johnny frowned into the depths of his cup, and then glanced up, bumping into her gaze. "Right after breakfast it will be."

"What do you mean?" Samantha asked.

"Didn't I tell you?" He took another swig of coffee and dumped the remainder down the drain. "I'm tagging along."

Michael sputtered into his coffee cup, then coughed.

Johnny stepped over and pounded him on the back. "Something wrong?"

With watery eyes, Michael shook his head and tried to knock his hand off him. Johnny pounded his back once more for good measure.

"I need more supplies for the house." Johnny leveled his gaze on Samantha. "Isn't that what you want? A fashionable remodeling on this place?"

"Yes." She rubbed her forefinger around the rim of the teacup. "But there's no need for you to take time off work. Michael can get what we need. After all, he's the foreman."

Johnny gritted his molars, the smile staying frozen on his face, his cheeks aching. "Oh, but I insist." Yanking the towel from around his neck, he rubbed his bare chest and sauntered from the room. "See you out front in ten."

At the appointed time, Johnny slouched in the driver's seat, revving the motor, his fingers drumming on the steering wheel. Watching Michael play gallant and assist his wife onto the front seat had his insides churning over like the engine. However, when he made to climb aboard and sit beside her, he put his foot down.

"Hey, man," he drawled. "It's a tight squeeze in front." He inclined his head over his shoulder and dropped his shades on his nose. "Climb in back. You don't want her to be uncomfortable, do you?"

Michael hesitated and then clambered in back, draping his designer jacket over the seat. Next moment, he shuffled forward, folded his arms on the back of the seat and poked his head between them.

"Can't do that, man." No way was he going to drive into town and have the blockhead blabbering in his ear. He pointed to the seatbelt. "Sit up and buckle up. It's the law."

"Of course."

Johnny figured he'd made a point that round. Stretching across Sam, he pulled the belt to buckle her in and, on the way back up bumped her breasts with his chin. Her breath fanned the nape of his neck. He tried to ignore the reaction of his body, but the damage was done. Soft and warm, he craved to bury his face in her bosom, drinking in her scent, touching, tasting, suckling ... He managed to shift away from the physical contact, but her delicate rose perfume stirred his senses. Memories flooded his mind. Memories of their wedding night, memories of all the nights since; when he touched, she touched, in the most erotic way ... he steeled his gut but couldn't control the leap of his pulse.

"Buckle up," he said, voice gruff, stretching the strap wide across her girth.

Samantha reached out to click it in place and her fingers brushed his. High voltage charged into her, and she quickly withdrew her hand, her heart racing.

"Thanks," she murmured, avoiding his eyes.

Johnny clicked the buckle in place.

For a breathless moment, she was tucked so close beside him, his heat sensitized her skin, and the cool spice of his aftershave tickled her nose. When he slid back to the driver's seat, she peeked at him from beneath her lashes. He adjusted the rearview mirror, released the brake and gripped the steering wheel with his hands. Strong, gentle hands. Hands that had explored every inch of her body in the most intimate way and made her blush from the crown of her head to the soles of her feet. She drew in a rush of air and, turning to look out the window, exhaled in a sigh, fogging up the pane.

The truck coasted down the track and onto the main road. Tension stretched taut between them, ready to snap at the first provocation. Sam shrank into her corner as far away from Johnny as possible, watching the vast desert whizzing by. In the distance, track home subdivisions were in the middle of construction, and she felt a sliver of ease. Not so isolated, after all.

"It's good of you, Jonathan, to be our chauffeur." Michael chuckled, blundering into their force field.

Johnny grunted and kept his focus straight ahead; tightening his grip on the steering wheel, he flexed his shoulder muscles.

Samantha sensed he'd like nothing better than to send Michael packing. But she couldn't have that. Michael was a buffer between her and Johnny. Without his noisy presence, she knew that one look from Johnny's smoky brown eyes and she'd succumb to his charm.

She couldn't do that.

Mustn't do that.

She'd fallen for his Irish malarkey two years ago and here she was married and pregnant. She clenched her hand, her fingernails biting into her palm. Was their marriage a counterfeit too, as that letter implied?

She would have to do some investigating, just to be sure; Michael could help her … search the internet at the library, call the city registry, do something. What she should've done was check the copy of their license in their safety deposit box at the Wells Fargo Bank in North Hollywood before rushing off that day. Since she'd been too upset to think clearly then, she could make up for it today at the library.

And if it was as the letter stated … she groaned.

"You, okay?" Johnny flicked his gaze over her.

"Great," she said, her voice overly bright.

He bunched his brow and turned his attention back to the road, saying nothing further.

Fine, she thought. *Fine!* Except, of course, it wasn't. Far from it.

However, this time around she wanted to make her decision with both eyes open, her heart and mind in sync. Johnny shifted gears, and his elbow brushed her thigh. Her pulse skidded. So much for controlling her emotions. Her heart had a will of its own.

"You're good at this chauffeur thing, Jonathan," Michael said in a conversational tone. "If you'd like a regular job with good benefits, I could—"

Johnny tightened his jaw, a nerve flogging his cheek.

"He's had practice," she interjected, deflecting the explosion brewing between the two men. "Chauffeuring."

The sound of Johnny's sharp intake of breath.

Disguised as a chauffeur, he'd gate crashed the wedding and claimed her as his bride. That seemed eons ago. Moistness pressed against her eyelids, and she blinked it away.

Michael snorted from the back seat.

"Worked, didn't it, Mikey?" Johnny said, his smooth words underlining a hard edge.

"Did it?" Michael gloated, his features reflected in the mirror. "Matter of opinion."

"Nice of you both to escort me to town," she blurted, fending off Johnny's next droll remark that'd stoke the already volatile situation.

Both men grunted in acquiescence. Samantha hid a smile.

"Not too bumpy for you back there, Michael?" she asked, glancing over her shoulder at him.

"Fi-i-ne," Michael said, bobbing up and down.

Johnny kept tabs on Michael through the mirror in the cab. When Samantha put her hand on the upholstery, the lovesick fool shuffled forward in his seat, attentive as a pup tossed a bone.

But when he placed his hand over hers, Johnny almost slammed on the brakes. Only by exerting extreme control over this inclination did he maintain normal speed. When he dared to squeeze her fingers, Johnny leaned on the horn, and Michael sprang away from her.

"It's a pleasure to take you into town, Samantha," bank-boy spouted, finding his voice much too quickly. "And wherever your heart desires."

Johnny smirked. *Laying it on a bit too thick, man.* But he kept that thought to himself. Ultimately, that might show his hand. Not an overly patient man, Johnny was fast learning to cultivate that virtue.

"I'll take you in my limo next time," the bozo offered.

There won't be a next time, buster, Johnny tossed the words around in his brain.

Samantha dared flutter her lashes at him. "Michael, how you do flatter a girl."

"Not just any girl," he murmured, his veiled gaze glued on her face.

Johnny had heard enough, and his innards somersaulted. Grim-faced, he focused on the approaching curve in the road, reminding himself that Michael Scott would be out on his backside before too long if he had anything to do about it. And he would. Very soon.

In the meantime, he'd put a stop to this *tete-a-tete*.

He swerved around the corner, tires screeching. Michael jostled back in place and Samantha slid into Johnny, nearly landing on his lap, her cotton dress riding up her thigh.

"You okay, Sam?" Johnny caught a glimpse of her shapely leg even though she was quick to straighten the material over her limbs. A sizzle of a beat, then he tossed over his shoulder, "Okay back there?"

"You did that on purpose," Michael accused, affronted.

"If you say so." Johnny curved his mouth in a satisfied grin.

Samantha snuggled back in her place, wondering what to make of Johnny. As each day passed, he became more puzzling, aloof. She took a deep breath and exhaled in force. As difficult as it might be, she determined to enjoy the day's outing.

A tense silence filled the cab, broken only by the hum of the motor while Johnny navigated the road for several more miles.

"Downtown Main Street at your service," Johnny finally announced, glimpsing the other man's reflection in the mirror with his mouth hanging open. "Something the matter, Scott?"

"It's no more than a pit-stop in the middle of nowhere." He took a comb from his pants' pocket, glanced in the mirror and slicked back his hair. "I could blink and miss it."

"If you don't like it " – Johnny flipped his sunglasses off and hooked them on his T-shirt pocket – "There's a bus across the street you can hop on."

"Wouldn't give you the satisfaction, leprechaun man." He stuffed the comb back in his pocket, snapped his shirt cuffs and adjusted his Pierre Cardin cravat. "This might be a prime location to check out the locals." He shot him a haughty nod. "With Samantha."

Johnny slid into a parking space and hopped out, striding around to help Samantha out, but the other had already vaulted from the back seat and beat him to it. Johnny gulped down his annoyance, his Adam's apple working overtime, and swiped his damp palms across his T-shirt sticking to his chest. Wouldn't do to make a scene in the middle of Main Street, but then again— Before he changed his mind and decked Michael on the chin, the other man sidestepped him, leading his wife on.

"Samantha, shall we?" Michael offered her his arm.

"Goodsprings, Nevada." She took his arm, strolling along the sidewalk, gazing at the storefront of Flossie's Ice Cream Parlor. "What a charming place." She peered at various photos displayed in the shop window and caught Johnny's dour reflection in the glass. "The old and new frozen in time."

Like her life, she thought, caught between her past and her future.

"Would you like an ice cream cone?" Michael asked.

She shook her head, not thinking she could stomach it … or anything right now. "Maybe later."

By this time, Johnny loomed on her other side, and he stood so close to her, his arm bobbed against hers. Sizzle shot into her, and she bristled, shifting a step away from him.

Johnny noticed her maneuver.

A strained silence coiled around them.

For a moment, Samantha stood stiffly between the two men, but then she pushed unpleasant thoughts aside. "Come on," she invited, looping her arm with Johnny's too. "I'm ready to go shopping."

But Johnny didn't move.

He shuttered his gaze, studying them. His heart pounded. Sweat broke across his chest. Air expanded in his lungs. He raised a fist, muffling the sound blasting from his mouth. He mocked a cough. Then, Johnny did the hardest thing possible and nearly burst a blood vessel in the process. He unhooked her hand from his elbow and handed her over to Michael, *carte blanche.*

"You two go along." A pause, a narrowing of his eyes, then, "I'll catch up with you later."

Startled, she stared at him, her features pinched in query. Before he could retract his idiotic words, she masked her uncertainty and turned to Michael. "I'd like to start with the library," she said, a slight quiver in her voice. "Is there one here?"

Aww, man. Maybe this psych stuff wasn't such a good idea.

"Sure." Johnny pointed to the brick building down the street. "The supplies could wait, if you'd like me to show you arou—"

"I wouldn't dream of coming between you and your supplies." She patted his arm and turned back to the enemy. "Michael, shall we go?"

Johnny watched them stroll away, his belly clenching and his mouth lined with sawdust. At that moment, she glanced at him over her shoulder and wiggled her fingers. "Bye."

He nodded and, bashing down bile rising in his throat, stalked in the opposite direction to the hardware store, every muscle in his body taut.

In the fastest time in the history of mankind, Johnny wheeled a cart laden with lumber, rolls of paper, paint brushes, electrical gadgets and an assortment of other construction supplies to the checkout counter. After he dumped the load in the back of the Chevy pickup, he trotted to the library and through the automatic doors, the air conditioning smacking his sweat-drenched body.

He scanned the interior. Once, twice. Not seeing them, he strolled up and down each row of shelves, searching. Finally, at the back of the room behind the last shelf, he caught them.

Chapter Twenty-Five

Michael had cornered Samantha between two rows of bookshelves, his hand splayed on the wall near her shoulder. Bending his head, he whispered something in her ear.

A giggle, and she pressed her hand against his chest.

Johnny blanched, his blood icing in his veins.

He'd lost.

Her.

His baby.

Their life together.

A future.

It finally smacked him between the eyes. He couldn't compete with money and class like that of the Scotts.

Then, a voice in his head whispered, *you goon, you've got money. Five million buckaroos.* So what? He didn't want to buy her or her love or their life. He wanted her to want him for who he was. Johnny Belen, from the wrong side of the tracks with dreams in his head, love in his heart and empty pockets. Yeah, he wanted her to want him. Period.

With his world crashing before his eyes, Johnny spun away and almost tripped over his own feet. Wait a minute. Samantha might not want him as her husband, and as much as that gutted his insides, there was a baby that would want him. Need him. He'd make sure his son or daughter knew him. He wouldn't forfeit his child, no matter what. He had five million dollars to make sure of that.

He pivoted, his hard gaze raking over them. "Am I interrupting anything?" Marching forward, he closed the gap, each step like lead. "Or are you two ready to leave?"

Michael pulled away, and Johnny collided with her clear gaze.

"You're back so soon, Johnny." She extended a home decorating magazine to him. "What do you think of this?"

He dismissed the trade, his eyes drilling deeper into her, demanding to read the truth. A suspended moment, and she snapped the journal closed, handing it to Michael. "I'd like to sign this out, please."

"Sure." Michael took it from her numb fingers and sauntered ahead to the checkout counter.

By the time they met him at the exit, there seemed to be an ocean of discontent dividing them.

Oblivious to the undercurrent between them, Michael said, "Ready for lunch?"

"Too much work to do," Johnny muttered. "We'll eat at the house."

Samantha's heart pitter-pattered in her chest, and she wondered what happened to make Johnny look at her with such icy disdain. Just a moment ago Michael had loomed over her, and, feeling claustrophobic, she'd tried to push him away. Now she jumped at the chance to escape the dour-faced Johnny. "I'd love to, Michael."

"Where to?" Michael took her arm and guided her out. "There must be a local hangout."

"How about the Bar & Grill?"

"Isn't that where Mira ... whatever works?" Johnny asked, walking a little behind the two, not missing a thing. "Aka The Pioneer Saloon and Café, aka The Tavern, aka The Pub."

"You remember?"

"Sure do," he said his gaze probing. "Not much gets by me, Mrs. Belen."

"The Bar & Grill it is." Michael walked forward, stopped, and glanced up and down the street. "Which way?"

An imperceptible sigh skimmed Johnny's mouth. "This way." He stomped ahead, leading the way. "I'd like to see if this woman is real or a figment of my wife's imagin—"

That did it. Samantha marched fast forward as quickly as her overladen condition allowed, grabbed his elbow and twirled him around. "Hey, I did not imagine that sweet lady."

Johnny raised his hands. "Okay. Don't get upset. If she's real, no problem." He tilted his head as if studying her. "But if she's not, we-ell ..."

"What are you implying?"

"Why nothing, sweetheart." He grabbed her hand and looped it through his elbow. She didn't pull away. Perhaps all was not lost. He glanced over his shoulder at Michael.

A perplexed look riddled the man's face as he wondered what just happened and glanced down at his empty hands. About time the tables turned in Johnny's favor. He lifted the corner of his mouth in a crooked smile. Now that he had Samantha on his arm, he'd make the most of it.

"Coming, Michael?"

Less than five minutes later, Johnny pushed the saloon-style doors open and escorted Samantha inside. Music blared, but the air was cool and clean due to the no smoking signs. While Michael paused outside admiring a pinstriped suit in the shop window next door, Johnny searched for an empty table. He spotted a booth by the window with a wide girth that would accommodate Samantha.

Ambling beside him, Samantha glanced about and waved, smiling. Johnny followed her gaze and the returning wave and grin from the person behind the bar. "You know the bartender?" he asked, surprised.

"There is the figment of my imagination." She chuckled and shuffled in the booth.

"That's Mira—"

"Mirabella," she said. "Tough as nails, sharp as a razor and quick as a whip."

"Gotcha."

"About time." She slanted him a glance from beneath her lashes, wondering if her words had a Freudian implication.

"Good thing she's on our side." He slid in the booth, facing her.

"Too true."

"Meaning?"

"Well, what with her super powers ..."

"Now wait a minute." He chuckled and felt a lightness in his spirit. And suddenly it was like old times, he and Sam teasing each other good- naturedly. "Don't get carried away."

"Remember the cherry pie." She shook her finger at him. "You gobbled it down and wanted more."

"Yeah." Wanting more was right. But not food. He gazed into her bright eyes and half parted lips. Wanting to bend down and capture them ... tasting her. "It was the best I've had," he admitted, tenderness stirring inside him for this woman who carried his child.

"And the clean house that I didn't take a broom to," she said. "I should've taken one to you, though, Johnny."

"Oh really?"

"Mmm." She gave him a pixie smile that turned his insides to mush.

He grunted and rubbed his cheek with his knuckles. He should've known it couldn't last. From beneath his brows, he paced the 'thorn' closing in and ready to gouge his side.

"Good." Michael hurried across the room, smoothing his wind-blown hair. "You found a table."

"We won't mind if you want to head back out," Johnny hinted.

205

"The hundred and twelve-degree temperature shouldn't faze a tough guy like you."

"Of course not." He slid in beside Samantha. "I promised Samantha a country-style lunch."

"More research?"

"Sure." He smiled into her eyes. "Local folklore and country cooking."

"Home cooking is what you mean, young man." Mirabella suddenly appeared beside their table, wiping her hands on her dime-sized apron that barely covered her cowgirl uniform.

"Yes, ma'am." Michael propped up to attention.

So, this was mamma's choice, Mirabella thought. She shook her head and glanced at heaven. What now?

You'll come up with something … a chuckle … out of this world. The message tickled her solar plexus.

Hah, hah, she transmitted back, a hint of sarcasm in her tone. Do I get double vacation time for this?

After the assignment, we'll discuss it.

Mirabella smirked to no one in particular. It might not turn out the way You'd like. Free will 'n all that.

It will be the best.

Hope you're right.

I know it.

And she did, too. He always got it perfect. Right now, though, she wasn't sure how it would happen. Samantha sat quietly staring out the window. Johnny's face reflected a storm brewing. Michael leaned back, resting his arm on the vinyl padding behind Samantha's shoulders and looking like he owned the premises.

"This place turn a profit?" he asked.

Samantha smiled and made the introductions. "The most amazing neighbor you'll ever meet, Michael. She's a wonder."

"I bet," said Johnny.

Mirabella gave him a stern look. "You placing bets on me, young man?"

"No, ma'am." Johnny suddenly felt like a schoolboy beneath her studious gaze, yet she looked no more than twenty herself. Yeah, twenty going on sixty, by her manner and speech. Wonder how she did it. He flashed her his rakish grin. "Just admiring my surroundings."

"Me included?"

Johnny chuckled. "Absolutely."

"'Bout time I got appreciated." She winked, belying the severity of her words.

"You are that, ma'am."

"You include your lovely and very pregnant wife in that sentiment?"

"Always, ma'am," he said, mesmerized by her brilliant smile.

She considered him for a moment longer from the corner of her eye, and thinking she'd put him on the spot long enough, patted his shoulder. "Good man." Then she turned to Michael, who was busy brushing imaginary dust off the table. Hmm, another germ-conscious human.

"We do okay in the profit department," Mirabella answered his question. "And the table's clean."

Michael glanced up and smiled, showing his dimple.

So, he can turn the charm on when it benefits him.

"I didn't mean to imply you didn't." Michael tilted his head at just the right angle. "I might buy this place."

"Not for sale." A young waitress walked up to their table, her dark curls bobbing around her face, her violet-blue eyes serious.

Michael crossed one leg over his knee and raked his wolfish eye over the girl. "Everything has its price."

Mirabella wanted to kick him.

"Ouch!" Michael placed a hand under the table and rubbed his shin.

Mirabella crinkled her eyes in amusement. Samantha had done it for her. "Some things, young man, don't carry a dollar sign."

"Like love." Samantha peeked at her husband, and her tremulous smile faded. He had his face behind the menu like he'd already dismissed the conversation circulating the table. Of course, she knew better. Alert, he caught every word and then some.

"Is there such a thing?" the girl asked, her eyes shadowed, a wistful twist to her mouth.

A silent moment, then they all erupted at once, except for Johnny.

"Of course," Samantha said.

"Nowadays?" She set three glasses of water on the table and took her order pad from her apron's pocket. "It's like looking for the proverbial needle in a hay stack."

So cynical for one so young, Mirabella thought. "Perhaps you should let it find you."

The waitress snapped her head up, a flicker of a smile on her mouth.

"Oh, it'll find you alright." Michael guffawed, wagging his foot. "Especially when the path is paved with crispy green bills."

"Doesn't last," Johnny muttered into the menu, finally voicing his thoughts.

Samantha's heart sank. Was that a message for her? That he didn't love her anymore? That he wanted their marriage over like that letter had implied? She set her own menu on the table, suddenly having no interest in food.

"Now that's where you're wrong, young man." Mirabella took him to task and turned to Samantha. "Isn't that right, dear?"

Near tears, Samantha shoved Michael from the booth. "Excuse me, I have to use the restroom."

"Janey here will take your orders," Mirabella said, looking directly at Michael.

He blinked at her in confusion.

A smooth operator this one. Too slick. The kind that eventually bumbled over himself. Mirabella chuckled. "I'll be behind the bar if you need anything." As for the other one, Johnny Belen, he had his insides in knots wondering where he stood with his wife, when all he had to do was … A customer caught her attention, and the thought drifted away.

Janey scribbled Johnny's order on her pad and turned to Michael. "What will you have?"

Michael wiggled his eyebrows and dimpled his cheek. "I'll start with one of you." He winked.

Johnny bolted upright. So, that was his game. He glanced at the waitress, but instead of taking offense, she giggled. "Not on the menu, today, sir." She fluttered her lashes at him.

"How about tonight?"

Johnny cocked his head, his eyes shuttered, his ears tuned in.

Janey smiled, not giving him a direct answer. When she reached out to take the menu from his hand, his fingers tangled with hers for a nanosecond. A definite signal.

"I'll take the house special," Michael said, watching the sway of her hips as she walked away.

Johnny had thought of Michael as the court jester, but a sleazy goon was totally another angle. How to tell Samantha was a tight fix. His shoulders slumped, and he slouched lower in the booth. She wouldn't believe him. Think he was badmouthing the friend of the family. He exhaled a sigh. He'd just have to wait it out. Watch for the right moment, then full speed ahead.

Glancing over his shoulder for Samantha, Johnny caught Mirabella smiling at him while shaking a concoction in the shaker. What was everyone so happy about? He wanted to smash chairs against tables and very possibly one or two over rich boy's head.

A sudden beeping noise pierced his thoughts, just as Michael pulled a miniature high tech transmitting device from his pocket. Looked like something a scientist would have to explain how to operate. Yet the bimbo must've figured how to use it, because he was talking into it. Hmm. Maybe not such a bozo after all.

"Willi—" Michael began and bit off his words. Flustered, he flung his head up and clashed with Johnny's cool gaze. "—er …

well, tell him what to do." Abruptly, he hung up and dropped the gadget back in his pocket.

Johnny slammed his lashes lower, his eyes slitting. Michael looked like he'd been caught with his hand in the cookie jar, but he'd bet Michael wasn't after that kind of dough.

"Business."

"Don't let me stop you." Johnny straightened up and stretched an arm along the back of the booth. "If you gotta go, you gotta go."

"You'd like that fine, wouldn't you?"

Johnny plastered an aggravatingly pleased grin on his mouth.

Michael glowered and set his elbows on the table. "I won't be going without Samantha."

"And hell can freeze over, Scott."

"Pull out your parka then. I feel a blizzard coming on," he baited. "Brr, in two days … with the right … er … wrong connections." Laughter burst from deep in his chest, and he slapped his hand on the table.

"Trying to tell me something, Scott?"

Michael shrugged. "Figure it out."

"Already done," Johnny fired back.

A tense moment, then Michael chuckled, the sound grating. "No, I think not."

"Think what you want, Scott."

Michael rubbed his hands together and opened his eyes wide. "For me to know and you to find out."

Johnny was nearly dumbfounded at his choice of words, and in other circumstances he would've burst out laughing. Not so now. He felt like a fish dangling on the end of a line, the hook embedded deep in his heart. Air pressure expanded in his lungs, and the words exploded from his mouth, "What's that supposed to mean?"

Michael raised his hand, blew lightly on his fingernails and buffed them across his shirt.

Johnny nailed the man with a fierce look. A blue streak poised to blast off his tongue, but Michael's next round hit its mark, neutralizing his hazardous thoughts.

"Little lady is a-comin'."

"Shut up," Johnny muttered between his teeth. Scott was up to no good, he sensed it in his gut. A hunch rarely missed. And he'd bet he'd been about to say 'Willie' before he faked it to 'well' during his staccato-style cell call. Something was going down in two days. And it involved Scott and Samantha. His gut ripped. He nearly groaned aloud, and he fisted his hands beneath the table just as Samantha drew near.

She smiled at Janey and exchanged a few words with Mirabella.

Mirabella tossed her head back and laughed, a deep, hearty sound that brought an unbidden curve to his mouth. He'd deal with Michael later. Then he grimaced. But what good would it do if Samantha had already made her choice?

Doubts tormented him long after she shuffled back beside Michael. He whispered something in her ear, and she burst out laughing. Johnny gripped the edge of the seat hard, the vinyl print pressing into his fingertips. Control, or he'd be up flooring the man with one swing.

"Order whatever—" Michael gestured with the menu and his glass went flying, spilling water onto the napkins and spraying Sam.

Startled, Samantha giggled.

"Sorry," Michael babbled.

"It's okay," she said, the smile lingering on her lips. "Fresh."

Could the man do no wrong in her eyes? A morose Johnny stared out the window at people strolling by, window-shopping or whizzing by in their jalopies. Ordinary. A normal day, in the normal life of a normal person. It seemed so easy, yet there was nothing normal about his life.

"Let me." Janey grabbed a dishcloth from her tray and mopped up the excess moisture from the table, her eyes straying from

Sam to Michael, then to Johnny. She slapped the rag back on her tray, her perplexed features reflecting that there was definitely something amiss with this trio.

Got that right, girlie, but not for much longer, Johnny thought. Not if he had anything to do about it, and he definitely did. And with that, Johnny took a napkin, reached across the booth and dabbed a moist spot from Samantha's pert nose. She acknowledged his gesture with a tremulous smile.

"You missed a spot." Michael flicked a drop of water from her chin with his finger and placed the moist tip in his mouth. "Tastes good."

A low growl sounded in Johnny's throat. The man was treading in a red flag zone, and unless he curbed his flaunts it was highly unlikely he'd get out of here in one piece.

Samantha reached across the table and brushed Johnny's arm, diffusing tension. His muscles turned iron hard beneath her fingers, and he glanced over his shoulder at the retreating waitress.

Sensing his withdrawal, she removed her hand. How could she reach this man of hers? He seemed so cold, so remote. Was there a chance for them? What would happen when he discovered she was a penniless rich girl from Beverly Hills? Would he still want her for whom she really was? Samantha Carroll, once endowed with wealth was now Cinderella poor. Would he turn out to be her Prince Charming come to the rescue or her croaking toad come to gloat? And how could he come to her rescue when he didn't have a penny to his name?

She sighed and pressed her hands to her temples.

"You okay, Sam?" Johnny asked, words jerking from his mouth.

She nodded and peeked at him from beneath her lashes. His jaw was like granite, his eyes brewing. Was he a wolf in lamb's clothing? Had it taken her two years to discover it? He was a married man. He had no business eyeing that waitress on her exit, and in front of her. Unless he already considered himself unmarried. She wrapped her quivery hands around her water glass, the condensation dampening her fingers.

She'd lost.

Lost Johnny.

Lost the chance at their future.

She took a drink, and liquid coolness slid down her throat. She set the glass back and slipped her hands beneath the table, patting her big belly.

Her baby.

She had her baby. She wouldn't relinquish her child. Regardless of how things stood between her and Johnny, she'd fight for her baby. She didn't have the funds to do it, but she'd think of something.

Turning her head slightly, she peered at Michael swirling the plastic straw in his water glass. A little boy look flashed across his face like he'd committed something naughty. He poked the ice at the bottom of the glass and slurped through the straw, appearing totally unconcerned.

"Michael, what are you doing?" She laughed, but she wasn't really amused. However, his antics distracted her from her troubling thoughts, and for that reason she gave him her undivided attention. And if Johnny wanted to behave like a boor, well, that was up to him.

"Daydreaming."

Samantha blinked, a flicker of a smile still on her lips.

"Of you."

"Always got some guff up your sleeve, don't you, Scott?" Johnny came to life, barely, the words grazing his mouth.

"For the right person." Michael ignored him and grinned at her.

Johnny set his jaw, and a nerve tore from his cheek to his temple. A tense beat, and words soft and smooth and controlled fell from his tongue, "How many right persons do you have?"

Turning up his nose, Michael bit the straw with his teeth and blew bubbles in the water. Johnny couldn't believe his eyes, and neither could she. Never mind that Michael was acting the fool beside her, she had to look at her options.

At twenty-nine, Samantha had to think of her future and her child's. If Johnny turned out to be the dud of the century ... her heart kicked in denial, but she didn't listen to it. Then, *you'd never have married him if he was a jerk.* She dismissed that, too. He could've changed. People do. For this last week, she'd be marking time and watching. Carefully.

The waitress approached with their orders and set a plate in front of her. The grilled salmon nestled atop a green salad should've had her taste buds bopping, but instead her mouth felt dry. She squeezed a wedge of lemon over the food, took a bite and forced the morsel down for baby's sake.

Michael wolfed down the steak and chug-a-lugged a can of Coke. Johnny, on the other hand, left his burger untouched and sipped from his water glass.

"Do you have ketchup?" Michael asked without missing a beat from chomping off another bite.

"Here you are, sir." The waitress took the plastic bottle from her tray and offered it to him, but it accidentally squirted.

"What the—" Michael jerked back in shock, tomato sauce dribbling from his face, then his features darkened in annoyance.

"I-I'm so sorry." Janey gaped at the ketchup trickling from his chin and splattering his shirt. Speechless, she snatched up the washcloth and mopped his shirt, but that only smeared it more.

"That will be all." Michael clamped his fingers around her wrist, his eyes chilling.

"I'm s-sorry," the girl stammered, a blush creeping up her neck and flushing her cheeks. "I didn't mean to squeeze the bottle."

"Right." Michael dismissed her apology, and realizing he still held her hand, let her go like he'd been zapped by a livewire.

The girl skittered back to the kitchen.

214

"Such incompetence," he grumbled. "I should make her pay to clean my shirt." His eyes strayed in the direction she'd gone. "And to think I flirted with her, thinking—"

"When was that Michael?" Samantha asked.

"Well, I-I don't remember exactly."

Johnny came to attention, his mouth splitting in a saucy grin. "Let me remind you."

"Not necessary." Michael spoke a tad too quickly, attempting to cover his blunder.

But Johnny was not about to be swayed. He saw his chance and chased it for all its worth. "While Samantha was in the bathroom."

"Is that right, Michael?" she asked, her eyes wide with innocence. "You hit on that girl behind my back?" Her hand fluttered to her mouth, concealing the twitch of a smile.

Michael shrugged, dismissing the incident as totally unimportant. "Wanted to give her a little attention." He loosened his cravat, and a sound, not quite a laugh and not quite a groan, trickled from his mouth. "City man, country girl. You know."

"I don't know, Michael." She folded her napkin neatly and placed it beside her plate. "Why don't you explain it to me?"

"Hrmph. I wanted to see how she'd relate to customers," he said, scrambling for words. "Thought I might give her a job—"

"Her duties?" Johnny couldn't help nixing his exit line.

Michael ignored him. "—in the restaurant casino ... uh ... dad and I are considering."

Samantha patted his arm. "How thoughtful of you."

Johnny sputtered. Samantha couldn't be falling for that line. Obviously she must, chatting him up the way she was. Yep. Hook, line, and *stinker* ... er ... sinker.

"You're serious about it?" she asked.

"Of course." Michael picked up a French fry and swiped it across a blob of ketchup that had fallen smack in the middle of his plate. "Your moth ... er ... my partner will be delighted."

"Michael, what're you saying?" she asked, snatching at his blunder. "My mother is involved in this?"

"Did I say that?"

Johnny had just taken a bite of his hamburger and was about to pierce a cherry tomato, but he changed his mind and pointed the fork at Michael. "Since you spilled the beanos, let's have the rest of it."

Shifting in his seat, Michael glanced around for an exit.

"Michael." Samantha stared him down.

"All right." He sighed. "The truth is—"

"You know the meaning of the word?"

Samantha shot Johnny a stern look.

Johnny motioned with his fork to proceed.

Michael gawked at him like he was a low life. Then, he settled back and turned his attention to her. "I-I wanted a partner and your mother, being the business woman that she is—"

"What does your father think?"

"He's ... uh ... leaving this transaction entirely up to me." He drummed his fingers on the tabletop. The cutlery clanged, and he dropped his hand onto his lap. "But h-h-he's had a yen to invest in these parts."

"Yen?" Johnny couldn't help jabbing. "Folk lingo that, sure."

A dark scowl from Michael. "Nobody asked you, carrot head."

Johnny grinned from ear to ear.

"Mom already has her hotel casino near the Nevada state line," Sam said, ignoring for the time being the men's impending squabble. "Just twenty minutes from here. She doesn't need another investment."

"She must think otherwise, for the Lucky Lou will be a major part of the transaction."

"What?" she leveled him with a laser-sharp look. "What exactly is going on?"

"Why don't you let her tell you, Samantha?" He picked up his fork, mashed fried potatoes, squirted ketchup in a circular design over them and forked them in his mouth.

"Because I'm asking you."

"Does he have to be here?" He inclined his head at Johnny and glowered.

"No."

"Yes," Johnny said.

Samantha touched his arm. "Johnny, would you mind if I have a few minutes alone with Michael?

Yeah, I do. Aloud he said, "If it 'll make you feel better, Sam." He dragged himself from the booth, branded the man with a fierce look, and then flicked his eyes over her. A second later, he strode to the bar and straddled a stool. Who was he after all? Just her husband, and soon to be her ex if he was reading the signals right.

"What'll it be?" Mirabella asked, placing a napkin on the counter.

"You don't want to know." He looked up, and her fathomless green gaze almost swept him away. Her smile washed over him like a soothing balm, and he found himself grinning back.

"How about something to drink for starters?"

He nodded. "Water with lots of bitter lemon."

"To match your mood?"

He chuckled. "That bad, eh?"

"Mmm." She poured him a tall glass of iced New Yorker and filled it with lime wedges.

He shook the kink from his shoulders, gulped the drink down in two shots and wiped his mouth with the back of his hand. "That hit the spot. Thanks."

She folded her arms on the counter and leaned forward, her eyes focused on his. "Things aren't always what they seem."

"No?" He tilted his head back at Michael and Samantha.

"No." She curved her mouth in that gentle smile that enveloped him in cotton wool.

"You coulda fooled me."

"Don't be." She winked and walked over to her next customer.

Johnny stared deep into the empty glass, wondering what Mirabella meant by her remarks. Had he been setting himself up, playing the fool?

Perplexed, he shook his head and swiveled off the stool. He pulled several bills from his pocket and set them on the counter. When he turned to go, she gave him the thumbs up signal. The corner of his mouth lifted in wry amusement, and he felt a lightness in his heart.

In two long strides, he loomed over Samantha and Michael, still deep in their discussion. "Finished, you two?" He grinned at the underlying meaning of his words and slapped a fifty on the table.

Samantha rummaged along the seat for her handbag and stuffed something inside, her hair camouflaging her face.

"I'm sorry, Samantha." Michael mumbled, nervously rubbing his thumb and index finger together.

"What mamma wants, she gets, isn't that it?" she murmured, a catch in her voice. "Never mind who gets hurt."

"What's the matter?" Johnny had long suspected mamma schemed to have her little girl reunited with bank-boy. A dry sound scratched his throat. The joke was on mamma. For the town had a *nouveau* rich dude, and his name was Johnny Belen. He brushed his knuckles across his chin. Alas, mamma didn't know that.

"None of your business, Belen," Michael said, his voice rising a notch.

"I'm making it my business."

"Stop it, the both of you," Samantha scolded, shuffling from the booth, her features pinched, her eyes glazed.

"Sam ..." Johnny said.

"Samantha ..." Michael said.

Ignoring both men, she waddled across the floor and out the

door, halting on the top step to get her bearings. A blistering heat wave smacked her in the face, and just having come from the air-conditioned tavern, she felt woozy. Her mouth was dry, and her throat was parched. She licked her lips and swallowed.

The horizon seemed to be darkening, yet the sky overhead was a hazy blue, the ground sunbaked. She squinted against the sun's glare and lifted her wrist to blot perspiration from her temples.

A hush of a footstep behind her.

A distant clap of thunder.

She stepped down, missed her footing and screamed, groping for anything to break her fall. She clutched empty air. She was falling, falling ... and all she could think of was her baby.

Chapter Twenty-Six

"No!" Johnny vaulted the distance between them and grabbed her before she crashed headlong down the stairs. Another heart-stopping moment followed as her excessive weight made him stagger, but he staggered backward away from the danger, bumping into Michael and stomping on his foot. "Call an ambulance, somebody!" He collapsed on the concrete and cushioned her against his chest, fear clawing into him.

She fluttered her eyes open. "Johnny." Then, she lowered her lashes and drifted off into oblivion.

With his fingers shaking, he unfastened several buttons on the front of her dress, ruffling the cotton to circulate air to her damp skin. His pulse pounded, and oxygen pressured his lungs to near explosive levels.

"I-i-is she go-going to be alr-right?" Michael stammered, ashen-faced.

"She ... they better be."

"Sh-she wanted to know." Michael drew back, favoring his sore foot. "Insisted."

"Shut up!" Johnny cut him a razor-sharp look. "If anything should happen to her or—" He shut his eyes tight against the sting pressing his lids. He couldn't lose her this way, or their baby. *No.* His insides screamed to heaven. *God, no!*

A gentle hand touched his shoulder. He got himself under control and glanced up at Mirabella's angelic face.

"They're going to be alright, Johnny," she said, tone reassuring.

"How can you be sure?" He brushed wisps of golden hair off Samantha's face and stroked her pale cheek with his fingertips.

"I believe. I know."

"I couldn't bear—." His voice broke and he rocked her in his arms. "I want to believe."

"You can," Mirabella said, her words soft as a dove's wing.

Just then, the ambulance siren pierced the afternoon lull in the downtown community and screeched to a stop. A medic hopped out, rushing to the scene while a second wheeled a gurney not far behind him. After checking her vital signs, the medics signaled it was okay to move her.

Johnny heaved her up in his arms and placed her upon the cot, holding her limp, cool hand. His heart clubbed his chest. Sweat poured from his pores and soaked his T-shirt. He didn't care. He sucked in a mouthful of air and willed his body heat to warm her chilled flesh.

"We've got her now," one of the attendants said.

Johnny nodded and tightened his fingers around hers, not letting go.

"Come along then."

After they rolled the stretcher into the ambulance, he climbed aboard, but before the door closed, Michael squeezed through.

"Get him out of here," Johnny growled.

Michael dug in his heels. "She's my fiancé."

Johnny shook his head. "She's my wife."

Confused, the attendants signaled the driver to drive on. "We'll sort this out at the hospital."

An hour later, Johnny still pacing the waiting room floor, paused to glance out the window, every cell in his body primed to explode at the least provocation. The sun had disappeared figuratively and literally from his vicinity—a desert flash storm doused the land, lightning tearing the sky … and his life.

Michael propped his backside on the edge of a chair and flipped pages in a magazine like a robot. Every time thunder rumbled, he jumped. Yo-yo man. Would've been comical in other circumstances, but to Johnny it compounded the burden on his shoulders. His legs nearly buckled, and he pressed his palms against the wall for support, his head bowed between his arms.

"Mr. Belen?"

"Yes." Johnny spun around so fast that for a second everything blurred, except for Michael about to stand. He gunned him a laser-sharp glare.

Michael collapsed back on the chair, gawking and pricking up his ears.

"I'm Johnny Belen," he said in a rush.

"Your wife would like to see you."

"Is she …"

The doctor touched his shoulder. "She's fine."

"The baby?"

"Kicking like a soccer player." The doctor smiled.

Johnny sent up a silent prayer, a flicker of a smile on his mouth.

"What made her faint, doctor?"

"Shock, most likely. Can result in shortness of breath … reduced oxygen to the brain." The physician checked his chart and made a note.

"Was your wife upset about anything?"

"I'm not sure," he said, a hitch in his throat, and walked down the corridor beside the M.D. "But I'm going to find out."

The doctor paused outside the unit, cautioning, "She's going to need rest and quiet for the next few days."

Johnny nodded and, with his insides chained to his ribs, pushed the door open. His heart vaulted in his throat. She lay on the bed swathed in blankets with her eyes closed and her face as pale as the whitewashed walls. In three long strides, he bridged the distance between them and stood at her side. Sensing him near, she fluttered her lashes open. Relief scored through him.

"Hi," he said.

"Hi." She breathed the word.

He claimed her hand and gave her fingers a gentle squeeze. "Doc said you can go home."

"Home." Her mouth quivered, and a tear spilled onto her cheek.

Johnny wiped it with the pad of his thumb. "What's wrong?"

She shook her head and a watery smile skimmed her lips. "Reaction I guess." She tried to push herself up but collapsed back on the pillows. A sound, not quite a laugh slipped from her mouth. "Might have to get Michael to help."

No, we won't, he thought, but said nothing.

A nervous giggle. "I'm so big now."

"I can handle you." He placed an arm around her shoulders and drew her to him, her head wedged beneath his chin. "One, two, three, oomph!"

With a moan she shuffled upright, and he swung her legs over the side of the bed. When she placed her hands on his shoulders, he wrapped his arms around her middle and lifted, setting her on her feet.

"Atta girl." His chin grazed her crown, and he caught a whiff of apple blossom shampoo through the medicinal smells in the room. He stroked her hair and then dropped his hands to her shoulders, drawing her closer into his embrace. "If anything had hap—"

"Thank God." She laid her head on his shoulder. "Nothing did.""I don't know what I—"

She raised her head, her eyes bright with tears, her lashes moist.

With a groan, Johnny devoured her with his mouth, and she clung to him like she'd never let go. Her moan of pleasure filled his mouth, and he thought he'd bust inside. He'd waited so long for this moment. Thought he'd lost her … lost all.

Never again.

"Dear God," he gasped, lifting his head and looking deep into her eyes. "I thought I'd never—" His mouth crushed hers, eclipsing his words, but not his ardor. Nectar … pure, unadulterated nectar. Ambrosia.

Groaning, he tightened his arms around her, curving her closer, but her tummy got in the way. She smiled, and he caught it on his lips. "Maybe baby wants attention, too?"

She reached up and stroked his cheek. "I thought it was ov—"

An avalanche of kisses smattered her face, and then he zoomed back to her mouth. The kiss rocked between them, communicating more than words could ever say. Reluctantly, Johnny broke the connection, his forehead touching hers, and fueled his lungs with oxygen.

"Time we were getting home, Mrs. Belen." A crooked smile settled on his mouth, and dipping his head, he stole another smooch.

"Yes, please, Johnny, take me home." She smiled. "Dogs and all."

She rubbed her cheek along his biceps and looped her arm through his.

With a spring in his step and joy in his heart that he'd thought he'd never feel again, Johnny escorted Samantha from the room and into the corridor. Several yards further, reality hit, and he skidded to a halt.

"Samantha, are you alright?" Michael hurried over to them, pawing at her arms and shoulders, and hooked his arm through hers.

"Fi-fine." Samantha peeked at Johnny from beneath her lashes. His face had that closed look again—remote as the Alps. Moments ago in the hospital room, the hunger in his eyes had her heart tripping and a thousand butterflies doing the tango in her stomach. She'd touched his cheek, his five o'clock shadow rough beneath her fingertips … a familiar sensation. And she'd felt warm and cozy in his arms.

Protected. Loved.

An illusion? Or a reality?

She brushed a hand across her eyes. For a fleeting moment, she'd believed she and Johnny had a chance and they'd make it. She must've been demented to think it was even remotely possible with Michael strutting his stuff and mamma not far behind.

"I'm sorry," Michael apologized profusely, pulling her from her thoughts. "If I knew it was going to upset you, I wouldn't have said—"

"What *did* you say, Scott?" Johnny thawed enough to ask, leading her outside.

"I-I-I—" Michael trotted along, clinging on her arm, his eyes darting between them.

She gave Michael a warning look.

"Secrets?" Johnny asked.

"No," she said, the word clipped. "No secrets, Johnny."

"Then, what's this about?"

Silent, she squeezed his arm and kept walking.

He locked his step in place. "Sam?"

"Not now, Johnny," she murmured, touching a hand to her forehead.

You dolt, Belen. She'd just had a shock that landed her in the hospital, and he stood in the parking lot grilling her. He should be on the rack receiving twenty lashes for his insensitivity. "Sorry, Sam." He patted her hand on the crook of his elbow. "I should be getting you home."

"Yeah," Michael agreed, then, catching Johnny's menacing look, darted his eyes about, searching for an out.

Johnny swatted the other man's hand off her, unlocked the Chevy and helped her up onto the front seat. If Michael didn't wise up, he'd be landing in a hospital room pronto. "Get in the truck, Scott," he barked.

Michael leaped onto the back seat.

A grim Johnny climbed up and slid onto the driver's seat.

Silence expanded, thickened … oppressed.

Michael fidgeted in his seat. "Samantha will tel—"

She clicked her seatbelt in place.

"Shut up, Scott." Johnny pounded his fist on the steering wheel. Michael jumped back. "You don't have to be so touchy, okay?"

Johnny felt tension biting into every sinew of his body. Ignoring his remark, he maintained his self-control. Just. Air pressuring his lungs blasted through his mouth. He turned the key in the ignition and eased the vehicle onto the flow of traffic, wondering what had brought Scott knocking on their door after two years.

The *how* he knew—mamma dear must've blabbed.

The *why* of it had him stumped.

It had to be more than stoking the discontent between Sam and himself.

A quick glance at her hugging the door intimated that she knew something.

Something she wasn't telling him.

Something Scott wasn't telling him.

Something Scott had told her that had created enough angst to land her in the hospital and endanger—

A fierce growl built in his throat, and he forced it down. He intended to find out what Michael had blabbered to her in the Tavern. In the meantime, he'd be on damage control—his life and marriage were on the line. Mamma-in-law and sour-puss in back could go fly a kite from the Stratosphere.

At that moment the clouds unleashed a fierce rain shower, and he swung the truck onto the main track. Windswept rain lashed the windshield, and he flipped the wipers on full speed. It came down so fast, bubbles formed on the ground, turning to puddles and flooding the road.

He slowed down and, peering through the liquid sheet, drove on in silence. Finally, after a seeming endless ride, he pulled into the kennel's parking lot, tires swishing and muddy water flying.

Johnny jumped out to the sound of yelping dogs. "Michael, see to the six pack, will you?" That 'd get the man out of range, and allow him a few minutes alone with Sam.

"I'll get wet."

"No?" Johnny scoffed. Shoving the back door of the Chevy open, he snatched his blazer and hurled it at him. "Now go."

Michael set his mouth in a mutinous line, but after a miniscule hesitation he threw his Cardin over his head and sprinted for the kennels.

Expelling a sigh, Johnny grabbed his plaid shirt from the back seat and placing it protectively around Sam, helped her down from the cab. He scooped her up in his arms and sheltering her with his body, lumbered for the house, her giggles teasing his ear.

"What's funny?" Somehow, he managed to adjust his hold on her, pull the key from his pocket and insert it in the lock.

"You," she whispered. "Carrying heavy me and making a dash for it like a quarterback."

"Did I score?" He turned the handle, shoved the door open with his shoulder, crossed the threshold and booted it shut with his heel.

"A loaded question, that."

"Mmm." He chuckled, staggering down the hall and into their bedroom. "To bed with you Sam."

"I'm not tired." She wriggled in his arms, her bulk nearly making him tip over, but, shifting a step, he stood strong.

"Doctor's orders." He set her on the mattress, the springs creaking beneath her weight. "Maybe we need to get a new bed. Too noisy, this one."

A purr sounded in her throat, and, depressing the mattress with her hands, she curved her lips in a smile. She let go, and the mattress squeaked again.

He caught her smile with one of his own, his eyes connecting to hers and a clear signal transmitted between them. Next second, he tossed his head and fine mist sprayed her face.

She laughed.

His heart lifted.

He could make her laugh, after all.

Playfully, she shoved his head back and brushed her hands down his torso. "You're soaked." She tugged at his shirt and then lower at his belt buckle. "Please get out of these wet clothes."

His hand clamped over hers, inadvertently pressing her fingers against him. He sucked in a sharp breath. "Stop that Sam or I'll be hopping in that bed with you." Every muscle in his body coiled. "If I do, you won't be sleeping any time soon."

Samantha glanced at their interlocked fingers, then at the straining zipper of his jeans. "Johnny ..." she raised her eyes, and he shuttered his.

"Sam ..." Abruptly, he released her hand and gripped her shoulders. "No."

At the stricken look on her face, he could've kicked himself. "What I meant is—"

"Never mind." She shook free from his hold and fumbled with the shirt he'd placed over her shoulders to protect her from the rain.

"Here, let me," he offered, but she slapped his hand away.

"I'm not an invalid. I can remove it myself, thank you very much."

He reached out and stroked her cheek with his thumb. "Sam, I can hardly breathe and not touch you." Placing his fingers beneath her chin, he raised it a notch so she had to look at him. She glanced every which way except at his face. "Sam, look at me."

Finally, she lifted her lashes. "Then, why?"

"Doctor said you had to stay in bed for a few days." A muscle ticked his jaw, and he cupped her cheek, her heat seeping into his fingers. "I want you and our baby to be all right.

"Oh, Johnny," she whispered, taking his hand between her own. "You don't have to worry," she said, brushing a tender kiss on his fingers and placing their entwined hands over her big belly. "We're fine."

"I intend for you to stay that way," he grunted, his jaw tight against the inferno inside him. "Now be a good girl and lie down."

After he settled her in bed, he propped on the edge and held her hand until she drifted off to sleep. Gently, he placed her hand beneath the blanket and brushed her brow with his lips. For a long moment, he just stood there looking at her, emotion stabbing his heart.

Curls framed her wan face. Her gold-tinted lashes brushed her cheeks. Freckles dusted her pert nose, tempting him to dip and touch each one with his lips. A silent groan ripped through him, but he held himself in check, lest he awaken her. Her mouth held the most color. A shade of pink, reminding him of the cactus rose he'd planted in the garden for her on Thanksgiving a few weeks ago. The telephone greetings from the in-laws ... er ... mamma monster had been the bitter glaze over the dinner he'd had to endure with Michael hovering over them in the kitchen. He grimaced. First of each month, the ding-a-ling had roses by the dozens delivered to Samantha and had doubled the order for Thanksgiving.

Johnny glanced over his shoulder, thinking said person would materialize any moment. Dismissing the foolish notion, he listened to the rhythm of his wife's breathing. The sound was soft and soothing. He brushed a wisp of hair off her brow, smoothed the blankets around her and walked to the door. Leaving it slightly ajar, he strolled to the living room.

Smack in the middle of Michael's rose garden.

Growling, he made to hurl the blooms out the window, but he thought better of it. He'd done that once and incurred Samantha's wrath. Johnny, coined the insensitive brute. So he'd water them instead. A sly curve tilted his mouth. He collected the bundles in his arms, marched to the bathroom and, dumping them in the bathtub, twisted on the tap. Seconds later, he turned the water off, walked back to the living room and opened all the windows.

Phew! fresh air.

A grin teased the corner of his mouth. Things had warmed up between Samantha and him these last few hours. He skimmed his hand across his lips and the grin vanished. A sign of things to come, or the calm before the storm?

An uncanny silence filled the house, broken only by the occasional gust buffeting the walls.

He sank in the rocking chair, dropped his head in his hands and massaged his scalp. Leaning back, he closed his eyes, and the motion rocked him into sudden awareness.

He couldn't delay any longer. The time had come. He had to come clean with Sam. Take his chances. Extend that trust he wanted from her. He'd begin by uprooting the seeds of strife Michael had scattered to wedge them apart, and then bulldoze doubts lingering between them into oblivion.

His eyes flew open, and he stared straight into the cold ashes of the grate. The gentle rocking soothed. It had been a wacko of a day, and he almost gave into slumber, but chill in the air and his damp clothes had goose bumps popping all over his body. He shook his shoulders and shuffled from the chair. After he shut the windows, he lit the fire.

Warmed by the flames, he tiptoed back to the bedroom to change into a pair of jeans and a flannel shirt. Samantha slept like a sweet princess. Adjusting his belt buckle, he curbed his yearning to get beneath the blankets with her and stalked out.

In the kitchen, he opened a cupboard and knocked down a couple of soup cans into his hands. He'd no sooner put the pot on the stove when the enemy burst through the door.

"I'm hungry as a hog." Michael rubbed his hands together and then blew air in his palms, warming them. "Brrr! It's coming down like a slot gushing coin."

Johnny frowned. "Shh."

Michael paused in the middle of removing his wet coat. "Did I really say that?" He chortled. "Hungry as a hog."

"You'll wake Sam."

"Guess I'm catching onto this country bumpkin slang quicker than I thought." He shrugged off his coat and draped it over the door.

"Scott, if you don't put a lid on it, I'll help you," he muttered.

"She asleep?" Michael mouthed as if he hadn't spoken.

Johnny stirred the soup. And stirred … and stirred.

Michael leaned over his shoulder. "Smells good."

"Help yourself." Johnny waggled his shoulders to clue him into stepping back.

Far and away back.

What was he up to with this buddy-buddy rap all of a sudden?

Johnny dodged him a glance and breathed a sigh of relief when he stepped aside. Saved him the trouble of bopping his noggin with a right hook.

Johnny closed his fingers in a fist and hiked a brow … no doubt that would hap—

"Thanks." Michael reached up and flipped a bowl from the cupboard into his palm. "I'm serious about an eatery in this area," he continued in a conversational tone. "It's growing faster than you can flick an ace outta your sleeve."

"You mean *your* sleeve." Johnny turned off the stove and carried the pot to the table.

"Well, okay." Michael chuckled. "Sure to turn a profit in no time."

"Sounds like a deal." The quicker Michael refocused on making a buck, the sooner he'd get him out of his house. "When you planning on cashing in?" Within the hour would work for Johnny.

"Glad you agree, Jonathan," he said, ignoring his second query.

"Why's that?"

"I want someone who knows the region to run the place for me." Michael paused, his chin propped on the bowl in his hand. "I thought you might be—"

"Not a chance." That explained his chummy overtures … tossing his smooth lines and reeling in anyone fool enough to fall prey to his promises. Johnny wouldn't be snared. But would Samantha get caught this second time around?

"You'd be making a heck of a lot more moolah than babysitting dogs."

"You don't know what I make, Scott."

Michael shriveled his brow. Finally, it must've hit him. He, who prided himself in knowing everything about his competitors, indeed did not know Johnny's net worth. "I know you don't make enough to keep her in style."

"You do?"

"It's evident by this—this—" He waved the bowl around, screwing up his face in distaste. "This dump."

"Cut the deck, Scott." He slammed the cupboard shut and stared Michael down. Time the gloves came off, and no better time than now with Samantha out of earshot. "What's your real agenda?" He pushed up his sleeves, leaned back against the counter and folded his arms across his chest. "I didn't swallow that tale about you studying the locals, etc."

Michael split his lips in a smile, not unlike a hyena's. "Too smart for your own good, Irishman."

"Really?"

"You should not have crashed my wedding to Samantha. Her mother and I had things pla—" He shrugged. "I'd hook Sam, bail mamma out, and catch the golden egg."

"The Lucky Lou."

"I'd take control" – he stroked his cheek with the bowl, replaying the plot in his mind – "toss mamma a percentage to keep her mum and—"

"—and squirm from under daddy's thumb," Johnny finished for him.

He gawked, affronted. "You know too much."

A wry grin tilted the corner of Johnny's mouth. "I worked the bank, remember?"

"You sure did," Michael agreed, his words slick.

The grin morphed to a smirk on Johnny's mouth. "Samantha's father?"

Michael shrugged and crossed to the table. "What he doesn't know can't hurt him."

"You lowlife," Johnny muttered, the words stinging his tongue. "Pretending to be an innocent, bumbling idiot."

Michael sneered. "Working though, isn't it." His eyes slitted, signaling his modus operandi was still engaged. "Mamma empathized, stroking my feathers … chicken soup 'n all. And the daughter" – he sighed, his hand over his heart – "who'd have thought it? She took me in under her roof … and … er … yours, and handed me a job." He guffawed. "You, Jonathan, are the stinger I can do without." He shook his head in mock sadness. "You simply have to go."

"Is that a threat?" Johnny cut back, his jaw taut, his eyes laser sharp.

"Did I say anything to you?" Michael glanced around the room. "No one here but you and me." He set the bowl on the table, sniffed the soup and straddled a chair. "In a court of law, it would be your word against mine."

"Got it all figured out, do you?"

"There's nothing you can do to stop me this time, leprechaun."

"I wouldn't be too sure." Johnny unfolded his arms and stuck his hands in the back pockets of his denims.

Michael bolted upright. "What do you mean?"

"Samantha's still married to me."

"That letter says otherwise—"

"How do you know—" Johnny took a menacing step closer, his words cold steel.

On his soapbox, Michael paid no heed and harped on, "Papa had me at his beck and call, jetting the globe … but eventually I got to it and made sure—"

"It was you."

"Hardly." Michael mocked a yawn with the back of his hand. "Money can buy inside info. People. Papers."

"So, you got some lackey to do your dirty work."

Michael sprang up, strolled to the window and propped his backside on the ledge. "If you say so."

Johnny stomped after him. "You actually paid some goffer to tamper with our wedding license?"

"Not *ours*," Michael chortled. "Yours and Samantha's."

"You're sick, Scott."

Michael laughed the louder.

Air filled Johnny's lungs, expanded in his chest and thrashed in his throat.

Swelling.

Gagging.

"Marriage … divorce, same difference." Michael shrugged, his face deadpan. "In my position, a name dropped here, a few bills greasing the right palm—" He broke off, his meaning clear. "Even bosom buddies will turn if the price is right."

Steady, Belen. "You have no morals, do you?"

"Have yours done you any good?" He drew his brows over the bridge of his nose. "You have a wife who's not really yours. You live like a pauper with no prospects for the future—"

Johnny grabbed him by his shirt collar. "Get out before I—"

"Shh!" Michael scoffed. "Or you'll wake our darlin' Sam."

"Then go real quiet like," he murmured, his words flint hard.

"Walk yourself out of my house before I rearrange your face and throw you out."

Michael sidestepped him, adjusted his collar and settled back

234

on the chair. "No can do." He propped his elbows on the table. "Soup's on."

Johnny hauled him up with such force, the chair went flying against the wall. "Out."

"Don't want to upset Samantha, do we?" Michael huffed, scrapping to get out of his grasp. "Not in her condition."

"You slime." Johnny shoved him from the kitchen, but Michael scuffled with him all the way to the door.

"Johnny!" The call floated down the hall, flashing a red alert on his wrestling the other man out.

He gripped Michael's shoulder with an iron hand, and the man groused out a sound of unease. A struggle raged within him—to pound him to a pulp or respond to Samantha's summons. Johnny ground his teeth, his jaw steel. There was no contest. Sam won hands down. But he had to control his anger and the situation in a way that would not adversely affect her and their baby.

Right now, she viewed Michael as an old friend who'd had a raw deal. Her sympathies were with the scumbag. If Johnny unveiled all, she wouldn't believe him, thinking he was bad-mouthing Michael. He couldn't blame her since he'd already made his feelings known about the idiot. Johnny squinted at him. He was no dummy. Michael Scott was playing them each against the other, including mercenary mamma.

He heaved Michael off his feet and deposited him back on the floor. "I'll be there in a sec', Sam." He stabbed the other man with a steely glare, signaling it wasn't over. "Your days here are numbered, Scott."

"Is that a threat, leprechaun?" Michael challenged, straightening his disheveled clothes.

"Did I say anything to you?" Johnny mocked a glance about the foyer. "Don't see anyone here but you 'n me." Chuckling, he sauntered down the hall and heard Michael suck in air and exhale in a gasp.

A deadly pause.

"You have more to lose than me, Irishman."

Johnny braked to a stop, the venom in the man's words like a dagger in his heart. Nearly gagging, he corded every muscle in his body and battled his demons. A second later, he rolled his shoulders and hurried to his wife.

Chapter Twenty-Seven

Samantha was struggling to fluff up the pillows when he walked in.

"Here, let me." He pulled her against his chest and adjusted the pillows behind her back. His rain-fresh scent was intoxicating, and a tremulous sigh breezed from her mouth.

"Something wrong?"

She shook her head into his shoulder.

"Why'd you call?" He settled her against the pillows and sat on the edge of the bed, holding her hand.

"I wondered if Michael had gotten in okay."

"Yeah." He patted her hand and slipped off the bed. "He's in the kitchen stuffing himself with chicken noodle soup. You want me to call him?"

She squinted at him. "Is something the matter?"

His face became a cold mask of indifference. "Since he ingratiated himself in our life, you haven't stopped throwing that goon in my face."

She wiggled her bottom in place, patted the blankets around her and paused, astonished.

"If it's him you want, then spit it out."

Her eyes grew wide. She blinked against the tears pressing on her lids, a reaction to her emotions being on the swing these last

237

few weeks. How could he doubt her so easily? Earlier at the hospital, she'd thought they'd finally made a breakthrough toward reconciliation. And now, to have him accuse her of wanting Michael scoured her already bruised heart. "Is that what you think?"

A tear glistened on the tip of her lash, then rolled down her cheek. He wiped it away with his knuckles and sank back on the bed, his hand covering her fingers fiddling with the blanket.

"I don't know what to think," he griped.

"Neither do I." She pulled her hand away, concentrating on outlining the quilt's design with her index finger. "You demanded an answer in regard to our marriage."

"What's wrong with that?"

"I'll tell you what's wrong with it." She shifted to a more comfortable position. "You should never have asked that."

"Why not?"

"Because you're supposed to know."

"Know what?"

Exasperated, she smacked the bed with her palm. "That I'd never damage our marriage or let anything break us up."

"You wouldn't?" He scooted closer.

"Of course not."

He frowned. "Why'd you keep throwing Michael in my face?"

"Because you made me mad."

"I did?" He flicked an unruly curl off his brow with his fingers, and she wanted to knock his hand away so she could do it. "Do I still make you mad?"

"More times than not."

"I do?"

"You do." She folded her hands over her big belly. "Why'd you behave like a bear with a sore head?"

He placed his hand over his heart, signaling his feelings. "I didn't want to lose you." He covered her fingers with his. "Especially to that bumbler."

238

"You do?"

"Do what?" He turned her hand over and stroked her palm with his fingers, sending tingles up her arm.

"Love me."

Johnny looked deep into her eyes. "Woman, would I have gone through that circus to marry you if I didn't?"

"Oh, Johnny." She wrapped her arms around his neck, pressing her cheek to his rough one. "I gave you my answer, then."

"You never doubted me, Sam?"

She coughed into his shoulder. "Doubts crossed my mind, but I didn't really believe them. Not with my heart."

He brushed her hair with his hand and hooked a lock behind her ear. "What kind of doubts?"

"I-uh- thought you might be after my money—"

"What?" He laughed, and it sounded more like a howl.

"You showed up so suddenly and were so determined to marry me when—"

"You were about to make the biggest blooper of your life." He smirked, pleased.

She grinned, happy. "True."

"True." Johnny lowered his head, his warm breath tickling her lips. A heartbeat, and he crushed her mouth with his in a kiss filled with longing, love, desire, impatience.

His heart booted his ribs. Passion ignited, and he wanted more, so much more. "Samantha," he breathed against her lips.

"Johnny." She sighed, her breath mingling with his.

He scrunched her hair in his palms and showered her face with countless kisses, nibbling his way down her chin. Taking a detour, he nipped her earlobe and blazed a path to her bosom, tasting … heaven.

Purring with pleasure, Samantha held his head to the spot, her fingers slicing through his hair. Careful not to apply his weight over her big tummy, he inched his way back up, branding her skin with love bites until he bumped into her mouth and found a haven.

239

A breathless moment, and he trailed his hand over her extended belly, caressing her full roundness and brushing across her navel. While his fingertips stroked, his mouth slid along the curve of her cheek, over her obstinate chin, down her neck, pausing at the pulse point on her throat.

Samantha tossed her head back to give him better access, her hands digging into the muscles of his shoulders. At fever pitch, Johnny worked his way back to her belly, his mouth colliding into his fingers vying for favor on her navel. His mouth won out.

While he dallied at the spot, she fondled the silky curls at his nape, the warmth of his love enfolding her in sweet sensation. Johnny played, caressed, tasted … then froze, his mouth staying fused on her stomach.

The child kicked.

He felt it.

And he almost cried.

Samantha sensed the flutter of the baby inside her and stroked his cheek, just as he glanced up. Tears shimmered in her eyes.

A million uncertainties flitted past, but one thing stood strong.

This moment.

This is what mattered.

He and Samantha together … together with their baby.

Raw emotion jolted him, and he cradled her face in his hands, pressing his mouth to hers. When he pushed her deeper into the pillows, emotion ignited to passion and he devoured her with his mouth, his hands, his body. Samantha met his ardor, and the mating rhythm played in their mouths, stimulating, exciting, arousing.

Finally, he panted against her lips, "Sam, I've got to stop now, or I won't be able to."

She held him to her. "No, please."

He was drowning in the feel, the taste of her … A thread of common sense thrust through the combustible fervor propelling him into its vortex. "For you," he gasped. "I must stop."

"No," she whimpered, her eyes glazed with emotion.

His hunger for this woman he married was unquenchable. His heart pumped like a countdown to blast off, and every muscle in his body coiled tight. He planted a fierce kiss on her parted lips, then rolled off her, his chest heaving, his body throbbing.

Flinging the blankets aside, he slipped under the covers fully clothed and pulled her close to his side, her head nestling against his heart.

Samantha slipped her hand beneath his shirt, caressing the spiral of hair on his chest, rising and falling like he'd run a marathon. When he'd kissed her so tenderly, she thought she'd come apart inside; his kisses honored, gave, took, loved ... her. This man she married loved her truly.

"I love you, Johnny Belen."

"I know that, now."

"Was there a time you didn't know?"

"Unimportant in the present circumstances," he murmured, avoiding an explanation.

"Johnny, did you doubt me?"

He caught her hand on his chest and brought it to his mouth, brushing his lips across each finger. "I ... uh ... thought you might have married me to get back at your mother." He licked each appendage, suckled, teased ... "And to get away from Michael Scott."

"You didn't," she gasped, but her shortness of breath had to do more with his ministrations than his words.

He blew on each fingertip, an erotic caress, and laid her hand over his heart. "Afterward, I thought you might have changed your mind. Wanted to leave me and go to mamma ... and to him."

"Johnny, you didn't?" she asked, aghast, feeling his heart thudding beneath her palm, echoing the chaotic beat of her own.

"The thought crossed my mind."

"Oh, Johnny."

"Him being a rich guy and all might have swayed you."

"You know me better than that."

"I did, I do, I will, Mrs. Belen." He curved his mouth into that sexy smile that had her pulse singing. "Always."

"I'm glad, Johnny." She snuggled closer to him.

He touched his lips to her temple. "I didn't really believe it. Not with my heart." His words echoed her confession of moments ago.

"You, Johnny Belen, are my only love."

"You be sure it's not a flash in the pan deal," he teased, a contented sigh rumbling from deep in his chest.

Samantha giggled. "After two years? I don't think so." An emotional tempest had torn her apart, but she'd landed in the safe haven of her husband's arms. She stroked the smattering of bronze hair on the back of his hand, her lighthearted banter taking a serious bent. "Johnny, I've lived the life of the rich and elite, if not the famous, and it didn't give me what I wanted." She drew his hand to her mouth and then held it against her cheek. "I've been happiest with you."

"And it will continue, Sammy mine."

"I wouldn't care if you didn't have a penny to your name." She chuckled. Of course, he didn't. Then, it hit her. Subconsciously, she'd been tagging a price on their love by pummeling him for a higher-end lifestyle these last two years. And almost lost him. True love never carried a dollar sign. She patted his hand. "Never mind, we'll make it" – she grinned – "Mr. so-called 'I'm tired as a toad with a limp doin' laps in quicksand.'"

He flung back his head and laughed. "You remember." Then he sobered. Inadvertently, he'd been ranking their love against cash flow by challenging her with a lower-end lifestyle. And nearly lost her. He brushed a hand across his brows. The real deal couldn't be measured in dough.

"Yes, I remember."

"The line was, 'tired as a toad doin' laps in quicksand.'"

242

"You were limping, Johnny." Her eyes grew wide, indignant. "I saw you when you walked to the tow truck."

"Aww, that was a pebble in my boot."

She shoved him, amusement crinkling the corner of her eyes. "Uh huh."

"I had to think fast. Didn't want you recognizing me right away and putting up a fuss."

"I don't fuss, Belen."

"Uh, huh." He hiked a brow.

Her mouth flirted with a smile. "I thought I could win an Oscar for my ugly duckling disguise at our wedding." The flirt turned to a full-fledged smile. "But you aced me out as the Academy Award winner." She burst into a fit of giggles, and he joined her, and it was like old times; lighthearted, fun.

When the laughter subsided, he tightened his arms around her and they listened to the rain falling on the roof.

"We're going to be okay, Sam."

"Mmm, I know, Johnny." She smoothed a wrinkle on his shirt and curved her fingers over his biceps. "I just know it."

"I wanted to have this place ready for you."

"It's okay."

"I don't know what happened with Willie, but I'm going to find out."

"We'll fix and pay as we go." She fluffed the pillows behind his head, making him more comfortable. "Going into debt is no fun."

"We're not going in the red, Sam." He looked at her, hard and steady. "In fact I want to tell—"

"Baby will be here soon and, oh!" She caressed her abdomen and he covered her hand, waiting for another kick. It came. She chuckled, and he caught the sound with his mouth. A sizzling moment later, she murmured, "I'll be in better condition to help with the kennels."

He placed a forefinger on her mouth, but she was on a roll

with her plans. "We can have a grooming salon, a pet supply store, sponsor dog shows and—"

His smacking kiss did the trick. When he came up for air, he caught merriment dancing in her eyes.

"Pawdicures are the in thing now." She grinned. "It'll be fun."

Johnny shook his head.

"What?"

"I ... uh ... have a confession to make."

"Wh-a-at?"

"I'm not ... uhm ... dirt poor."

To his utter amazement, she took him to task. "Johnny Belen, of course you're not. You're my husband, the father of my child, my true love." She gave him a tender smile. "That's richer than rich."

At her words, his heart flipped and soared. How could he have doubted this woman who loved him, carried his child, had just confessed to not minding sloshing in the trenches to make the kennels a success? He slapped his forehead, wanting to kick himself from here to the North Pole. He'd allowed childhood insecurities ... not being good enough, not measuring up, shunned by the rich and glam ... to resurface and blind him to the truth.

To the treasure he had.

Held in his arms.

Next to his heart.

He swiped a hand across his eyes.

Snobbery could hit both sides of the tracks. It had him hood-winked for a time, thinking it was a rich man's affliction; but he took first prize as blockhead from the poor side of town, the way he'd reacted to Samantha's desire for a better life. He must've been the dolt of the century. She wanted a better life with him, Johnny, not Michael Scott. Without his Sam, he would be a poor man indeed, and it had nothing to do with the size of his bank account.

"That's the best wealth in the world, Sam." He grinned. "The other kind is mighty useful, though."

A puzzled look flashed across her face, then she opened her mouth wide. "Oh my gosh, you don't mean—"

"Yep, I do mean."

"How?" She wobbled up, and he rearranged the blanket that had fallen to her waist.

"My Good Samaritan act paid off at—"

"Don't kid me, Johnny." She laughed, slanting him a wary gaze.

"Scout's honor." He held up two fingers and crossed his heart.

She grabbed his arm, shaking him with her excitement. "How much?"

"Five mil."

"Nooo."

"Yeees."

She flung her arms around him, her laughter ringing off the pinewood beams of the ceiling. The sweetest sound Johnny had ever heard.

"That's wonderful because I ... uh ... don't have a penny," she mumbled the words so quietly, he strained to hear.

"Because ..." he prompted.

"I'm the pauper, Johnny." She fell back on the pillows. "Mother gambled away the family fortune." Sadness glazed her features, and he wanted to say something to comfort her, but didn't know what, so he just listened. "She needed a fast buck—"

"Michael."

She nodded. "To bail her casino from going belly up."

He stroked her palm and, not wanting to hurt her, didn't voice the suspicion circling his mind. It appeared mamma had reengaged her plot devices to serve Sam on a platter to the bimbo once again. He scratched his brow. From what the bimbo babbled in the kitchen, though, it sounded like he had the upper hand in executing the game plan.

Johnny snorted his displeasure, and drew her closer into his embrace.

"She's hawked it to the rafters." She hiccupped and laid her head on his shoulder. "It's in much worse shape than two years ago, and she's got the family estate—" Unable to go on, she pressed her fingers to her mouth.

"Shh, it's going to be okay," he crooned.

"My own mother wanted to sacrifice my happiness to bail herself out of her I.O.U.s." She closed her fingers over his hand. "That didn't work, so now she's after dad; she's making good on her threat to divorce him and force him to sell the Bel Air estate" – she sniffed – "the family home. She's after half the take of the liquid assets."

"That's extreme, Sam, even for your mamma."

"Michael flaunted a copy of the divorce papers at the Tavern." There was a catch in her voice and she swallowed, giving vent to the whimper in her throat. "Mamma's signed, a-a-and daddy hasn't yet … Michael said he doesn't know if his heart can stand it, so waiting—"

Johnny pursed his lips as more pieces of the puzzle fell into place.

"I should've called since Thanksgiving, but with the remodeling and the baby so near I—"

"You can't go blaming yourself, Sam." He patted her hand, a line carving his forehead. "What else did Scott blab?"

"Knowing mamma's scrambling to keep the biz from collapsing, he offered to help."

"Oh yeah," Johnny jeered.

She gripped his hand tight. "I-i-if I can get her to sell him the casino at cost, he'll work on mamma to rescind—"

"The divorce," he bit out. "Convenient."

"I-I don't know how I can, Johnny," she murmured. "Mamma's so hard headed."

"What's the note on the debt?"

246

"Don't know for sure. In the millions, though."

Johnny reclined against the headboard and, draping an arm around her shoulders, tucked her in the crook of his shoulder. His windfall must've gouged mamma's financially strapped biz and hurled her within a hair of bankruptcy. "Yet she's managed to stay afloat," he said, raising an eyebrow.

"Oh, mamma's always got an ace or two up her sleeve."

"Like the bucko you hired?" He inclined his head toward the kitchen, thinking a subtle hint might clue her in. More than likely, Michael had been stacking mamma's balance owing with under the table loans. Once he had her cornered, he'd squeeze her out one way or the other. A grim line settled on his mouth. Fair or foul didn't crease the jerk.

"Oh, I don't think so." A faint smile curved her mouth. "Mamma keeps her secrets under wraps until she's ready to make her move … er … roll her dice."

"Your father's been blindsided?"

She nodded. "Pop thinks he's about to retire with money to burn." She folded and refolded the edge of the blanket in pleats. "I don't know how to tell him."

"I see." Johnny rubbed his chin on the crown of her head, smelling the fresh shampoo scent of her hair.

"Do you Johnny? Really?" She bunched the blanket in her fist. "Would you underwrite mamma's banknote to give pops some peace of mind? If he knew mamma siphoned his life savings on the turn of a card" –she hiccupped, tears tightening her throat— "and filed for div—" Her words cracked.

"Is that all there is to it, Sam?"

"Isn't that enough?" She sniffed. "I was hurt for the longest time and mad at my mother, but I kind of understand—"

"I don't."

"Sometimes people do things when they feel threatened. Later regret it." She winced, still not totally convincing even herself. "I can't see how she could again though, Johnny." She touched her swollen abdomen thinking of their child. "Unless she convinced herself it was for my own good." She rubbed her cheek on his shoulder, the flannel of his shirt soft upon her skin. "But turning on daddy is really below the line. Scummy."

Johnny clamped his mouth shut before he blasted something that might upset her further.

"But I have to forgive her." Sam pressed her fingers to her temples. "I want our baby to grow up in a happy family—" The words tripped in her throat, and she pulled the blanket up to her chin. "I thought she'd started to make up for it, but now, I don't understand." She shuddered, and he tightened his arm around her shoulders.

"Will you help her, Johnny?" she murmured. "Maybe we can nix this and save dad a lot of heartache." A wistful smile skimmed her lips at the pun but quickly vanished.

"I'll see what I can do." Johnny caressed her cheek with his fingers, something still niggling the back of his brain. Where mamma was concerned, there were too many question marks and not enough dots. As for Michael, he'd played the sympathy card to weasel his way into their home, snow Sam under and use the divorce angle as his wildcard. He'd covered his bases.

"Anyone want to play scrabble?" Michael shouted from the living room as if nothing untoward had occurred between him and Johnny in the kitchen.

"No!" Sam and Johnny said in unison.

Sam curled into the crook of his arm. "Wish he'd leave soon, Johnny. He grates on my nerves."

Mine too, he thought and nodded. "Glad you finally realize it."

She tilted her mouth in a tender smile and, placing her hand over his heart, fluttered her lashes closed. Adjusting the blanket around her shoulders, he held her like he had the greatest gift in his arms.

Johnny wanted to protect her from the double deal he suspected was brewing between mamma and Michael. And although he'd have to hoof the turf for a while longer, he was determined to bust it wide open. Soon. A ripple of dread snaked across his shoulders blades. He glanced at his wife cuddled close to him. Nothing would hurt her or their baby. He'd make sure of that. Even if it cost him all he had.

Quietly, he withdrew from the bed, but she reached out and clasped his hand. "Johnny?"

"Mmm."

"When ..." She shifted beneath the blankets, her lashes fanning her cheeks. "When did you hit the jackpot?"

"When I married you, Sam."

A smile flittered on her mouth.

His neck muscles constricted, trapping oxygen in his throat. Johnny knew the wisecrack merely delayed the inevitable. His pulse pounded.

The grenade was about to detonate in his face.

"The money," she murmured, her voice drowsy.

He knew what she meant.

He remained silent for so long, she dragged her eyes open. "Johnny?"

"I can explain, Sam."

"Explain?" She blinked, perplexed.

"It was on the way to church."

Samantha let go of his hand, rubbing sleep from her eyes and fuzz from her brain.

"Totally unexpected."

"T-two years ago?" She brushed hair from her brow and squinted up at him. "You've been loaded all this time? And you kept it from me?"

Blood drained from his face, and he bet he could hear the proverbial pin drop even with the backdrop of the raging elements. His heart cracked. He'd come so close to losing her. Then, just for a few hours, he'd come out of left field and hit a home run in the matrimonial stakes. It must've been a foul at the bottom of the ninth, and he was about to strike out.

Game over?

"That was on our wedding day."

He nodded, and his stomach did a wheelie.

"You didn't tell me."

He shook his head.

He could use an ally right about now. Where was Mirabella?

"Oh, Johnny, why?"

He shrugged. "I'm not sure." Suddenly what he'd imagined as her ulterior motives for marrying him were unfounded. His foolishness was about to sabotage his marriage unless he backpedaled with on-target answers. But, God help him, he didn't know what to say that would right the wrong she thought he'd done her.

Trust.

That's what he wanted from her. How was he going to get it when he'd withheld it from her at the start?

"You didn't trust me," she said, her voice seeming to come from a distance.

"No. It wasn't like that—"

"Yes."

"I'm sorry, Samantha."

"So am I, Johnny." She flipped the covers off and struggled to stand.

"Let me help you."

Samantha held her hand up to ward him off. "I can manage." Wobbling on her feet, she made a grab for the headboard to regain her balance, but Johnny reached for her, supporting her against his chest. For a split second, she stayed touching him, then pushed away from him.

"I started to believe what you said." A heavy pause. "Believe you." An ache jabbed in the vicinity of her heart, and the hurt vibrated through her body. "About love, trust and family." Her whimper grazed the air. She squared her shoulders, ignoring the splintering in her chest. She'd take care of herself and her baby.

She'd get a job. Mirabella would help her … maybe work the 'Bar 'n Grill' with Janey. The time had come for Samantha Belen to learn to manage for herself.

Without husband Johnny Belen.

Without friend Michael Scott.

And without gambling mamma.

"I never lied to you, Sam."

"No. Just withheld resources that could've given us a better life." *But you withheld facts about your financial status, girlie,* a small voice prompted from inside her. *To test him. Find out his true colors as you termed it. Well, trust played both sides of the fence. You want trust, you gotta give it first.* She shook her head, silencing the voice. "You had us living like mice in a matchbox for two years when you had the means to—" She collapsed on the bed and covered her face in her hands. Tears didn't come. She'd used them up.

"I tried to tell you several times."

"Not good enough."

"That's not fair."

"Why isn't it?" she asked, her voice faltering, her gaze accusing. "You don't keep something like that from your wife unless—"

"Unless what?" he demanded, his features drawn.

"Unless you don't trust."

"Trust who?"

"Me."

"And you did?

"Did what?"

A force of air ejected from his mouth, his control stretched to the limit. "Trust me."

Sam waved her hands about. "We're not talking about me, Belen."

"Maybe we should, Sam." Johnny gulped down the acid rising in his throat and felt the burn in his chest. "Uptown girl can do no wrong?"

251

"Huh!" She pounded the bed with her small fist. "I'm not even a midtown or even a downtown gal now."

Her words knifed his ribs, and his chest seemed to cave for a second. "Poor boy Belen—"

"Hardly that," she countered.

"—s' always off beam."

"Oh, you impossible, stubborn Irishman." She fidgeted with the bedding. "I don't know how I could've—"

"Could've what?" He slitted his gaze, his words smooth, cool.

"Never mind."

"Fine." He challenged her mutinous look with his own.

"Fine!"

He stood his ground amidst the minefield in their bedroom for another tense moment. "You want some chicken soup, if *Mikey* didn't gobble it all?"

Silence.

Finally, she shook her head, and hair fell over her face, concealing her features. A sigh, and she swatted the strands off her shoulder. "I thought my ... *our* life, just for a few hours today, was on track." She blinked, and her eyes dulled with disillusionment. "But it crashed."

"And I with it," Johnny muttered, but a sudden bang muffled his words and distracted them from their argument.

"Michael."

"Yeah."

"You're worse than mother and Michael."

Johnny winced, her brittle words lacerating his insides.

"At least mother had a legitimate reason. Her life was in ruins."

Spikes skewered his gut, icing his heart and numbing him all over.

"And Michael." She waited a moment for her quivery lip to still. "His approach may have been a little underhanded—"

"A little, huh!" Johnny thawed enough to fire back.

"But I think he does care about me." Trance-like, Samantha

seemed to look right through him. She'd been so close to happiness, and then to lose it at a word ... a word from Johnny, whom she loved, had trusted.

"I have to go." She tottered several steps to the door, their argument echoing in her mind ... her heart. She winced. Perspiration dampened her palms, and, sucking in a breath, she gripped the doorframe.

A second ... two ticked by.

"Michael," she called, knowing she had to think, pray this through.

"Don't do this, Sam," Johnny said, a note of desperation in his voice.

"I-I-I have to." She glanced over her shoulder at him, her face ashen, her eyes glacial pools.

He couldn't very well hog tie her to him and never let go. That would get him arrested and leave the playing field wide open for the caffler. "You don't know everything—"

"I know enough."

She combed her fingers through her hair, and he almost reached for her but checked the motion. He felt helpless.

Powerless.

Didn't she realize from the get go that the letter had been a con staged by Michael and mamma for self-serving purposes? To break them up—branding him the bad guy and her the jackpot bride deluxe for mamma's choice second time 'round?

It destroyed him not to blast it from the top of his lungs, but the timing was off. He had to keep mum. With the baby so near, he didn't want to stoke the inferno of discontent between them, and thus play into 'enemy' hands. Best he could do now was watch, wait, and strike a knockout on target. And he would, he promised himself. Nothing less would do.

"On my way, Samantha," Michael hollered from the living room.

Samantha glanced around. "Where's my Bible?"

Johnny toured the room with his gaze and picked it up from behind the bedside lamp. "What do you want your Bible for?"

"Answers."

At precisely that moment, the doorbell rang, and Johnny curled his top lip. Was it possible? Saved by the bell. It would've been amusing in other circumstances. Not now. Not with every muscle in his body knotted against the raw ache assaulting his insides.

Chapter Twenty-Eight

"You have visitors," Michael said, poking his face around their bedroom door.

Samantha walked to him.

Johnny stood rigid as the plywood patching the walls.

When the other man grasped her elbow to escort her out, Johnny shot forward ready to battle, then reined in. Couldn't rush it. His instincts told him that much, and the gouge in his gut confirmed it.

"Mirabella, Janey." Samantha stepped away from Michael and extended her hand in greeting. "What a perfect time for a visit."

"That it is." Mirabella smiled, and caught sight of Johnny standing by the bedroom door. Hmm, troubled waters brewing. He had his arms raised above his head, one hand gripping the top of the doorframe, his other behind his back. Looked like he wanted to topple the building on Michael's head like Samson had done to the Philistines.

Not a good idea, Mirabella. Samson went down with the building. Don't want that to happen here.

She glanced at heaven and nodded. Message received. Help!
Apply what I've taught you.

This is getting a little outta my league.

He chuckled. *Hardly.*

Oh, come on.

His grin broadened. *You know I'm there for you, always.*

Yeah. She tilted her mouth in a knowing smile, and her whole face sparkled.

Samantha opened her eyes wide, and then blinked several times. The Good Samaritan coming to her rescue on the freeway flashed through her memory. She shook her head. Stress. That must be it.

"Please sit down," she invited, motioning to the living room with her hand. At that moment, Michael hooked his arm through hers and his other through Janey's, escorting them both to the sofa beside the blazing hearth.

"We were passing by, and Mirabella suggested we visit," the young girl murmured, her gaze straying to Michael.

"With goodies to boot." Mirabella patted her shoulder.

"Beats soup and crackers." Michael stood at attention, ogling the basket Janey held in her hand. "Let me help you with that, ma'am," he offered, playing gallant gentleman. And then he snatched the basket from her grasp and sampled a cookie. "Mmm, good." His eyes seemed to be gobbling Janey instead.

The girl smoothed her skirt, and a nervous laugh bounced from her lips. "You sound like the folk 'round here."

"Like to blend right in."

Janey glanced at his designer slacks and cardigan and caught the glint of the gold chain around his neck and matching bracelet encircling his wrist. "Not highly likely, Mr. ..."

"Scott." A wolfish smile split his mouth. "But Michael, please." He plopped down on the cushions, bopped up and down once and placed the hamper on his lap. Then, he patted the place next to him. "I feel like we're old friends." Popping a chocolate éclair in his mouth, he chewed and rolled his eyes. "Exquisite."

Janey blushed and sat on the edge beside him. At the same instant, he bounced to his feet, looped the handle over his wrist and traipsed for the kitchen. "I'll be right back." He hurried away, whiffing at the basket like a Cocker Spaniel.

"Janey, why don't you go and help him," Mirabella said in a soft, yet persuasive tone. "If I remember, plates are in the top right-hand cupboard."

Samantha chuckled. "You're right." Now, how did she know that? They'd only had a couple of mugs when Mirabella had brought them the cherry pie nearly three months ago. Miraculously, the house had become so clean it sparkled. Samantha squinted at her.

A pause, and she shook her head, dismissing her foolish musings.

"Anyone like a drink?" Johnny released his viper grip on the door and ventured in, leaning casually against the wall. Time he played host. After all, it was still his home. For how much longer he didn't know, but for now it was his zone.

Mirabella turned the sweetest look toward him, and it was like a heavy weight lifted from his shoulders. He returned her smile. And it actually came from his heart.

"I make a nice cup of tea," Mirabella said. "If Samantha won't mind my using her kitchen." She turned and drew Sam into her luminous gaze.

"Mirabella, tea would be like heaven right now."

Mirabella glanced from one to the other. "Wouldn't it now." The words glided from her mouth, but neither heard. "You just sit there, dearie, and rest." A nod at Johnny. "That husband of yours can keep you company 'til we trot back." Noticing he held the Book in his hand, she lifted a shapely brow. "Good reading."

Johnny came to, realizing he was still gripping Sam's Bible between his fingers. "I don't know." He pushed himself away from the wall and slammed it on the coffee table.

"I guarantee it," Mirabella whispered. "A really *Good Book*." A covert glance from beneath her golden lashes, and she twirled, seeming to fly from the room. "This'll only take a minute."

Heavy silence filled the room. The walls seemed to be closing in, suffocating. Samantha fidgeted and avoided looking straight at Johnny.

"I won't bite." He pinned her on the spot with his rock brown gaze but made no move to bridge the gap between them.

She shuffled forward on the sofa and made to stand.

"Going somewhere?" he clipped, stepping in front of her.

"I feel hot." She placed a hand at the collar of her blouse and fluffed the fabric, allowing air to circulate her skin. "I'm going to open a window."

"Sit down," he said, his words tight. "I'll open it for you."

His tension was like a tangible, viable force drawing her to him like a magnet, and she settled back, rubbing her arms.

"Fresh air will do you ... er ... both of us good." He raised the window several inches and a gust whirled an icy snap into the room.

"I'm not helpless." She reclined against the cushions and closed her eyes.

"Not with dancing boy marking every step you take." He tapped the pane of glass, and it rattled. Something else that needed mending. He smirked at the intimation in his thoughts.

Samantha lifted her lashes and stared him full in the face, her eyes frosty. "I'm glad I have a friend like Michael to call in time of need."

Johnny snorted. "You should know the half of it."

"What's that supposed to mean?"

"Nothing."

"Then I'll ask Michael."

"Ask me what?" Michael strolled back in the room, stuffing his mouth with a strawberry tart and reaching for another from the plate Janey held in her hands. "Mmm, delicious, Janey."

A hint of hot pink tinted the girl's cheeks, and she lowered her lashes.

"High tea," Mirabella proclaimed, rolling in the trolley with a silver tea set upon it. "As the British say." She curved her lips in a sweet smile.

Steam rose from the teapot, and cinnamon spice wafted to them.

"Oh my, how lovely." Samantha glanced at Mirabella then at Janey.

"Where'd this come from?" She crinkled her brow. "I don't have a tea set like that anywhere in the house."

"You do now, sweetie." Mirabella adjusted her square spectacles and offered her a cup.

Samantha gaped, her mouth falling open, then slammed it shut. The eyeglasses, the gentle yet commanding voice, the squeaky-clean image … her guardian trucker flashed across her mind. Oh my gosh, could it have been Mirabella?

"Your tea, dear," Mirabella said in her motherly voice.

Sam came to and took the cup from her extended hand. "Thank you." She took a sip, and the fruity spice soothed her wild imaginings. Of course, that's all it was. Fanciful thinking.

She cradled the cup between her palms, and warmth seeped into her fingers. Just then, Michael plopped down beside her with such gusto, the cup shook in her hand and hot liquid spilled over the rim and onto the saucer, startling her totally back to the present.

"Oopsy daisy," Michael said, causing everyone to sputter a giggle.

Except Johnny.

Unabashed, Michael chuckled, taking the teacup from her fingers and setting it on the coffee table. Then, he took her hand in his and raised it to his lips. "So sorry, my lovely Samantha."

A split second before his lips fused on her skin, Johnny leaped and yanked him off the couch, a right hook smashing his jaw. Michael thumped to the floor, groaning.

"I told you to stay away from my wife," Johnny muttered, each word like another strike.

Janey set the pastry plate on the table and rushed to Michael, while Samantha struggled from the sofa to offer her help.

"Must you be such a boor, Belen?" she asked, her words spiking into his heart.

"Yeah." When their life and their future was at stake. Heck, how'd he turn out to be the bad guy again? Resigned, he backtracked to the window, propped his hip on the ledge and watched the proceedings from beneath his bunched brows. He'd struck out again. Unable to get a foothold on home base, it looked like he was losing the game for good. He huffed in a breath and let it whoosh from his tightlipped mouth. In another week or so he'd be clear of this, one way or another. Yet a thorn stabbed through the twister inside him.

He scraped his fingers over the stubble on his jaw and dismissed the unsettling feeling. Shifting his gaze, he smacked into Mirabella's kindly eyes. A split second zinged by, and she winked. If he hadn't punched that pompous jackass, she would've done it for him. She poured a cup of tea and brought it to him, her face beaming like a golden halo.

Don't give up. The message vibrated in his heart.

Was he imagining things? He ran a hand across his eyes.

Janey knelt beside the bimbo and stroked his hair, cooing words of comfort. The creep lapped it up like a cunning fox.

Samantha held his hand.

Johnny bit iron between his molars.

Couldn't she see beneath his sophisticated façade? Michael was under the impression that he'd clear mamma's note and in return play with Samantha. Bile surged in his belly, stinging his throat and corroding his tongue. On the verge of hauling Michael up and chucking him out on his rear to the dogs, Johnny hardened every muscle of his body, and the gale scaled to a category five typhoon inside him. With extreme caution, he set the teacup on the trolley. He needed something stronger than this delicate brew.

Something with bite … fire.

Not having anything in the house to quench the raging in his gut, he thought a change of scene might help. "I'm going out."

Samantha's head snapped up, her eyes locking with his in an unforgettable moment.

Time suspended.

"Mirabella, a damp cloth please," she murmured, still connected to his gaze. The moment she blinked and turned back to Michael, the force field shattered between them, but didn't dissipate. "Michael's breaking out in a sweat."

Johnny stomped out and pulled the front door nearly off its hinges, then slammed it shut behind him.

When Samantha heard the truck's engine roar, her heart sank. She handed the towelette to Janey who eagerly mopped Michael's brow. She collapsed on the rocker, rocking to and fro. What had just happened?

Johnny had walked out, that's what.

Her temples pounded, her palms damp. She shut her eyes and then popped them open. She swallowed, the taste bitter. Soon as her guests left, she would pack her bags.

****

Johnny was drowning his sorrows in a glass of Volcanic Sparkler when Mirabella materialized beside him at the Tavern.

"How you doin'?"

"Don't ask." He tipped the tall glass and guzzled a mouthful, the fire burning his throat from hot sauce rather than hard liquor.

"But I am." She crinkled her eyes at him. "Asking."

He shrugged and took another gulp from the tumbler. "Take a guess."

"I don't need to." She propped herself on the stool next to his, bracelets jingling on her wrist. "It shows."

He finally glanced her way. Her eyes were like laser beams

piercing straight into his heart. Instead of pain, he felt a healing balm. "Mirabella, what ... who are—"

"Buy a girl a drink?" She tilted her lips in that timeless smile, and Johnny blinked, giving her an answering grin.

"You drink?"

"Sure." She chuckled. "Sparkling water."

Johnny nodded to the bartender. A pause and, "Where's Janey?"

"Took her home," Mirabella murmured. "That child's had a heck of a life." A twinkle entered her eye. "But her world's about to go kaboom in the best way possible."

At that moment, the bartender placed her order on the counter, and she smiled her thanks, pushing the glass away and picking up the bottle.

"Such a doubting Thomasina about—" Mirabella took a swig from the bottle, her gaze distant. "Why, it's all about love." She set the bottle on the bar and smacked her lips. "When in doubt" – she glanced up – "ask Him."

He chuckled, pleased. *Thank you, Mirabella.*

"You're welcome, Sir."

"You say something?" Johnny asked.

Mirabella giggled, took the bottle and tapped his glass, "Cheers!"

"Yeah, mud in your eye." Johnny swallowed and screwed up his face as the liquid flame blistered his throat. The wild Desert Tepins were indeed the world's hottest peppers, topping chilis, jalapenos—and then he got whacked—a triple wallop on the head, and he sputtered, "Who's with Sam?"

Mirabella lifted a smooth eyebrow.

"No!" The word detonated from his mouth. Since Mirabella sat here beside him and Janey was home, that only left Michael. That slime was alone with his wife. Johnny leaped off the stool, hurled several bills on the bar and tripped through the door in his hurry to get to her.

"S'long, handsome," Mirabella whispered after him. This

assignment was nearly over, and she could sigh in relief. Fantasize about sunshine, beaches, cute guys ...

A hearty laugh from above.

"I work hard," she said.

And you love it.

"Must you remind me?"

Now and then.

"Okay, okay." But she grinned.

****

The moon hung in the star-studded sky, but Johnny didn't notice. He didn't notice the storm had lifted and cleared the night. He gripped the wheel in his hands and floored the gas pedal, barreling down the road like a thousand demons were chasing him.

After what seemed like eons, he swerved into the driveway, tires screeching, and vaulted out. He jogged down the track, bounded the stairs in one leap and shouldered the front door. It didn't budge. Frowning, he rammed it with his body.

Nothing.

"Samantha, open the door," he belted out.

Silence.

"I know you're in there." He pounded, and the door rattled on its hinges. "Sam, open the door, now!"

The night breeze rustled palm fronds at the side of the house, the sound mingling with his agitated breathing. Unsavory images plagued his brain. He grabbed the doorknob and shook it so hard it nearly dislocated. A suction of oxygen, and he pressed his forehead against the door.

Control, Belen, control.

He counted to three. Stuffing his hands in his pockets, he searched for the house keys and came up empty. He slapped his hand to his forehead, groaning. In his rush to exit earlier, he must've left them on the mantel above the fireplace. He'd meant to hide a spare set in a safe place outside but hadn't done it yet.

Think, Belen, think.

He clambered across the porch, leaped down the stairs and raced to the back of the house, skidding on the gravel. A blast of air from his lungs misted in the cool night, and relief coursed through him.

The bathroom window was open a crack. He jumped up but couldn't reach the ledge. A glance about, and he dragged the trashcan beneath and climbed on top. He teetered but managed to clamp his hand on the ledge and shove the window wider. He shimmied up the wall and dragged himself through the opening, head first. It was a tight squeeze, and halfway through his rump caught on the frame. Wiggling to and fro, he finally fell through, sprawling on the floor with a thud. He picked himself up, dusted himself off and reeled from the scent of roses still floating in the bathtub.

He thrust the door open and stomped down the hall. "Samantha!"

Not a sound, not even a skitter of a mouse.

Hair on his nape bristled.

And he knew.

She was gone.

But still, a sliver of hope lingered in his heart. He rushed into their bedroom and flung the closet door open.

Empty.

Hope died.

Johnny collapsed on the bed, his head dropping into his hands. He shoved his fingers through his hair, the weight of the world crushing him. A sliver of a whisper, "Lord, help me."

A sudden sound, and his head shot up. He listened for it again, but it didn't repeat. House noises. To be sure, he dragged himself up and into the living room. A quick glance around confirmed his worst fears.

Samantha had run off with Michael Scott.

He pounded the wall with his fist, emotion ravaging him—anger, sadness, resentment, love, loss. Spinning, he swatted his hand across the coffee table with such force, plates and teacups went flying, the Book beneath the plate of pastries flipping open. A growl rumbled from deep inside him. He slithered down the wall and splattered to the floor, pain stripping him raw.

His wife, his child, his marriage.

Gone.

Stolen.

Everything he'd believed in, been naive to believe in, had deserted him.

Silent moments hurled by, and he floundered between anger and dejection. He flung his head up and swept the room with his dazed gaze. He wanted to wring Michael's neck, shake Samantha until she rattled. And as for him— His eyes crossed on the open Book on the coffee table. He snatched it up.

Samantha's Bible.

Bitterness corroded his tongue. About to fling it against the wall, he tightened his grip on it instead. Samantha didn't go anywhere without her Bible. For her to have left without it meant they'd left in a hurry. Why?

He had no answers.

He felt lost. Powerless.

He flipped the pages. Samantha said she found answers in this Book. What did she mean? He leafed through the pages so fast they blurred. Then he stopped, perspiration seeping from his every pore, his breathing heavy.

You're a fool, Belen.

He whacked it back on the table, his eyes glued on the open page.

He squinted at the words, and then a jolt popped him awake.

The kennels. The house. The truck. The money.

He groaned, a guttural sound ripping from deep inside him.

All the material success was nothing without Samantha even if his intentions were good … doing it for her.

A dog howled in the night, and it was like it was proclaiming his defeat.

Anguish slashed his insides, and sweat soaked his shirt. At a loss of what to do, how to right his life, Johnny bent his head and prayed. He sucked in a deep breath and exhaled in a rush, blinking away emotion misting his eyes.

Another dog yelped.

Then he laughed, the sound loud and clear as revelation illuminated his heart, filling him with new hope.

Another woof in the night, then another, and pretty soon a canine chorus filled the air.

Johnny snapped up his head, listening. Could it be that instead of destruction, it could be restoration? He staggered to his feet and gripped the window ledge so hard his knuckles ached.

How did this come about? The last two years of his life flashed through his mind, and fierce feelings tore through him. What remained was love. His love for her. And, if he dared believe, her love for him.

And by gosh, he dared.

A tornado of air blasted from his lungs, and he rolled up his sleeves, marching to the kitchen. He brewed a cup of coffee, set it on the table and straddled a chair. After couple of sips, a grin flirted on his mouth.

Two years ago, he'd been wedged between monster mamma and bozo boy, and it had seemed hopeless but—the grin widened across his mouth—he'd caught the girl and married her.

Could history replay itself?

He took a gulp of the bittersweet brew and nearly scalded his throat. Feeling no pain, he slapped his palm on the table. He wouldn't go down without a scuffle. He'd fight for his family. But he needed a strategy. A foolproof plan.

The digital on the stove flashed two a.m. There were no flights out of Vegas for another five hours. If he drove to L.A. like a maniac, he wouldn't get there much earlier. Michael either drove back to Beverly Hills with Sam or hopped on the last flight out of McCarran Airport. Either way, Johnny had a few hours in his favor, and he'd use them for all their worth.

After an hour of pacing back and forth through the house, trying to formulate a plan, he flung himself on the couch. Samantha's delicate scent lingered on the cushions and wrapped around him like a soft caress. Erotic memories tantalized his mind, stirring his blood, his heart, with longing. Heat infused his body. He broke out in a cold sweat; dark images tormented his mind.

Samantha and Michael.

A fierce growl erupted from his lungs. He wouldn't dare. Could Michael be so diabolical? She was nearly nine months pregnant for heaven's sake. Finally, tossing and turning, he fell into a fitful sleep.

****

Sun filtering through the window warmed his face. Johnny cracked an eye open and glanced at his wristwatch. Five a.m. He groaned and made to turn over.

A shockwave hit.

The empty gouge in his gut stung, and everything vibrated through his memory banks. A feeling of impending doom chilled his body. His eyes flew open, and he shot off the couch.

An hour later, Johnny slung his carryon bag over his shoulder and paced the airport terminal while waiting for the first flight out to Los Angeles. To pass the time, he dropped a coin in a slot machine. No kling, kling. No flashing lights. A gurgle of laughter sounded from deep in his throat. His gambling luck had run out.

And so had his options in the battle to reclaim his life, marriage, a future with what was his. All through the night, he'd rumbled with his thoughts and hadn't come up with a clear-cut plan.

In the natural, it seemed a lost cause.

In the gaming circuit, a long shot.

In the faith realm, a possibility.

War raged in his mind. Believe or doubt.

He glanced at the Swiss watch on his wrist and got in line to board the Southwest aircraft, knowing he was about to face the biggest challenge of his life. Combat the enemy—monster mamma, her entourage and high roller Scott. Could he pull it off a second time and reclaim what was rightfully his … Samantha and their baby?

Fear ripped through him.

He found his seat, stored his bag in the bin above and settled back.

Buckling up, he stared out the window while the airliner taxied down the runway.

He had a choice.

Just as the aircraft was airborne, Johnny chose to believe … and the spirit of the fighting Irish rose up inside him. And he knew what he had to do.

Chapter Twenty-Nine

After his plane landed at LAX, Johnny jogged through the terminal, rented a Chevy sports coupe and burned rubber on the Golden State 5 to the strains of *Hark the Herald Angels Sing*. When he spotted the Wilshire/Beverly Hills off-ramp, he glanced in his rearview mirror, signaled and changed lanes to exit.

"Breaking news!" The radio newscaster's voice replaced the Christmas melody and jolted Johnny from his despondent thoughts. "Robbery in progress. Wilshire and Westwood. Advise motorists to stay clear from vicinity."

Johnny smirked. "Welcome to L.A."

"Woman hostage going into labor. Bank manager, Scott, assures us that ..." Static crackled, drowning the remainder of the newsflash.

Johnny's heart froze, and then splattered a crazy rhythm in his chest.

Dear God, could it be Samantha? Seconds later, he jackknifed into the Carroll's driveway and slammed on the brakes. "Nah." He shook off his foolish fears. Talk about a long shot. It couldn't be. Too coincidental.

The roiling in his belly sent another SOS.

Right on cue, the front door of the estate flew open and banged shut behind Amelia Carroll. Amazing how she navigated the stairs in spiked heels at record speed, then nearly rammed into his car before she realized she had company.

"Belen, is that you?"

He shoved the passenger door open. "Get in!"

"My baby girl's a host—"

"It is Samantha." He felt like someone had taken a vacuum and sucked his insides out. Twisting on the ignition, he backed out through the double wrought-iron security gates, the tires screaming on the pavement.

"And Michael Scott," Mrs. Carroll murmured.

A foreboding silence filled the cab.

Johnny changed gears, floored the gas pedal and focused on the road ahead. His mouth was set, a nerve battering his cheek.

"It's not as it seems." Sam's mother gave him a wary glance, her words perforating the tension between them.

"No?" He arched a derisive brow. "Suppose you tell me how it is, mmm?"

"I'm too distraught."

"Give it a go." Johnny tightened his jaw against bitter feelings resurfacing. Most of his arguments with Sam had stemmed from mamma thinking him an unsuitable husband for her socialite daughter. "You were never at a loss for words when you badmouthed me to Sam."

"Wh-why I never." She squirmed in her seat and glanced out the window.

"You did."

"Well, maybe a little." She turned back and twisted her purse strap around a scarlet tipped finger. "I encouraged her to go for someone more established in his life." A peek at him from beneath her mascara-laden lashes. "You can understand my concern as a parent." A pause then, "You're almost one."

"Let's call a spade a spade, shall we?" he muttered, his words loaded with sarcasm. "You schemed to have her marry money. Lots of it."

"That would've helped." She fanned her fingers across her neck. "In the circumstances, I figured one day she'd thank me."

"What 'stances we talkin' 'bout?"

"Got carried away with the gambling," she said in an offhand way.

"She admits it," Johnny mocked in awe.

"Sure, why not?" She played with a button on her silk suit with her fingertips. "I wanted the best for Sammy, and marrying the right man—"

"Scott."

"He seemed a good catch at the time."

A traffic light changed to red, and Johnny screeched to a stop, gripping the wheel. "What do you mean, at the time?"

"After I realized Sam wanted you—"

"She wanted me?"

"Oh, Belen," she said in an exasperated tone. "Of course she did, does. And once my little girl makes up her mind about something, come hell or high water, she'll stand by it."

A lump of emotion took permanent residence in his throat. He pummeled out a breath. Hell and high water had flooded their path, washing Michael Scott on their doorstep.

"I decided to stop smashing a brick wall" – she tossed her head – "and gracefully stepped aside, letting her live the life she chose."

"You still didn't approve." The green light flashed, and he pressed the pedal, zooming through the intersection.

"No." Mrs. Carroll clung onto the seat edge with one hand and her seat belt with the other.

A police car swerved behind them, siren blaring and red light flashing. Like a law-abiding citizen, Johnny made to pull over and then changed his mind. The cop chase would get them to the bank faster.

"And so you got in cahoots with Scott and had him tracking Samantha to Goodsprings."

"He did what!"

"Don't pretend you knew nothing about it."

"This might come as a surprise to you, young man, but I didn't."

"Nothing you'd do would surprise me, Mrs. Carroll," he bit out.

"I did not sic Michael on Samantha."

Johnny snorted at her choice of words.

"I had other ... er ... things to concentrate on." She placed her purse on her lap and tapped her fingernails on it.

The sound aggravated his already major migraine, and he bit out, "Your casino bellying up, for one?"

"How'd you know?"

He tossed her a dubious look and received a dodgy one back.

"Michael Scott," they said in unison.

"That slippery slug—" She seethed. "Imagine my thinking him a suitable catch for my darling."

"Imagine that."

After a lengthy pause, she bounced back with her undeniably practiced charm. "Now tell me, what was Michael doing in glitz city? Besides chasing after my beautiful, married and very pregnant daughter."

"Maybe not so married."

"What do you mean?"

A heavy sigh. "That's another story." Was there a flea's hair of a chance meddling mamma could be blameless in Scott's second round dupes? "He was scouting for a casino restaurant." With her track record, highly unlikely. He dealt her another quick glance, and shook his head.

"I know the one he's after." She squeezed her purse between her fingers, nearly bursting its contents.

He hoped she imagined it was Scott's throat. An image he found immensely satisfying.

"Mine," she blasted the word like a rifle shot. "The Lucky Lou."

272

He'd known as much, but wanting insider info he tossed his head back and laughed. "Going after a losing hand?"

"Not that funny, I can assure you."

"Okay, so, assure me," he said tongue in cheek.

"After Sam married you," she said, and the 'you' sounded like an accusation. "I figured I could still cut a deal with golden boy. For a share of the biz, he'd bail me out of my financial pit."

"What happened?"

"He got greedy." She hesitated, and then blurted, "Angling to capitalize on your marriage woes, he wanted the girl and the dough."

A rude noise bounced from his throat while he glanced at the street signs ahead.

She stuck her chin out, indignant. "He threatened to take over … wanted control—"

"And you don't?"

She raised her perfectly plucked eyebrows, then grinned. "Too smart for your own good, John boy."

"Aww, gee, thanks." Johnny shot her a covert glance. Sincere or bumping up his ego? "Why target the Lou instead of purchasing another?"

"Michael Scott talks a good story, but daddykins controls the purse strings. So long as he's still breathing, Herbert Scott won't relinquish an inch of his banking interests, especially to his son." She jutted her bosom and bared her teeth. "*Mikey* thought he'd lowball me by cracking a quick and easy deal. In the forefront of the real estate buzz, he'd be set to collect a windfall of profits."

"What made him a better catch then?" he blurted, the pricking of his pride forced the words out.

"The golden goose—"

"What, the egg not good enough for you?" Johnny mouthed back.

Amelia gave him a stern look beneath her brows, but her top lip twitched just a tad. "In any case" – she dismissed his wisecrack with a wave of her hand – "having the boy in the family would've given me the cookie jar ... er ... piggy bank," she confided, her tone a notch lower than normal. "Although he had to go to daddy first, I could control Michael and, therefore, work big daddy without him being the wiser."

"And Sam?"

"She 'd have everything I never had as a girl."

"Maybe she didn't want what you wanted?"

"It's obvious she didn't." A nervous chuckle; surprising coming from the stylish Mrs. Carroll. "That didn't come out as I intended."

"Yeah." Johnny let that one go, glad they'd missed the a.m. traffic rush. Checking the rearview mirror, he spotted the traffic cop closing in.

"How dare that boy try to woo my daughter, my *married* daughter, behind my back just to get his paws on her inheritance." Mrs. Carroll sniffed, grossly embellishing the drama she was creating. "Trying to get to me through Sammy is treading the edge." A smug expression glossed her features. "If he doesn't wise up, he'll come tumbling down."

"Don't underestimate him," Johnny said. "Michael may act the bumbling idiot, but he's no fool." He should know.

Mrs. Carroll poo-pooed the idea. "What an awfully boring life he must live to chase after another man's wife and then want to pounce on a losing business." She adjusted the cuff of her Chanel jacket and fluttered her lashes. "Don't you think?"

Johnny shook his head.

"Why persist like a gamester on a losing streak unless—"

"He had a score to settle," Johnny thought aloud, recent events clicking into place like a jigsaw puzzle.

"For?"

"Being jilted."

"At the altar." Mrs. Carroll giggled, then smothered the sound with her fingers. "Made to look the fool, eh?"

Frowning, Johnny scratched his unshaven cheek.

"Hardly intentional, but in his mind a betrayal nonetheless," she murmured, a serious undertone to her words.

"And?" Johnny prodded.

"Humiliating in his station in the community," she added. "That explained why daddy sent Mikey globetrotting for a couple of years. By the time he returned, the media frenzy flapped out and Michael could show his face about town, most hard pressed to recall the jilting incident of two years ago. Everyone, of course, except Michael."

Danger signals flared in Johnny's brain, his pulse pumping record highs. How far would the man go to feather his bruised ego?

"And?" he fired, startling her to continue piecing the story together.

"He'd ... uh ... want" – her giggle turned into two, then three, before she swallowed the nervous sound – "to pay back ..."

"... those whom he thought ..." Johnny picked up the tale and tossed it back to her.

"... were to blame," she mumbled.

"What d'ya know?" He slapped his hand on the steering wheel. "We're finally on the same page."

She wrung her hands. "Two years ago, I thought a rich son-in-law sounded the ticket to greener pastures." She attempted a grin, but it fizzled on her mouth. "I was desperate."

"Now you're not?

She hedged. "More."

Johnny grunted.

"Sam would have none of it." She clasped her hands in her lap, an odd gesture of acceptance for monster mamma. "She wanted to marry a poor Irishman instead."

"Gee, thanks."

A reluctant smile brushed her lips. "Thank God—"

"You know Him?"

"Who?"

275

"God."

"W-well, not personally, but I have heard—" She crinkled her brow. "Hmm, Samantha has prattled about a Jesus who—" Her voice broke and she veiled the moment in a cough. "I-I did ask Him to keep Sam and the baby safe, even though I—"

"Go on," Johnny invited, but Mrs. Carroll veered away from that topic. He could've told her it was easy to know Him. Those few words he'd prayed earlier that morning would change anyone's life no matter who they were or what they'd done.

A chuckle vibrated from deep in his chest, when he heard Mrs. Carroll 'go on' with her tale.

"Anyway, I'm glad I have a husband who was smart enough to skim profits over the years. He bailed us out in the nick of time, just before the wedding."

"So, Sam didn't have to go through that fiasco—"

"Well, no, but—"

"Mrs. Carroll, you'd have pawned your daughter off to the highest bidder in any case." In his estimation, monster mamma just sprouted horns.

"It does sound horrible," she murmured, then brightened. "You crashed the nuptials" – she tittered, a sliver of sound – "and all's well that ends well ... Shakespeare."

A growl rumbled from deep in his throat. "It's not over yet."

"Right again, Irish boy." She pressed her mouth in a tight line, and then bleated, "I thought we were on easy street, then whammo! Some fool popped us for five million on a slot machine." She fanned her face with a nervous hand. "We got so far in the hole this time, bankruptcy's been jabbing us for two years."

"Enter Michael—round two."

A soft snarl scratched Mrs. Carroll's throat. "The creep."

Johnny raised a brow and waited for more.

"The Lucky Lou" – she patted her thickly sprayed hair in place – "was named after my great grandfather, the quickest hand in the west. At cards." She snickered at that and then splayed her hand, studying her lacquered nails. "I should've invited you and Sam to stay over for your honeymoon, but I was sore at—"

"Her marrying me."

"I panicked. The more she refused, the more I pushed that dodo onto her." She sighed. "But she dug her heels in, saying she'd rather live in the poorhouse with you than hook up with that stuffed shirt."

"Yet she almost did marry the designer shirt."

"Well, uh …"

"There's more," Johnny muttered. "Time to come clean, Mrs. Carroll."

Mrs. Carroll flapped her hands as if what she was about to say was totally unimportant. "She pushed me to the edge, and I threatened if she didn't marry Michael, I'd … uh … leave her father."

"Blackmail?"

Mrs. Carroll sniffed, but her eyes were drier than the desert.

Heat flushed his face, and he nearly exploded. He blasted the air from his mouth, diffusing the pressure in his lungs. "How's his heart?"

She shot him a puzzled look. "Whose?"

"Your husband's."

"Solid," she said, pleased. "Why—"

"And the divorce proceedings?"

Mrs. Carroll fidgeted on the seat. "Of course, I didn't mean it." She giggled, but it came out brash.

It wasn't so long ago that she was slaving at the sink, suds up to her elbows, washing pots and pans in the hotel kitchen. She'd married Sam's father by maneuver. A catered event at the National Realtors Convention in Vegas … a very drunken Harold put to bed by a little doll of a gal … she curled her lip at the memory, then the curl softened to a smile.

A real estate mogul didn't cross her path every day. A little lust thrown in with her good looks, and she'd pulled it off. Had him hooked, and a baby on the way didn't hurt her cause, either. She'd married money, recouped the Lou that was about to be auctioned off and tried to make a home for them as best she could. She couldn't help it if she had a cunning business mind and spent most of her waking hours counting cash and plotting how to make more.

She gulped. Precious little of it now, though.

At fifty-nine, Amelia Carroll wasn't ready to go to pasture, and when she did, she'd go with a bang, not a whimper. The Michael Scotts of the world she could squash beneath her stiletto. She grinned and flicked her thumb across her chin.

"I was doing it for her," she murmured, as if that absolved her sin.

Johnny grunted.

"She thwarted my plans and married her Irishman anyway."

Her words filled his heart with tenderness for his wife. If anything should happen to her … ruthlessly he shackled his thoughts.

"A shocker for Michael," she added.

Johnny reached on the dashboard and pulled out the divorce doc Sam had placed in her Bible. "He's got one for you, mamma-in-law." He tossed her the paper.

"What's this?" She perused the document. "Why that swine—" Clicking her bag open, she took out a tissue and dabbed her cheeks. "Slinging dirt—"

"Must've stung, having mother and daughter both turn him down flat."

A smile struggled for place on her mouth but didn't make it. She stuffed the doc inside her bag. "Belen, what am I to do?"

"Duck."

She didn't even hear him, working her lip between her teeth. "He's vindictive."

A chuckle flew from his lips at her woebegone expression. "Not to worry. You can handle the likes of Michael."

She brightened. "You think so?"

"I certainly do." He shot into the other lane as a Mercedes cut him off. "How goes the business now?"

"We're about to go bust." She brushed an imaginary tear from her eye. "It's my little girl's future holding, and my grandbaby's."

"Still refusing to sell?"

"Holding out for a miracle."

"I'll see what I can do," he murmured below his breath.

She chuckled, missing his words. "Did I actually say that?" Then she sobered. "It certainly won't come from Michael."

"Nope." A blare of a horn drowned out the word.

"Sam doesn't know him like I do."

"But I do, Mrs. Carr ... Amelia," he said loud and clear, giving her a high five with his hand.

"Yeah, I bet you do." She laughed, patting his arm, and then quickly withdrew her hand. "You will let me do the honors when the time comes?"

Johnny grinned. "With pleasure."

"I'm beginning to like you, John Belen."

"That's good ma'am, because I'm aiming to stay your son-in-law for a long time to come." He squinted, rubbing his knuckles across his chin. *You'll like me a whole lot better knowing the five mil that fleeced the Lou landed in my lap.* Johnny chuckled.

"What's funny at a time like this?" She made a wad with the Kleenex, dropped it in her purse and snapped it shut.

"Nothing." A muscle socked his jaw. Nothing would ever be amusing again if anything should happen to his Sam and their baby. "I have to get Sam safely out of there."

"You'll have to beat me to it, sonny boy." She set her chin like the Rock of Gibraltar.

Johnny swerved into the right lane, floored the gas pedal and, a moment later, squealed around the corner with the bank in sight ... and the cop on his fender.

Chapter Thirty

Johnny skidded to a stop in the outdoor mall parking and leaped out. Cops swarmed the bank building, and media personnel rushed to and fro, Choppers circled overhead, and curious bystanders gawked from across the street.

A second set of tires squealed, and Mrs. Carroll slid from the Chevy and stood next to Johnny. The traffic officer bounded from his vehicle and caught on at a glance, the traffic violation forgotten.

"My wife's in—"

"Sorry." The law officer blocked his way. "This is a restricted area."

"My daughter—"

"Sorry, ma'am."

"She's pregnant ..." Johnny blurted, his belly churning.

"My first grandchild—"

"There's an ambulance standing by." The officer pointed behind him. "And the S.W.A.T. team's on its way."

"I have to get to her," Johnny said, his voice desperate.

"You wanna help your wife, mister?" the officer bit out. "Stay outta our way." Another lawman waved him over to the squad car, and he jogged away.

"I have to find a way." Johnny raked both hands through his hair.

Mrs. Carroll grabbed his elbow and pulled him aside.

"I must get to her." He yanked his arm free from her hold. "I can't stand here and do nothing."

"You won't have to." She slung her purse strap over her neck and shoulder, her eyes glinting with purpose. "Follow me. There's another way into the bank. Michael let that slip once when he was trying to impress me." Hurrying away from the action, she skirted the building toward the side entrance. "Let's hope the luck o' the Irish is with you, and it isn't sealed."

A grim-faced Johnny nodded.

"Got a flashlight in that car of yours?"

"Yeah." He was already racing to his car before she finished speaking. After he rummaged in his duffel bag for the light, he grabbed the miniature first aid kit and, on instinct, the Bible from the dashboard, pocketing it as he ran. In less than thirty seconds, he was back in the game with mamma leading the way.

She prowled behind a trash bin concealing the slit of a dirt path between the Global Bank Exchange and the Toys-R-Us shop. A tense moment, and motioning him to follow she squeezed between the two walls. "I hope this leads to the bank's main floor."

"You hope?" Johnny swiped his hand across his nape. "You don't know?"

"I've never crawled on my hands and knees into a bank before." She fluttered her lashes against the sheen of tears in her eyes … real this time.

Johnny clamped down on his teeth, his jaw iron hard.

Danger and an unpalatable outcome taunted if they didn't make it on time. Of course, neither voiced the dreaded thought.

"Keep faith." Johnny pressed a reassuring hand on her shoulder to jack up her courage … and his.

She patted his hand, took a deep breath and the air blasted from her mouth. "I'm going after my daughter and granddaughter." She slapped him with a watery smile. "I have a feeling it's going to be a girl."

A wan grin brushed his mouth and then vanished. The thought of Samantha delivering their baby in the midst of a bank robbery had ice chunks grooving his spine. "Right behind you."

Mrs. Carroll flung off her jacket, kicked off her pumps and fell flat on her face in the dirt. Her bracelets jangled. Slipping them off her wrist, she shoved them at him, and he stuffed them in his jacket's pocket. A quick glance beneath the building, and she ventured forth into the dark abyss. Johnny hit the ground behind her and flicked on the flashlight.

A few moments later, she stopped and listened. Not a sound except their breathing. She rapped the floorboards above her head with her knuckles. When she heard the hollow sound, she gave him the thumbs up signal and jiggled the board. After several tries, she mouthed in exasperation, "It won't budge."

"You sure this is the spot?"

"Yes."

Johnny set the flash down, cocked an ear for any noise, and then, lacing his fingers around the First Aid box, swung at the floor with a swift uppercut, knocking it out. Pulling it off, he wiggled his way upward into the vault. An eye scan indicated it was locked and bolted. The robbers hadn't hit yet. Monster mamma handed him the flashlight, and when she clutched his other hand, he hauled her up beside him.

"This'll be their next target," he murmured, scoping the area.

Just then, the combination lock clicked from the other side, and he motioned her to take cover behind the metal shelves.

"Hurry it up," someone commanded in a tense whisper.

Johnny flicked off the flash and pressed himself flat against the wall beside the door.

The vault partition yawned wide and concealed Johnny in shadow. After nudging the numb teller to step inside with the point of his weapon, the thief tossed a couple of burlap bags on the floor. Johnny squinted, then gaped at the flaming CKR logo emblazoned on the cloth. It matched the feed sacks at the kennels.

"Shovel the dough in the sacks and be quick 'bout it," the robber ordered, twitching his neck.

Trembling from head to toe, the blonde turned to grab a stack of bills from the shelf, caught sight of Johnny and sucked in a sharp breath.

Johnny pressed a finger to his lips.

In record time, the girl stuffed the bags with the loot, and then Johnny signaled her to stand back. The moment the burglar stepped forward to pick them up, Johnny slugged him over the head with the First Aid Kit. He keeled onto the floor, his gun sliding across the tiles and stopping at mamma's feet. She snatched it up and leaped from her hiding spot, the firearm shaking in her hands.

"Watch where you're pointing that thing," Johnny mouthed and turned to the teller. "How many more are out there?"

She raised a wobbly finger.

Mrs. Carroll pulled the silk scarf from around her neck and tossed it to her. "Tie pretty boy up, will you, honey. He'll have a doozer of a headache when he comes to."

Johnny extricated the handgun from his mother-in-law's itchy fingers and held it by his side. "Stay here."

She gave him a "you're nutso if you think I'm going to stay out of the action" look and swept up the First Aid Kit from the floor. "We're about to sting this operation, boy." She shoved up her sleeves. "Let's move out."

A saucy grin flirted on his mouth, and then he fell flat on his belly, cautioning her to stay low. He crawled to the nearest desk, and she followed, huddling beside him to stake out the bank floor. The other culprit brandished his revolver about, forcing the hostages to stand against the wall with their hands behind their necks.

A scream filled the air, and he knew it was Samantha. He made to leap out, but Mrs. Carroll grabbed him by his shirt flaps and pulled him down. "Don't give us away, now, John."

The robber cocked his head and backtracked to the vault, stopping mere inches from them.

Johnny stilled.

Mrs. Carroll held her breath.

"Hey, in there." He shifted from one foot to the other, his weapon pointed at the frightened people. "Hurry it up!"

Johnny bunched his brow.

Mrs. Carroll breathed.

The man's New York twang sounded familiar. A low growl built in his throat. He pushed the gun into Amelia's hand and leaped for him. The Bible tumbled from his pocket the precise moment the stooge's gun went off, blasting a hole in the ceiling and dinging the fan before clattering to the floor. Johnny kicked the weapon aside and slugged the pot-bellied man on the jaw with the flashlight. The culprit whacked onto the floor, groaning and clutching his jaw.

In a flash, Mrs. Carroll snagged the wayward weapon from the floor, tossed it to Johnny and choked the gun she was holding between her fingers. "It's over buster."

"Willie." Johnny stripped the mask from his face. "You disappoint me." He shook his head. "Skipping out on me on the 5 Freeway ... mismanaging the kennels ... trippin' out with biz capital." A pause. "Aww, man, going 'poof' like that was not a nice thing to do."

Willie had the grace to blush.

"And I bet the ... er ... workhand you planted at the kennels is snoozing in the vault."

"I can come clean." Willie made to get up, but Johnny shoved him back down with his boot. "He paid me real good ... I needed the dough ... figured you'd be hitched by the time we got to church ... later more cash to keep mum 'bout the forged—"

"Go on," Johnny said, the words bullet hard.

"Scott came up with this other idea and—" Willie sputtered on his words.

"What does that weasel have to do with this?" Mrs. Carroll loomed above him, double barrels loaded and pointing at his chest.

"He-e ..." Willie shuffled back against the wall, waving her away.

She lowered her thick lashes, concealing the glint in her eyes. "Doesn't take a rocket scientist to figure out what that conniving two-bit loser was up to." She swished the gun in her hand. "But do carry on ... I'm curious to know all the facts."

"H-he had a system goin'." Willie's eyes dodged from one to the other. "H-he laundered the bank loot through me to the kid" –he inclined his head toward the vault— "who buried it at the kennels."

"The loose dirt behind the door of the dog shed," Johnny murmured, but nobody heard him.

"Stealing from his own daddy's bank." Amelia set her scarlet painted mouth in a disapproving line.

"I got a measly cut from the buried treasure," Willie whined.

"You couldn't take the money and run." Amelia sized him up and down, her words more a statement than a query.

Willie scowled. "Scott got it all on video, in case one of us double-crossed him."

"Copy that, Willie boy." Amelia glanced up at the surveillance camera in the corner of the ceiling.

"Scapegoat." He pointed to Johnny. "Wanted to pin the job on—"

"Burlap sacks make good evidence," Johnny muttered.

"You knew the layout of the bank." Willie's Adam's apple bopped, his lip twitched. "This stick-up and the dough stashed at the kennels would lay it on you, thicker than Aunt Jemima's pancake syrup." He chortled, and his belly jiggled. "A disgruntled ex-employee ... revenge ... you'd be in the slammer for several years."

"Leaving the way clear for him to infiltrate—that toad's gonna be toast," Amelia murmured. "How dare he try to implicate my son-in-law in a burglary, and in his daddy's bank." She slapped Johnny on the shoulder, and he staggered back a step, a twitch of amusement on his mouth. "And plot to seduce my little girl and oust me from my casino."

Mamma drew oxygen into her lungs, and her bosom lifted.

Willie gawked.

She glared back, air whooshing from her mouth.

Willie shuffled his rear back against the wall, his fingertips brushing across the Book on the floor.

Ignoring Willie, mamma noticed the teller stepping timidly from the vault, and beckoned with the firearm. "Come 'ere." When the girl tiptoed closer, she smacked the handgun in her palm. "Think you could hold onto that while I attend to my daughter?"

The girl nodded and turned the weapon on Willie. "D-don't move."

"Point it down, little lady, not at me." He curled his fingers around the Book without realizing it.

Like an avenging tigress, Mrs. Carroll stomped through the bank in her dirt-streaked designer clothes, torn stockings and grimy feet. "John boy, my jangles."

Puzzled, Johnny shook his head.

She held up her wrist. "A little socialite armor wouldn't hurt ... bolster my shield."

A hint of a grin, and he pulled the gold bracelets from his pocket and placed them in her palm. Without missing a step, she slipped them on her wrist and flashed her charismatic smile. "Someone call the police, we got the bad guys."

Applauding, the captives stepped back and revealed Samantha lying on the floor.

Johnny and mamma jostled each other in their rush to get to her, barely noticing the police storming the front door.

"Anybody hurt?" The officer's voice boomed, triggering a pandemonium eruption.

The hostages shook their heads. "Just scared." Someone in the back started to cry. "Mighty scared," another added. "Terrified."

Nodding, the grim-faced policeman focused on a tall, fair-haired man peeking from behind two fat ladies. "You have something to add?"

"N-no." Michael shook his shoulders and stepped forward. "If I can be of assistance—"

"Is there a doctor in the house ... er ... bank?" Mrs. Carroll called, her voice rising an octave. "Michael, make yourself useful and see what's keeping him."

He nodded but didn't move, his mouth hanging open.

"My grandbaby is on its way."

The officer spoke into a transmitter. "We need a doctor, pronto."

Johnny fell to his knees beside Samantha and shrugged off his jacket. Quickly folding it, he placed it beneath her head, his thumb brushing her cheek.

"Johnny, is that you?"

"Yeah, it's me, sweetheart." Johnny closed his hand over hers and gulped down emotion threatening to choke him. A second later, she tensed and gripped his arm as a contraction racked her body.

A cry burst from her lungs.

"Breathe, Sammy, breathe," mamma said, gasping for air.

Samantha panted, digging her fingers into Johnny's forearm.

"Oh my gosh." Mamma paced back and forth. "She's coming. Baby's coming." Frantic, she turned every which way, and then whacked Michael on the head. "Heat some water, get towels, scissors ..." She panted herself. "And take that pretty girl" – she gestured to the dark haired girl rushing through the door, her coat flapping, and searching for someone – "with you."

The girl turned to the woman next to her. "Go on, Janey. He needs you."

After Janey followed Michael into the kitchenette, Mirabella floated to a stop beside Johnny. She touched his shoulder, and he glanced up.

"Mirabella, what are you doing ... how'd you know—"

Mirabella smiled that eternal smile.

Bewildered, he shook his head and turned back to Sam as another contraction convulsed her body.

"The heart knows," Mirabella whispered, but he didn't hear, too wrapped up in comforting his wife. "How far apart?"

He examined his wristwatch, perspiration glazing his forehead and dribbling down his temples. "Three minutes."

"Let me." Mirabella knelt down beside him, pulled Samantha's coat aside and lifted her dress above her knees. "Johnny, get me some towels." She inclined her head toward Michael and Janey returning from the staff lounge with the supplies. "Spread them under Samantha." Gently, she smoothed the damp hair off her brow. "Samantha, honey, I want you to help me."

Samantha opened her glazed eyes.

"I have to see how much you've dilated."

Samantha raised her legs a little higher and allowed Mirabella access. "Oh, my," she said with joy. "I see the head. Push Samantha, push."

A raw groan ripped from her, and she pushed the baby further down the birth canal.

"It's almost here." Mirabella cheered her on.

"Where's that doctor?" The police officer shoved his cap off his head and mopped his moist forehead with the cuff of his sleeve.

"That's what I'd like to know," Amelia Carroll huffed, leaning over Mirabella's shoulder.

Johnny held Samantha's hand and cooed words of comfort, sweat soaking his shirt.

"Push again, love," Mirabella encouraged. "Once more. Twice. A little harder. That's it. She's almost here ... I have her head ... push one more time, real hard."

Samantha did.

The baby slid out into Mirabella's waiting hands. "I've got her."

"M-Michael, scissors." Mrs. Carroll stretched out her hand, without taking her eyes off the baby.

He stumbled closer with Janey glued to his side and handed mamma the cutting shears from the First Aid Kit.

Mamma passed the scissors to Johnny. At Mirabella's nod, he cut the umbilical cord. Emotion pummeled his insides and expanded his chest with unspeakable joy. His eyes stung.

The baby belted out a cry, and everyone laughed in relief. Even the two handcuffed robbers trudging by glanced over, and Willie raised the Book in his hand in a victory signal. For a split second, his eyes connected with Johnny's, then he shifted and slammed into Mirabella.

Mirabella pierced him with her laser sharp gaze as if she could see deep into his soul.

"Let's get outta here," he mumbled, tripping over his feet in his hurry.

"Never seen two perps so eager to get into police custody." The officer chuckled, pacing their exit and that of his two men flanking them.

"Doctor's here," one called over his shoulder, catching sight of the M.D. leaping from the ambulance.

"Don't need him, now," Mrs. Carroll announced smugly and transfixed on her granddaughter, her eyes glazed with tears. "Are they all that small?"

Mirabella placed the infant on Samantha's breast and wrapped the flaps of her coat around the babe. "Some tea might be nice, don't you think?" she whispered to Mrs. Carroll.

Reluctantly, mamma followed Mirabella to the staff kitchen, but kept glancing over her shoulder at the baby. Nearly bumping into Michael standing like a statue not two feet away, she narrowed her eyes and gave him the once over. "I'd like to know how you'll get yourself out of this one, Michael Scott."

"I-I-I don't know what you're talking about." But he didn't move; shock had him shackled to the spot.

She shook her head. "And to think I wanted him in the family."

Mirabella chuckled and inclined her head toward Johnny holding Samantha and their baby in his arms. "Never hurts to have a rich relative in the family."

Mrs. Carroll gazed at her granddaughter and dabbed her eyes with the cuff of her sleeve, her bracelets jangling. "She's the treasure."

"First and foremost." Mirabella looked deep into her eyes, and her radiant smile touched mamma's heart. A wink, and she rubbed her thumb and index finger together.

Mrs. Carroll's mouth fell open, her eyes big as saucers. "No!"

Mirabella nodded. "At the Lou."

A shriek of laughter. "I didn't lose it. The dough's in the family."

"It certainly is."

"Why that ne'er-do-well has the luck o' the Irish with him, after all."

A cherubic grin curved Mirabella's mouth. "I wouldn't put it quite like that."

But Mrs. Carroll didn't hear, already calculating net profits. "I always knew my Sam would land on her feet. She's a girl after mamma's smarts."

"Of course."

"I'll have to phone Harold. He's never going to believe all this," she rattled on with nervous energy. "Always saying I have a wild imagination. He'll be thrilled with his granddaughter."

"Yes, he will," Mirabella murmured, but Mrs. Carroll had already pulled her cell phone from her purse, punching in the number.

While the phone rang, Amelia glanced around for Mirabella,

then shrugged, thinking she must've gone back to join the crowd. By the third ring, reality hit, and she paled; then her lips broadened to a smile, albeit with reservation.

She was a grandma.

Joy tickled her heart, and then she gripped the mobile tight. She'd have to mend her ways ... do something with the family business ... er ... give a percentage of proceeds to charity ... help the homeless ... Her gossipy socialite friends would think she'd lost her mind. She muffled a giggle. They'd also be green with envy. She waggled her shoulders. Atone for past sins ... set an example for her granddaughter ... go to church ... she gulped ... eventually she'd get there ... of course, she had to go for the Christening— "Granddaddy, congrats to you ... er ... us, Harold ..."

Mirabella lounged atop the defunct ceiling fan, amused at the dealings of the human heart trying to make sense of life. Swatting a tinsel streamer dangling in her face, she winked at heaven, delighted at the outcome.

Johnny and Samantha determined to build a marriage on divine decree: 'What therefore God hath joined together, let no man ... er ... meddling mamma put asunder.'

He chuckled.

A grin glowed on Mirabella's lips. "Mission accomplished."

Affirmative, Mirabella.

She chomped on a gumdrop, blinking her moist lashes. "I'll miss this one."

You won't have time.

Alert, Mirabella did a good work on the gumdrop between her teeth.

What with the Christmas Holidays, things have become hectic on the Earth realm.

"Uh, uh." She swallowed and popped another gummy in her mouth.

"Not before I get my vacation time."

A telling pause.

"We had a deal." She tossed her braid over her shoulder and flew about. "I'm so looking forward to sun bathing and …"

A rush of air ruffled Johnny's hair, and goosebumps chilled his body. He turned around and saw Mrs. Carroll and Janey passing out hot tea in paper cups. He rolled his stiff shoulders. The prickles on his skin relaxed, and a peace, so profound he couldn't explain it, settled around his heart. "Thank you, Lord. All's well."

"With Him it always is."

Johnny twisted behind him, but no one was within speaking range. A sudden breeze, light as an angel's wing, brushed him again. And he knew. "Thanks, Mirabella," he whispered, smiling.

Samantha hugged their daughter close to her heart and took his hand, placing it protectively over their baby. Then she covered his hand with hers, and her tired eyes glittered with happiness. "I do, Mr. Belen."

Emotion filled his heart to explosive levels, and he blinked the sting from his eyes. Johnny dipped his head, placed a kiss on their child's head, then on Sammy's lips. "I banked on it, Mrs. Belen."

Epilogue

Mirabella, decked in beach gear from across the ages, sat cross-legged on the judge's desk and sipped a bottle of sparkling Water Lite. Tilting the sun hat off her brow, she peered over her Dolce & Gabbana sunglasses. "You interrupted my vacation for this?"

Figured you didn't want to miss it.

"Hear ye, hear ye, all rise …" the bailiff droned on. The judge in his black robes walked into the courtroom and sat down. "All sit."

"Kinda cute, don't you think?" Mirabella murmured. "Draped in all that flowing fabric."

Behave.

"Defendants, please rise."

A somber looking Michael, Willie and his sidekick stood facing the judge.

"Mr. Herbert Scott," the judge announced, glancing at him parked on the front bench, "has filed no charges against his son Michael Jay Scott and his two accomplices."

Dressed in an expensive three-piece pinstriped suit and a gold watch chain looped across his breast pocket, daddy Scott turned to his wife propped beside him, sniffing and dabbing her eyes. "Gertrude, shut up."

"However, even with blank bullets, such juvenile antics could result in tragedy." The judge glared at the three culprits from beneath his bushy brows. "Therefore, I sentence you to six months ... uh ... hard labor at the Canine Resort Kennels in Goodsprings, Nevada." The judge blinked, dumbfounded at what he said.

Mirabella grinned. "That was your doing."

Mmm.

Beaming, mamma sat wedged between Johnny and Samantha, cooing to her granddaughter nestled in her arms. "That translates to shoveling dog poop for the next six months."

They burst out laughing.

Mirabella giggled, then swallowed the tinkle of sound.

A message flashed through.

"Uh, uh. No. Oh no." She shook her head vehemently. "I've got three days left at this oh, soooo cool, trendy spot and I intend to enjoy every minu—"

That young couple will need you.

Mirabella glanced at Johnny and Samantha. "They look happy to me."

He chuckled. *Not them.*

Mirabella fluttered her lashes, her eyes open wide as understanding dawned in her spirit. "You don't mean—" she took a swig of her drink and gulped— "Michael and that cute lil' waitress? Oh, puh-lease!"

I do.

Mirabella waved the bottle in her hand as if the assignment was a piece of cake. "Any agent can handle those two."

Uh, uh.

"Why not?" She flicked a frizzy curl off her shoulder and adjusted the sunglasses on her nose.

You have inside info.

"I'll share—"

Mirabella.

"Okay." She sighed, and then brightened. "I'll go after six months."

Can't wait.

"Why not?"

You know how impatient humans are.

"Aww, have a heart."

I do.

And, of course, He did.